DREAMS
A LITERARY ANTHOLOGY

DOVER THRIFT EDITIONS

Edited by
Bob Blaisdell

W0081357

DOVER PUBLICATIONS
GARDEN CITY, NEW YORK

DOVER THRIFT EDITIONS

GENERAL EDITOR: SUSAN L. RATTINER
EDITOR OF THIS VOLUME: MICHAEL CROLAND

Bibliographical Note

This Dover edition, first published in 2023, is a new selection reprinted from standard texts. Misspellings, minor inconsistencies, and other style vagaries derive from the original texts and have been retained for the sake of authenticity. The selections from the Bible are from the King James Version. A new Introduction has been specially prepared for this edition.

International Standard Book Number

ISBN-13: 978-0-486-85111-2
ISBN-10: 0-486-85111-7

Manufactured in the United States of America
85111701   2023
www.doverpublications.com

Contents

II. Mythology, History, and Religion

III. Philosophy and Psychology

IV. Poetry and Drama

V. Memoirs and Essays

Introduction

And they said one to another, Behold, this dreamer cometh.
—Genesis, XXXVII

This is an anthology of dreams, literary and personal. Whether the selections are familiar or not, they are startling, amazing, troubling, or amusing. The selections are about the experience of dreams from within by the characters or the authors. Sometimes the dreams foretell the future, and sometimes they reveal the past. Almost always they dreadfully or comically reveal the dreamer's naked self.

All of the selections date from at least a hundred years ago, that is, up to when Dr. Sigmund Freud's theories wonderfully created worldwide controversies about the extent of the revelatory nature of dreams. Dreams have probably never been seen or written about in the same way since Freud's influential entry into the discussion, but he is not the star of this volume; more truly he is its child. The American poet and transcendentalist Ralph Waldo Emerson took a flying leap into dream theory before Freud was even born and landed, perhaps, as far as Freud did decades later. "My dreams are not me; they are not Nature, or the Not-me: they are both," writes Emerson. "They have a double consciousness, at once sub- and ob-jective. We call the phantoms that rise, the creation of our fancy, but they act like mutineers, and fire on their commander; showing that every act, every thought, every cause, is bipolar, and in the act is contained the counteraction. If I strike, I am struck; if I chase, I am pursued."[1] The unselfconscious hero of dreamwork, if there is one, is Joseph, the Old Testament's

---

1 See Emerson's "Demonology," page 162.

undaunted dream interpreter, whose life takes wonderful and terrible turns through his God-given talent to decipher dreams.

This anthology might remind us that Freud himself was awakened to his theories through nineteenth-century novels and classical Greek literature. Queen Jocasta's dream interpretation of her husband's nightmare in Sophocles's *Oedipus the King* anticipated Freud's interpretation 2,400 years later: "fear not that you will wed your mother. Many men before now have slept with their mothers in dreams. But he to whom these things are as though nothing bears his life most easily." So in Oedipus's case, *Jocasta was wrong*. It's easy to get dreams wrong, explains another heroic woman, Penelope, in Homer's *The Odyssey*: "dreams verily are baffling and unclear of meaning, and in no wise do they find fulfillment in all things for men. For two are the gates of shadowy dreams, and one is fashioned of horn and one of ivory. Those dreams that pass through the gate of sawn ivory deceive men, bringing words that find no fulfillment. But those that come forth through the gate of polished horn bring true issues to pass, when any mortal sees them." There is no telling which gate your dream has passed through, so interpreters beware! Just ask Agamemnon about his dream in the midst of the Trojan War (see page 92).

I have included skeptics of dreams as well as those who marvel at dreams' literary usefulness. First a critic, the sharp mocker G. K. Chesterton: "There can be comparatively little question that the place ordinarily occupied by dreams in literature is peculiarly unreal and unsatisfying. When the hero tells us that 'last night he dreamed a dream,' we are quite certain from the perfect and decorative character of the dream that he made it up at breakfast. The dream is so reasonable that it is quite impossible."[2] On the other hand, the religious philosopher Sir Thomas Browne, a contemporary of the seventeenth-century Metaphysical poets, notes that "in one dreame I can compose a whole Comedy, behold the action, apprehend the jests and laugh my selfe awake at the conceits thereof." The ever clever Robert Louis Stevenson swears that his famous stories have come to him in dreams, created by "Brownies," and far exceed his own creative imagination: "Who are the Little People? They are near connections of the dreamer's, beyond doubt; they share in his financial worries and have an eye to the bank-book; they share

---

2 See Chesterton's "Dreams," page 153.

plainly in his training; they have plainly learned like him to build the scheme of a considerate story and to arrange emotion in progressive order; only I think they have more talent; and one thing is beyond doubt, they can tell him a story piece by piece, like a serial, and keep him all the while in ignorance of where they aim. Who are they, then? and who is the dreamer?"[3] This harkens to the most marvelous critic and creator of dreamlike literature, Jorge Luis Borges, the twentieth-century Argentine who was a great admirer of Stevenson. Borges—who is not represented in this collection because of copyright reasons—reflected that for him writing is like dreaming and dreaming is like writing. He told a friend, "What's difficult about writing a nightmare is that the nightmare feeling does not come from the images. Rather, as Coleridge said, the feeling gives you the images."[4]

Novelists repeatedly dramatize the thin or transparent door between waking and dreaming in their characters' lives. Charles Dickens writes in *Oliver Twist*: "There is a kind of sleep that steals upon us sometimes, which, while it holds the body prisoner, does not free the mind from a sense of things about it, and enable it to ramble at its pleasure. So far as an overpowering heaviness, a prostration of strength, and an utter inability to control our thoughts or power of motion, can be called sleep, this is it; and yet, we have a consciousness of all that is going on about us, and, if we dream at such a time, words which are really spoken, or sounds which really exist at the moment, accommodate themselves with surprising readiness to our visions, until reality and imagination become so strangely blended that it is afterwards almost a matter of impossibility to separate the two."[5]

Meanwhile in nineteenth-century Russia, Fyodor Dostoyevsky describes the peculiar and penetrating lucidity of dreams in *Crime and Punishment*: "Raskolnikov had a fearful dream. He dreamt he was back in his childhood in the little town of his birth. He was a child about seven years old, walking into the country with his father on the evening of a holiday. It was a grey and heavy day, the country was exactly as he remembered it; indeed he recalled it far more vividly in his dream than he had done in memory."[6] The twenty-first-century

---

3 See Stevenson's "A Chapter on Dreams," page 203.

4 Willis Barnstone. "Thirteen Questions: A Dialogue with Jorge Luis Borges." *Chicago Review*. Winter 1980.

5 See Dickens's *Oliver Twist*, page 26.

6 See Dostoyevsky's *Crime and Punishment*, page 28.

novelist Karl Ove Knausgaard seems to have achieved Raskolnikov's hallucinatory vividness of dreams in the fictional recreation of his life in the *My Struggle* series.

* * *

After various second thoughts, I have organized the dreams by loose groupings of genre. At first I arranged the selections chronologically. In that order, there seemed to be a similarity or overlapping of eras and places that confused rather than illuminated the dreams. When I retreated to alphabetization, the accidental bedfellows of Dickens, Dickinson, Doolittle, and Dostoyevsky and Poe, Pound, and Pushkin threw me off, making the dreams seem abruptly *dis*connected and resistant to continued musing. The landscapes were so different that it was like traveling from the Arctic to the equator at the turn of a page. The genre categories make the comparisons and contrasts more natural and less discombobulating. (Their order may have come to me in a dream.) The selections are arranged alphabetically within each section:

   I. Novels and Short Stories
  II. Mythology, History, and Religion
 III. Philosophy and Psychology
  IV. Poetry and Drama
   V. Memoirs and Essays

Some of the pieces' placements are debatable. You, reader, are welcome to move Ovid's passage from *Metamorphoses*—originally in Latin verse and rendered here in English prose—from Mythology to Poetry or Voltaire's "Of Dreams" from Philosophy to Essays. You could make a Nightmares category and include Guy de Maupassant's "The Horla," Charles Lamb's "Witches, and Other Night-Fears," or even Emily Brontë's shriek-worthy dream by Mr. Lockwood in *Wuthering Heights*. I have noted a few of the nightmarish episodes in the short introductions to the selections—as warning or invitation.

I have included two complete short stories, one each by Anton Chekhov and Franz Kafka. I could be persuaded that Kafka read Chekhov's "Sleepy," anxiously went to bed, and dreamed up his own version of a doctor's nightmare. The selections from the novels seem unusually capable of standing on their own, with the briefest of contextual summaries. Even without the surrounding hundreds of pages, characters' reactions to and experiences of dreams in *Les Miserables, Jane Eyre*, and *Anna Karenina* are so dependent on their immediate telling that they have an independence from the rest of the novel.

The essayists and memoirists have been my favorite discoveries or rediscoveries, Lamb and William Hazlitt among them. Personal essays have evolved not a jot since their early nineteenth-century glory days. "We are not hypocrites in our sleep," Hazlitt observes. "The curb is taken off from our passions, and our imagination wanders at will. When awake, we check these rising thoughts, and fancy we have them not." Hazlitt anticipates Freud: "Infants cannot disguise their thoughts from others; and in sleep we reveal the secret to ourselves."[7]

Just as insightful, perhaps, are comic passages by Jerome K. Jerome and William Dean Howells. Howells's heyday came in late nineteenth-century America, and though he is little read today, we should remember that he can be as funny as his friend Mark Twain: "Every one knows how delightful the dreams are that one dreams one's self, and how insipid the dreams of others are. I had an illustration of the fact, not many evenings ago, when a company of us got telling dreams. I had by far the best dreams of any; to be quite frank, mine were the only dreams worth listening to; they were richly imaginative, delicately fantastic, exquisitely whimsical, and humorous in the last degree; and I wondered that when the rest could have listened to them they were always eager to cut in with some silly, senseless, tasteless thing, that made me sorry and ashamed for them. I shall not be going too far if I say that it was on their part the grossest betrayal of vanity that I ever witnessed."[8]

The poets, as is their wont, dart their way into the core and souls of the dream experience. Hilda Doolittle, writing as H.D., catches the way our dreams set their own limits:

> I should have thought
> in a dream you would have brought
> some lovely, perilous thing,
> orchids piled in a great sheath,
> as who would say (in a dream),

---

7 See Hazlitt's "On Dreams," page 171.
8 See Howells's "I Talk of Dreams," page 176.

"I send you this,
who left the blue veins
of your throat unkissed."[9]

I owe credit to the biggest and best anthology of at least semiliterary dreams, *The World of Dreams* by Ralph Louis Woods (1947). Woods's selections introduced me to several religious works, Freud's contemporaries and rivals, and philosophers about whom I was ignorant. Among them is Zhuangzi, also known as Chuang Tzŭ, who has offered readers for two millennia the Daoist mind bender about the butterfly: "Once upon a time, I, Chuang Tzŭ, dreamt I was a butterfly, fluttering hither and thither, to all intents and purposes a butterfly. I was conscious only of following my fancies as a butterfly, and was unconscious of my individuality as a man. Suddenly, I awaked, and there I lay, myself again. Now I do not know whether I was then a man dreaming I was a butterfly, or whether I am now a butterfly dreaming I am a man."[10]

A list of other inspiring or useful works about literary dreams is in the Selected Bibliography.

Bob Blaisdell
New York City
January 2023

---

9 See H.D.'s "At Baia," page 140.
10 See Zhuangzi's *Zhuangzi*, page 127.

I. Novels and Short Stories

Anonymous

The Arabian Nights ("The Ruined Man Who Became Rich
Again Through a Dream")
c. 800–1200

*A hopeful dream leads the hero on a foreign adventure. The anonymous
collection of Middle Eastern folk stories known as* The Arabian Nights
or One Thousand and One Nights *is full of comic, exciting, and
magical tales. In this one, Shahrazad, the fictional teller, shows us that
only through misfortune does the protagonist discover happiness in his
own home.*

There lived once in Baghdad a wealthy man and made of money,
who lost all his substance and became so destitute that he could earn
his living only by hard labour. One night, he lay down to sleep,
dejected and heavy-hearted, and saw in a dream a Speaker who said to
him, "Verily thy fortune is in Cairo; go thither and seek it."

So he set out for Cairo; but when he arrived there, evening overtook him and he lay down to sleep in a mosque.

Presently, by decree of Allah Almighty, a band of bandits entered
the mosque and made their way thence into an adjoining house;
but the owners, being aroused by the noise of the thieves, awoke and
cried out; whereupon the Chief of Police came to their aid with his
officers. The robbers made off; but the Wali entered the mosque and,
finding the man from Baghdad asleep there, laid hold of him and beat
him with palm-rods so grievous a beating that he was well-nigh dead.
Then they cast him into jail, where he abode three days; after which
the Chief of Police sent for him and asked him, "Whence art thou?";
and he answered, "From Baghdad." Quoth the Wali, "And what
brought thee to Cairo?"; and quoth the Baghdadi, "I saw in a dream

One who said to me, Thy fortune is in Cairo; go thither to it. But when I came to Cairo the fortune which he promised me proved to be the palm rods thou so generously gavest to me."

The Wali laughed till he showed his wisdom-teeth and said, "O man of little wit, thrice have I seen in a dream one who said to me: 'There is in Baghdad a house in such a district and of such a fashion and its courtyard is laid out garden-wise, at the lower end whereof is a jetting-fountain and under the same a great sum of money lieth buried. Go thither and take it. Yet I went not; but thou, of the briefness of thy wit, hast journeyed from place to place, on the faith of a dream, which was but an idle galimatias of sleep." Then he gave him money saying, "Help thee back herewith to thine own country."

And Shahrazad perceived the dawn of day and ceased to say her permitted say.

Now when it was the Three Hundred and Fifty-Second Night, she said, It hath reached me, O auspicious King, that the Wali gave the Baghdad man some silvers, saying, "Help thee back herewith to thine own country"; and he took the money and set out upon his homewards march. Now the house the Wali had described was the man's own house in Baghdad; so the wayfarer returned thither and, digging underneath the fountain in his garden, discovered a great treasure. And thus Allah gave him abundant fortune; and a marvellous coincidence occurred.

Charlotte Brontë

Jane Eyre
1847

Charlotte Brontë was the eldest of the three literary Brontë sisters. In Chapter 21, the narrator—and title character—tells us of the fearful dream foretelling her future.

Presentiments are strange things! and so are sympathies; and so are signs; and the three combined make one mystery to which humanity has not yet found the key. I never laughed at presentiments in my life, because I have had strange ones of my own. Sympathies, I believe, exist (for instance, between far-distant, long-absent, wholly estranged relatives asserting, notwithstanding their alienation, the unity of the source to which each traces his origin) whose workings baffle mortal comprehension. And signs, for aught we know, may be but the sympathies of Nature with man.

When I was a little girl, only six years old, I one night heard Bessie Leaven say to Martha Abbot that she had been dreaming about a little child; and that to dream of children was a sure sign of trouble, either to one's self or one's kin. The saying might have worn out of my memory, had not a circumstance immediately followed which served indelibly to fix it there. The next day Bessie was sent for home to the deathbed of her little sister.

Of late I had often recalled this saying and this incident; for during the past week scarcely a night had gone over my couch that had not brought with it a dream of an infant, which I sometimes hushed in my arms, sometimes dandled on my knee, sometimes watched playing with daisies on a lawn, or again, dabbling its hands in running water. It was a wailing child this night, and a laughing one the next: now it nestled close to me, and now it ran from me; but whatever mood the apparition evinced, whatever aspect it wore, it failed not for seven successive nights to meet me the moment I entered the land of slumber.

I did not like this iteration of one idea—this strange recurrence of one image, and I grew nervous as bedtime approached and the hour of the vision drew near. It was from companionship with this baby-phantom I had been roused on that moonlight night when I heard the cry; and it was on the afternoon of the day following I was summoned downstairs by a message that some one wanted me in Mrs. Fairfax's room. On repairing thither, I found a man waiting for me, having the appearance of a gentleman's servant: he was dressed in deep mourning, and the hat he held in his hand was surrounded with a crape band.

"I daresay you hardly remember me, Miss," he said, rising as I entered; "but my name is Leaven: I lived coachman with Mrs. Reed when you were at Gateshead, eight or nine years since, and I live there still."

"Oh, Robert! how do you do? I remember you very well: you used to give me a ride sometimes on Miss Georgiana's bay pony. And how is Bessie? You are married to Bessie?"

"Yes, Miss: my wife is very hearty, thank you; she brought me another little one about two months since—we have three now—and both mother and child are thriving."

"And are the family well at the house, Robert?"

"I am sorry I can't give you better news of them, Miss: they are very badly at present—in great trouble."

"I hope no one is dead," I said, glancing at his black dress. He too looked down at the crape round his hat and replied—

"Mr. John died yesterday was a week, at his chambers in London."

"Mr. John?"

"Yes."

"And how does his mother bear it?"

"Why, you see, Miss Eyre, it is not a common mishap: his life has been very wild: these last three years he gave himself up to strange ways, and his death was shocking."

"I heard from Bessie he was not doing well."

"Doing well! He could not do worse: he ruined his health and his estate amongst the worst men and the worst women. He got into debt and into jail: his mother helped him out twice, but as soon as he was free he returned to his old companions and habits. His head was not strong: the knaves he lived amongst fooled him beyond anything I ever heard. He came down to Gateshead about three weeks ago and wanted missis to give up all to him. Missis refused: her means have long been much reduced by his extravagance; so he went back again, and the next news was that he was dead. How he died, God knows!—they say he killed himself."

I was silent: the tidings were frightful.

Emily Brontë

Wuthering Heights
1847

In Chapter 3, Mr. Lockwood, the confident narrator who has rented a domicile from the mysteriously surly Mr. Heathcliff, spends a night in Heathcliff's snowbound house.

I began to nod drowsily over the dim page: my eye wandered from manuscript to print. I saw a red ornamented title "Seventy Times Seven, and the First of the Seventy-First. A Pious Discourse delivered by the Reverend Jabez Branderham, in the Chapel of Gimmerden Sough." And while I was, half-consciously, worrying my brain to guess what

Jabez Branderham would make of his subject, I sank back in bed, and fell asleep. Alas, for the effects of bad tea and bad temper! What else could it be that made me pass such a terrible night? I don't remember another that I can at all compare with it since I was capable of suffering.

I began to dream, almost before I ceased to be sensible of my locality. I thought it was morning; and I had set out on my way home, with Joseph for a guide. The snow lay yards deep in our road; and, as we floundered on, my companion wearied me with constant reproaches that I had not brought a pilgrim's staff: telling me that I could never get into the house without one, and boastfully flourishing a heavy-headed cudgel, which I understood to be so denominated. For a moment I considered it absurd that I should need such a weapon to gain admittance into my own residence. Then a new idea flashed across me. I was not going there: we were journeying to hear the famous Jabez Branderham preach, from the text "Seventy Times Seven"; and either Joseph, the preacher, or I had committed the "First of the Seventy-First," and were to be publicly exposed and excommunicated.

We came to the chapel. I have passed it really in my walks, twice or thrice; it lies in a hollow, between two hills: an elevated hollow, near a swamp, whose peaty moisture is said to answer all the purposes of embalming on the few corpses deposited there. The roof has been kept whole hitherto; but as the clergyman's stipend is only twenty pounds per annum, and a house with two rooms, threatening speedily to determine into one, no clergyman will undertake the duties of pastor: especially as it is currently reported that his flock would rather let him starve than increase the living by one penny from their own pockets. However, in my dream, Jabez had a full and attentive congregation; and he preached—good God! what a sermon; divided into *four hundred and ninety* parts, each fully equal to an ordinary address from the pulpit, and each discussing a separate sin! Where he searched for them, I cannot tell. He had his private manner of interpreting the phrase, and it seemed necessary the brother should sin different sins on every occasion. They were of the most curious character: odd transgressions that I never imagined previously.

Oh, how weary I grow. How I writhed, and yawned, and nodded, and revived! How I pinched and pricked myself, and rubbed my eyes, and stood up, and sat down again, and nudged Joseph to inform me if he would *ever* have done. I was condemned to hear all out: finally, he reached the *"First of the Seventy-First."* At that crisis, a sudden inspiration descended on me; I was moved to rise and denounce

Jabez Branderham as the sinner of the sin that no Christian need pardon.

"Sir," I exclaimed, "sitting here within these four walls, at one stretch, I have endured and forgiven the four hundred and ninety heads of your discourse. Seventy times seven times have I plucked up my hat and been about to depart—Seventy times seven times have you preposterously forced me to resume my seat. The four hundred and ninety-first is too much. Fellow-martyrs, have at him! Drag him down, and crush him to atoms, that the place which knows him may know him no more!"

"*Thou art the man!*" cried Jabez, after a solemn pause, leaning over his cushion. "Seventy times seven times didst thou gapingly contort thy visage—seventy times seven did I take counsel with my soul—Lo, this is human weakness: this also may be absolved! The First of the Seventy-First is come. Brethren, execute upon him the judgement written. Such honour have all His saints!"

With that concluding word, the whole assembly, exalting their pilgrim's staves, rushed round me in a body; and I, having no weapon to raise in self-defence, commenced grappling with Joseph, my nearest and most ferocious assailant, for his. In the confluence of the multitude, several clubs crossed; blows, aimed at me, fell on other sconces. Presently the whole chapel resounded with rappings and counter rappings: every man's hand was against his neighbour; and Branderham, unwilling to remain idle, poured forth his zeal in a shower of loud taps on the boards of the pulpit, which responded so smartly that, at last, to my unspeakable relief, they woke me. And what was it that had suggested the tremendous tumult? What had played Jabez's part in the row? Merely the branch of a fir-tree that touched my lattice as the blast wailed by, and rattled its dry cones against the panes! I listened doubtingly an instant; detected the disturber, then turned and dozed, and dreamt again: if possible, still more disagreeably than before.

This time, I remembered I was lying in the oak closet, and I heard distinctly the gusty wind, and the driving of the snow; I heard, also, the fir bough repeat its teasing sound, and ascribed it to the right cause: but it annoyed me so much, that I resolved to silence it, if possible; and, I thought, I rose and endeavoured to unhasp the casement. The hook was soldered into the staple: a circumstance observed by me when awake, but forgotten. "I must stop it, nevertheless!" I muttered, knocking my knuckles through the glass, and stretching an arm out to seize the importunate branch; instead of which, my fingers closed on the fingers of a little, ice-cold hand! The intense horror of nightmare came over me: I tried to draw back my arm, but the hand clung to it, and a most melancholy voice sobbed, "Let me in—let me in!" "Who are you?" I asked, struggling, meanwhile, to disengage myself. "Catherine Linton," it replied, shiveringly (why did I think of *Linton*? I had read *Earnshaw* twenty times for Linton) "I'm come home: I'd lost my way on the moor!" As it spoke, I discerned, obscurely, a child's face looking through the window. Terror made me cruel; and, finding it useless to attempt shaking the creature off, I pulled its wrist on to the broken pane, and rubbed it to and fro till the blood ran down and soaked the bedclothes: still it wailed, "Let me in!" and maintained its tenacious gripe, almost maddening me with fear. "How can I!" I said at length. "Let *me* go, if you want me to let you in!" The fingers relaxed, I snatched mine through the hole, hurriedly piled the books up in a pyramid against it, and stopped my ears to exclude the lamentable prayer. I seemed to keep them closed above a quarter of an hour; yet, the instant I listened again, there was the doleful cry moaning on! "Begone!" I shouted. "I'll never let you in, not if you beg for twenty years." "It is twenty years," mourned the voice: "twenty years. I've been a waif for twenty years!" Thereat began a feeble scratching outside, and the pile of books moved as if thrust forward. I tried to jump up; but could not stir a limb; and so yelled aloud, in a frenzy of fright. To my confusion, I discovered the yell was not ideal: hasty footsteps approached my chamber door; somebody pushed it open, with a vigorous hand, and a light glimmered through the squares at the top of the bed. I sat shuddering yet, and wiping the perspiration from my forehead: the intruder appeared to hesitate, and muttered to himself. At last, he said, in a half-whisper, plainly not expecting an answer, "Is any one here?" I considered it best to confess my presence; for I knew Heathcliff's accents, and feared he might search further, if I kept quiet. With this intention, I turned and opened the panels. I shall not soon forget the effect my action produced.

Heathcliff stood near the entrance, in his shirt and trousers; with a candle dripping over his fingers, and his face as white as the wall behind him. The first creak of the oak startled him like an electric shock: the light leaped from his hold to a distance of some feet, and his agitation was so extreme, that he could hardly pick it up.

"It is only your guest, sir," I called out, desirous to spare him the humiliation of exposing his cowardice further. "I had the misfortune to scream in my sleep, owing to a frightful nightmare. I'm sorry I disturbed you."

"Oh, God confound you, Mr. Lockwood! I wish you were at the—" commenced my host, setting the candle on a chair, because he found it impossible to hold it steady. "And who showed you up into this room?" he continued, crushing his nails into his palms, and grinding his teeth to subdue the maxillary convulsions. "Who was it? I've a good mind to turn them out of the house this moment?"

"It was your servant Zillah," I replied, flinging myself on to the floor, and rapidly resuming my garments. "I should not care if you did, Mr. Heathcliff; she richly deserves it. I suppose that she wanted to get another proof that the place was haunted, at my expense. Well, it is— swarming with ghosts and goblins! You have reason in shutting it up, I assure you. No one will thank you for a doze in such a den!"

"What do you mean?" asked Heathcliff, "and what are you doing? Lie down and finish out the night, since you *are* here; but, for heaven's sake! don't repeat that horrid noise: nothing could excuse it, unless you were having your throat cut!"

"If the little fiend had got in at the window, she probably would have strangled me!" I returned. "I'm not going to endure the persecutions of your hospitable ancestors again. Was not the Reverend Jabez Branderham akin to you on the mother's side? And that minx, Catherine Linton, or Earnshaw, or however she was called—she must have been a changeling—wicked little soul! She told me she had been walking the earth these twenty years: a just punishment for her mortal transgressions, I've no doubt!"

Scarcely were these words uttered when I recollected the association of Heathcliff's with Catherine's name in the book, which had completely slipped from my memory, till thus awakened. I blushed at my inconsideration: but, without showing further consciousness of the offence, I hastened to add, "The truth is, sir, I passed the first part of the night in—" Here I stopped afresh—I was about to say "perusing those old volumes," then it would have revealed my knowledge of their written, as well as their printed, contents; so, correcting myself, I went on, "in spelling over the name scratched on that window-ledge. A monotonous occupation, calculated to set me asleep, like counting, or—"

"What *can* you mean by talking in this way to *me*!" thundered Heathcliff with savage vehemence. "How—how *dare* you, under my roof?—God! he's mad to speak so!" And he struck his forehead with rage.

I did not know whether to resent this language or pursue my explanation; but he seemed so powerfully affected that I took pity and proceeded with my dreams; affirming I had never heard the appellation of "Catherine Linton" before, but reading it often over produced an impression which personified itself when I had no longer my imagination under control. Heathcliff gradually fell back into the shelter of the bed, as I spoke; finally sitting down almost concealed behind it. I guessed, however, by his irregular and intercepted breathing, that he struggled to vanquish an excess of violent emotion. Not liking to show him that I had heard the conflict, I continued my toilette rather noisily, looked at my watch, and soliloquised on the length of the night: "Not three o'clock yet! I could have taken oath it had been six. Time stagnates here: we must surely have retired to rest at eight!"

"Always at nine in winter, and rise at four," said my host, suppressing a groan: and, as I fancied, by the motion of his arm's shadow, dashing a tear from his eyes. "Mr. Lockwood," he added, "you may go into my room: you'll only be in the way, coming downstairs so early: and your childish outcry has sent sleep to the devil for me."

"And for me, too," I replied. "I'll walk in the yard till daylight, and then I'll be off; and you need not dread a repetition of my intrusion. I'm now quite cured of seeking pleasure in society, be it country or town. A sensible man ought to find sufficient company in himself."

"Delightful company!" muttered Heathcliff. "Take the candle, and go where you please. I shall join you directly. Keep out of the yard, though, the dogs are unchained; and the house—Juno mounts sentinel there, and—nay, you can only ramble about the steps and passages. But, away with you! I'll come in two minutes!"

I obeyed, so far as to quit the chamber; when, ignorant where the narrow lobbies led, I stood still, and was witness, involuntarily, to a piece of superstition on the part of my landlord which belied, oddly, his apparent sense. He got on to the bed, and wrenched open the lattice, bursting, as he pulled at it, into an uncontrollable passion of tears. "Come in! come in!" he sobbed. "Cathy, do come. Oh, do— *once* more! Oh! my heart's darling! hear me *this* time, Catherine, at last!" The spectre showed a spectre's ordinary caprice: it gave no sign of being; but the snow and wind whirled wildly through, even reaching my station, and blowing out the light.

Miguel de Cervantes

Don Quixote (Chapter 23: Of the Wonderful Things the
Incomparable Don Quixote Said He Saw in the Profound
Cave of Montesinos, the Impossibility and Magnitude of
Which Cause This Adventure to Be Deemed Apocryphal)
1605

Don Quixote *remains a thoroughly modern novel, despite the fact
that Cervantes wrote it at the beginning of the seventeenth century.
How could one explain the deluded hero Don Quixote's story of his
adventure in the cave except how his servant and sidekick Sancho Panza
takes it—as an elaborated, embellished dream? Don Quixote declares
that "a profound sleep fell upon me, and when I least expected it,
I know not how, I awoke and found myself in the midst of the most
beautiful, delightful meadow that nature could produce or the most lively
human imagination conceive. I opened my eyes, I rubbed them, and
found I was not asleep but thoroughly awake." A vivid dream prompts
one's imagination to expand and order it, and yet, as Don Quixote
says, what has happened to him in the cave took place for days, so how
could it have been a* dream? *Panza's mockery does not trouble him.*

It was about four in the afternoon when the sun, veiled in clouds,
with subdued light and tempered beams, enabled Don Quixote to
relate, without heat or inconvenience, what he had seen in the cave
of Montesinos to his two illustrious hearers [i.e., Sancho Panza and
Don Quixote's cousin], and he began as follows:

"A matter of some twelve or fourteen times a man's height down
in this pit, on the right-hand side, there is a recess or space, roomy
enough to contain a large cart with its mules. A little light reaches it
through some chinks or crevices, communicating with it and open
to the surface of the earth. This recess or space I perceived when I was
already growing weary and disgusted at finding myself hanging suspended by the rope, travelling downwards into that dark region
without any certainty or knowledge of where I was going, so I resolved
to enter it and rest myself for a while. I called out, telling you not to
let out more rope until I bade you, but you cannot have heard me.
I then gathered in the rope you were sending me, and making a coil
or pile of it I seated myself upon it, ruminating and considering what
I was to do to lower myself to the bottom, having no one to hold
me up; and as I was thus deep in thought and perplexity, suddenly

and without provocation a profound sleep fell upon me, and when I least expected it, I know not how, I awoke and found myself in the midst of the most beautiful, delightful meadow that nature could produce or the most lively human imagination conceive. I opened my eyes, I rubbed them, and found I was not asleep but thoroughly awake. Nevertheless, I felt my head and breast to satisfy myself whether it was I myself who was there or some empty delusive phantom; but touch, feeling, the collected thoughts that passed through my mind, all convinced me that I was the same then and there that I am this moment. Next there presented itself to my sight a stately royal palace or castle, with walls that seemed built of clear transparent crystal; and through two great doors that opened wide therein, I saw coming forth and advancing towards me a venerable old man, clad in a long gown of mulberry-coloured serge that trailed upon the ground. On his shoulders and breast he had a green satin collegiate hood, and covering his head a black Milanese bonnet, and his snow-white beard fell below his girdle. He carried no arms whatever, nothing but a rosary of beads bigger than fair-sized filberts, each tenth bead being like a moderate ostrich egg; his bearing, his gait, his dignity and imposing presence held me spellbound and wondering. He approached me, and the first thing he did was to embrace me closely, and then he said to me, 'For a long time now, O valiant knight Don Quixote of La Mancha, we who are here enchanted in these solitudes have been hoping to see thee, that thou mayest make known to the world what is shut up and concealed in this deep cave, called the cave of Montesinos, which thou hast entered, an achievement reserved for thy invincible heart and stupendous courage alone to attempt. Come with me, illustrious sir, and I will show thee the marvels hidden within this transparent castle, whereof I am the alcaide and perpetual warden; for I am Montesinos himself, from whom the cave takes its name.'

"The instant he told me he was Montesinos, I asked him if the story they told in the world above here was true, that he had taken out the heart of his great friend Durandarte from his breast with a little dagger, and carried it to the lady Belerma, as his friend when at the point of death had commanded him. He said in reply that they spoke the truth in every respect except as to the dagger, for it was not a dagger, nor little, but a burnished poniard sharper than an awl."

"That poniard must have been made by Ramon de Hoces the Sevillian," said Sancho.

"I do not know," said Don Quixote; "it could not have been by that poniard maker, however, because Ramon de Hoces was a man of yesterday, and the affair of Roncesvalles, where this mishap occurred, was long ago; but the question is of no great importance, nor does it affect or make any alteration in the truth or substance of the story."

"That is true," said the cousin; "continue, Señor Don Quixote, for I am listening to you with the greatest pleasure in the world."

"And with no less do I tell the tale," said Don Quixote; "and so, to proceed—the venerable Montesinos led me into the palace of crystal, where, in a lower chamber, strangely cool and entirely of alabaster, was an elaborately wrought marble tomb, upon which I beheld, stretched at full length, a knight, not of bronze, or marble, or jasper, as are seen on other tombs, but of actual flesh and bone. His right hand (which seemed to me somewhat hairy and sinewy, a sign of great strength in its owner) lay on the side of his heart; but before I could put any question to Montesinos, he, seeing me gazing at the tomb in amazement, said to me, 'This is my friend Durandarte, flower and mirror of the true lovers and valiant knights of his time. He is held enchanted here, as I myself and many others are, by that French enchanter Merlin, who, they say, was the devil's son; but my belief is, not that he was the devil's son, but that he knew, as the saying is, a point more than the devil. How or why he enchanted us, no one knows, but time will tell, and I suspect that time is not far off. What I marvel at is, that I know it to be as sure as that it is now day, that Durandarte ended his life in my arms, and that, after his death, I took out his heart with my own hands; and indeed it must have weighed more than two pounds, for, according to naturalists, he who has a large heart is more largely endowed with valour than he who has a small one. Then, as this is the case, and as the knight did really die, how comes it that he now moans and sighs from time to time, as if he were still alive?'

"As he said this, the wretched Durandarte cried out in a loud voice:

> O cousin Montesinos!
> 'Twas my last request of thee,
> When my soul hath left the body,
> And that lying dead I be,
> With thy poniard or thy dagger
> Cut the heart from out my breast,
> And bear it to Belerma.
> This was my last request.

"On hearing which, the venerable Montesinos fell on his knees before the unhappy knight, and with tearful eyes exclaimed, 'Long since, Señor Durandarte, my beloved cousin, long since have I done what you bade me on that sad day when I lost you; I took out your heart as well as I could, not leaving an atom of it in your breast, I wiped it with a lace handkerchief, and I took the road to France with it, having first laid you in the bosom of the earth with tears enough to wash and cleanse my hands of the blood that covered them after wandering among your bowels; and more by token, O cousin of my soul, at the first village I came to after leaving Roncesvalles, I sprinkled a little salt upon your heart to keep it sweet, and bring it, if not fresh, at least pickled, into the presence of the lady Belerma, whom, together with you, myself, Guadiana your squire, the duenna Ruidera and her seven daughters and two nieces, and many more of your friends and acquaintances, the sage Merlin has been keeping enchanted here these many years; and although more than five hundred have gone by, not one of us has died; Ruidera and her daughters and nieces alone are missing, and these, because of the tears they shed, Merlin, out of the compassion he seems to have felt for them, changed into so many lakes, which to this day in the world of the living, and in the province of La Mancha, are called the Lakes of Ruidera. The seven daughters belong to the kings of Spain and the two nieces to the knights of a very holy order called the Order of St. John. Guadiana your squire, likewise bewailing your fate, was changed into a river of his own name, but when he came to the surface and beheld the sun of another heaven, so great was his grief at finding he was leaving you, that he plunged into the bowels of the earth; however, as he cannot help following his natural course, he from time to time comes forth and shows himself to the sun and the world. The lakes aforesaid send him their waters, and with these, and others that come to him, he makes a grand and imposing entrance into Portugal; but for all that, go where he may, he shows his melancholy and sadness, and takes no pride in breeding dainty choice fish, only coarse and tasteless sorts, very different from those of the golden Tagus. All this that I tell you now, O cousin mine, I have told you many times before, and as you make no answer, I fear that either you believe me not, or do not hear me, whereat I feel God knows what grief. I have now news to give you, which, if it serves not to alleviate your sufferings, will not in any wise increase them. Know that you have here before you (open your eyes and you will see) that great knight of whom the sage Merlin has prophesied such great things; that Don Quixote of La

Mancha I mean, who has again, and to better purpose than in past times, revived in these days knight-errantry, long since forgotten, and by whose intervention and aid it may be we shall be disenchanted; for great deeds are reserved for great men.'

"'And if that may not be,' said the wretched Durandarte in a low and feeble voice, 'if that may not be, then, my cousin, I say "patience and shuffle"'; and turning over on his side, he relapsed into his former silence without uttering another word.

"And now there was heard a great outcry and lamentation, accompanied by deep sighs and bitter sobs. I looked round, and through the crystal wall I saw passing through another chamber a procession of two lines of fair damsels all clad in mourning, and with white turbans of Turkish fashion on their heads. Behind, in the rear of these, there came a lady, for so from her dignity she seemed to be, also clad in black, with a white veil so long and ample that it swept the ground. Her turban was twice as large as the largest of any of the others; her eyebrows met, her nose was rather flat, her mouth was large but with ruddy lips, and her teeth, of which at times she allowed a glimpse, were seen to be sparse and ill-set, though as white as peeled almonds. She carried in her hands a fine cloth, and in it, as well as I could make out, a heart that had been mummied, so parched and dried was it. Montesinos told me that all those forming the procession were the attendants of Durandarte and Belerma, who were enchanted there with their master and mistress, and that the last, she who carried the heart in the cloth, was the lady Belerma, who, with her damsels, four days in the week went in procession singing, or rather weeping, dirges over the body and miserable heart of his cousin; and that if she appeared to me somewhat ill-favoured or not so beautiful as fame reported her, it was because of the bad nights and worse days that she passed in that enchantment, as I could see by the great dark circles round her eyes, and her sickly complexion; 'her sallowness, and the rings round her eyes,' said he, 'are not caused by the periodical ailment usual with women, for it is many months and even years since she has had any, but by the grief her own heart suffers because of that which she holds in her hand perpetually, and which recalls and brings back to her memory the sad fate of her lost lover; were it not for this, hardly would the great Dulcinea del Toboso, so celebrated in all these parts, and even in the world, come up to her for beauty, grace, and gaiety.'

"'Hold hard!' said I at this, 'tell your story as you ought, Señor Don Montesinos, for you know very well that all comparisons are odious, and there is no occasion to compare one person with another; the peerless Dulcinea del Toboso is what she is, and the lady Doña Belerma is what *she* is and has been, and that's enough.' To which he made answer, 'Forgive me, Señor Don Quixote; I own I was wrong and spoke unadvisedly in saying that the lady Dulcinea could scarcely come up to the lady Belerma; for it were enough for me to have learned, by what means I know not, that you are her knight, to make me bite my tongue out before I compared her to anything save heaven itself.' After this apology which the great Montesinos made me, my heart recovered itself from the shock I had received in hearing my lady compared with Belerma."

"Still I wonder," said Sancho, "that your worship did not get upon the old fellow and bruise every bone of him with kicks, and pluck his beard until you didn't leave a hair in it."

"Nay, Sancho, my friend," said Don Quixote, "it would not have been right in me to do that, for we are all bound to pay respect to the aged, even though they be not knights, but especially to those who are, and who are enchanted; I only know I gave him as good as he brought in the many other questions and answers we exchanged."

"I cannot understand, Señor Don Quixote," remarked the cousin here, "how it is that your worship, in such a short space of time as you have been below there, could have seen so many things, and said and answered so much."

"How long is it since I went down?" asked Don Quixote.

"Little better than an hour," replied Sancho.

"That cannot be," returned Don Quixote, "because night overtook me while I was there, and day came, and it was night again and day again three times; so that, by my reckoning, I have been three days in those remote regions beyond our ken."

"My master must be right," replied Sancho; "for as everything that has happened to him is by enchantment, maybe what seems to us an hour would seem three days and nights there."

"That's it," said Don Quixote.

"And did your worship eat anything all that time, señor?" asked the cousin.

"I never touched a morsel," answered Don Quixote, "nor did I feel hunger, or think of it."

"And do the enchanted eat?" said the cousin.

"They neither eat," said Don Quixote; "nor are they subject to the greater excrements, though it is thought that their nails, beards, and hair grow."

"And do the enchanted sleep, now, señor?" asked Sancho.

"Certainly not," replied Don Quixote; "at least, during those three days I was with them not one of them closed an eye, nor did I either."

"The proverb, 'Tell me what company thou keepest and I'll tell thee what thou art,' is to the point here," said Sancho; "your worship keeps company with enchanted people that are always fasting and watching; what wonder is it, then, that you neither eat nor sleep while you are with them? But forgive me, señor, if I say that of all this you have told us now, may God take me—I was just going to say the devil—if I believe a single particle."

"What!" said the cousin, "has Señor Don Quixote, then, been lying? Why, even if he wished it he has not had time to imagine and put together such a host of lies."

"I don't believe my master lies," said Sancho.

"If not, what dost thou believe?" asked Don Quixote.

"I believe," replied Sancho, "that this Merlin, or those enchanters who enchanted the whole crew your worship says you saw and discoursed with down there, stuffed your imagination or your mind with all this rigmarole you have been treating us to, and all that is still to come."

"All that might be, Sancho," replied Don Quixote; "but it is not so, for everything that I have told you I saw with my own eyes, and touched with my own hands. But what will you say when I tell you now how, among the countless other marvellous things Montesinos showed me (of which at leisure and at the proper time I will give thee an account in the course of our journey, for they would not be all in place here), he showed me three country girls who went skipping and capering like goats over the pleasant fields there, and the instant I beheld them I knew one to be the peerless Dulcinea del Toboso, and the other two those same country girls that were with her and that we spoke to on the road from El Toboso! I asked Montesinos if he knew them, and he told me he did not, but he thought they must be some enchanted ladies of distinction, for it was only a few days before that they had made their appearance in those meadows; but I was not to be surprised at that, because there were a great many other ladies there of times past and present, enchanted in various strange shapes, and among them he had recognised Queen Guinevere and her dame Quintañona, she who poured out the wine for Lancelot when he came from Britain."

When Sancho Panza heard his master say this he was ready to take leave of his senses, or die with laughter; for, as he knew the real truth about the pretended enchantment of Dulcinea, in which he himself had been the enchanter and concocter of all the evidence, he made up his mind at last that, beyond all doubt, his master was out of his wits and stark mad, so he said to him, "It was an evil hour, a worse season, and a sorrowful day, when your worship, dear master mine, went down to the other world, and an unlucky moment when you met with Señor Montesinos, who has sent you back to us like this. You were well enough here above in your full senses, such as God had given you, delivering maxims and giving advice at every turn, and not as you are now, talking the greatest nonsense that can be imagined."

"As I know thee, Sancho," said Don Quixote, "I heed not thy words."

"Nor I your worship's," said Sancho, "whether you beat me or kill me for those I have spoken, and will speak if you don't correct and mend your own. But tell me, while we are still at peace, how or by what did you recognise the lady our mistress; and if you spoke to her, what did you say, and what did she answer?"

"I recognised her," said Don Quixote, "by her wearing the same garments she wore when thou didst point her out to me. I spoke to her, but she did not utter a word in reply; on the contrary, she turned her back on me and took to flight, at such a pace that crossbow bolt could not have overtaken her. I wished to follow her, and would have done so had not Montesinos recommended me not to take the trouble as it would be useless, particularly as the time was drawing near when it would be necessary for me to quit the cavern. He told me, moreover, that in course of time he would let me know how he and Belerma, and Durandarte, and all who were there, were to be disenchanted. But of all I saw and observed down there, what gave me most pain was, that while Montesinos was speaking to me, one of the two companions of the hapless Dulcinea approached me on one without my having seen her coming, and with tears in her eyes said to me, in a low, agitated voice, 'My lady Dulcinea del Toboso kisses your worship's hands, and entreats you to do her the favour of letting her know how you are; and, being in great need, she also entreats your worship as earnestly as she can to be so good as to lend her half a dozen reals, or as much as you may have about you, on this new dimity petticoat that I have here; and she promises to repay them very speedily.' I was amazed and taken aback by such a message, and turning to Señor Montesinos I asked him, 'Is it possible, Señor Montesinos, that persons of distinction under enchantment can be in need?' To which he replied, 'Believe me, Señor Don Quixote, that which is called need is to be met with everywhere, and penetrates all quarters and reaches everyone, and does not spare even the enchanted; and as the lady Dulcinea del Toboso sends to beg those six reals, and the pledge is to all appearance a good one, there is nothing for it but to give them to her, for no doubt she must be in some great strait.' 'I will take no pledge of her,' I replied, 'nor yet can I give her what she asks, for all I have is four reals; which I gave (they were those which thou, Sancho, gavest me the other day to bestow in alms upon the poor I met along the road), and I said, 'Tell your mistress, my dear, that I am grieved to the heart because of her distresses, and wish I was a Fucar to remedy them, and that I would have her know that I cannot be, and ought not be, in health while deprived of the happiness of seeing her and enjoying her discreet conversation, and that I implore her as earnestly as I can, to allow herself to be seen and addressed by this her captive servant and forlorn knight. Tell her, too, that when she least expects it she will hear it announced that I have made an oath and vow after the fashion of that which the Marquis of Mantua made to avenge his nephew Baldwin, when he found him at the point of death in the heart of the mountains, which was, not to eat bread off a tablecloth, and other trifling matters which he added, until he had avenged him; and I will make the same to take no rest, and to roam the seven regions of the earth more thoroughly than the Infante Don Pedro of Portugal ever roamed them, until I have disenchanted her.' 'All that and more, you owe my lady,' the damsel's answer to me, and taking the four reals, instead of making me a curtsey she cut a caper, springing two full yards into the air."

"O blessed God!" exclaimed Sancho aloud at this, "is it possible that such things can be in the world, and that enchanters and enchantments can have such power in it as to have changed my master's right senses into a craze so full of absurdity! O señor, señor, for God's sake, consider yourself, have a care for your honour, and give no credit to this silly stuff that has left you scant and short of wits."

"Thou talkest in this way because thou lovest me, Sancho," said Don Quixote; "and not being experienced in the things of the world, everything that has some difficulty about it seems to thee impossible; but time will pass, as I said before, and I will tell thee some of the things I saw down there which will make thee believe what I have related now, the truth of which admits of neither reply nor question."

Anton Chekhov

"Sleepy"
1888

The Russian short story writer, doctor, and playwright describes the torment of a young servant girl whose masters do not allow her time to sleep while she cares for a colicky baby and manages the household chores: "The cradle creaks plaintively, Varka murmurs—and it all blends into that soothing music of the night to which it is so sweet to listen, when one is lying in bed. Now that music is merely irritating and oppressive, because it goads her to sleep, and she must not sleep; if Varka—God forbid!—should fall asleep, her master and mistress would beat her." This story is presented in its horrifying entirety.

Night. Varka, the little nurse, a girl of thirteen, is rocking the cradle in which the baby is lying, and humming hardly audibly:

> "Hush-a-bye, my baby wee,
> While I sing a song for thee."

A little green lamp is burning before the ikon; there is a string stretched from one end of the room to the other, on which baby-clothes and a pair of big black trousers are hanging. There is a big patch of green on the ceiling from the ikon lamp, and the baby-clothes and the trousers throw long shadows on the stove, on the cradle, and on Varka. . . . When the lamp begins to flicker, the green patch and the shadows come to life, and are set in motion, as though by the wind. It is stuffy. There is a smell of cabbage soup, and of the inside of a boot-shop.

The baby is crying. For a long while he has been hoarse and exhausted with crying; but he still goes on screaming, and there is no knowing when he will stop. And Varka is sleepy. Her eyes are glued together, her head droops, her neck aches. She cannot move her eyelids or her lips, and she feels as though her face is dried and wooden, as though her head has become as small as the head of a pin.

"Hush-a-bye, my baby wee," she hums, "while I cook the groats for thee . . ."

A cricket is churring in the stove. Through the door in the next room the master and the apprentice Afanasy are snoring. . . . The cradle creaks plaintively, Varka murmurs—and it all blends into that soothing music of the night to which it is so sweet to listen, when one is lying in bed. Now that music is merely irritating and oppressive, because it goads her to sleep, and she must not sleep; if Varka—God forbid!—should fall asleep, her master and mistress would beat her.

The lamp flickers. The patch of green and the shadows are set in motion, forcing themselves on Varka's fixed, half-open eyes, and in her half slumbering brain are fashioned into misty visions. She sees dark clouds chasing one another over the sky, and screaming like the baby. But then the wind blows, the clouds are gone, and Varka sees a broad high road covered with liquid mud; along the high road stretch files of wagons, while people with wallets on their backs are trudging along and shadows flit backwards and forwards; on both sides she can see forests through the cold harsh mist. All at once the people with their wallets and their shadows fall on the ground in the liquid mud. "What is that for?" Varka asks. "To sleep, to sleep!" they answer her. And they fall sound asleep, and sleep sweetly, while crows and magpies sit on the telegraph wires, scream like the baby, and try to wake them.

"Hush-a-bye, my baby wee, and I will sing a song to thee," murmurs Varka, and now she sees herself in a dark stuffy hut.

Her dead father, Yefim Stepanov, is tossing from side to side on the floor. She does not see him, but she hears him moaning and rolling on the floor from pain. "His guts have burst," as he says; the pain is so violent that he cannot utter a single word, and can only draw in his breath and clack his teeth like the rattling of a drum:

"Boo—boo—boo—boo . . ."

Her mother, Pelageya, has run to the master's house to say that Yefim is dying. She has been gone a long time, and ought to be back. Varka lies awake on the stove, and hears her father's "boo—boo—boo." And then she hears someone has driven up to the hut. It is a young doctor from the town, who has been sent from the big house where he is staying on a visit. The doctor comes into the hut; he cannot be seen in the darkness, but he can be heard coughing and rattling the door.

"Light a candle," he says.

"Boo—boo—boo," answers Yefim.

Pelageya rushes to the stove and begins looking for the broken pot with the matches. A minute passes in silence. The doctor, feeling in his pocket, lights a match.

"In a minute, sir, in a minute," says Pelageya. She rushes out of the hut, and soon afterwards comes back with a bit of candle.

Yefim's cheeks are rosy and his eyes are shining, and there is a peculiar keenness in his glance, as though he were seeing right through the hut and the doctor.

"Come, what is it? What are you thinking about?" says the doctor, bending down to him. "Aha! have you had this long?"

"What? Dying, your honour, my hour has come. . . . I am not to stay among the living . . ."

"Don't talk nonsense! We will cure you!"

"That's as you please, your honour, we humbly thank you, only we understand. . . . Since death has come, there it is."

The doctor spends a quarter of an hour over Yefim, then he gets up and says:

"I can do nothing. You must go into the hospital, there they will operate on you. Go at once . . . You must go! It's rather late, they will all be asleep in the hospital, but that doesn't matter, I will give you a note. Do you hear?"

"Kind sir, but what can he go in?" says Pelageya. "We have no horse."

"Never mind. I'll ask your master, he'll let you have a horse."

The doctor goes away, the candle goes out, and again there is the sound of "boo—boo—boo." Half an hour later someone drives up to the hut. A cart has been sent to take Yefim to the hospital. He gets ready and goes. . . .

But now it is a clear bright morning. Pelageya is not at home; she has gone to the hospital to find what is being done to Yefim. Somewhere there is a baby crying, and Varka hears someone singing with her own voice:

"Hush-a-bye, my baby wee, I will sing a song to thee."

Pelageya comes back; she crosses herself and whispers:

"They put him to rights in the night, but towards morning he gave up his soul to God. . . . The Kingdom of Heaven be his and peace everlasting. . . . They say he was taken too late. . . . He ought to have gone sooner. . . ."

Varka goes out into the road and cries there, but all at once some-one hits her on the back of her head so hard that her forehead knocks against a birch tree. She raises her eyes, and sees facing her, her master, the shoemaker.

"What are you about, you scabby slut?" he says. "The child is crying, and you are asleep!"

He gives her a sharp slap behind the ear, and she shakes her head, rocks the cradle, and murmurs her song. The green patch and the shadows from the trousers and the baby-clothes move up and down, nod to her, and soon take possession of her brain again. Again she sees the high road covered with liquid mud. The people with wallets on their backs and the shadows have lain down and are fast asleep. Looking at them, Varka has a passionate longing for sleep; she would lie down with enjoyment, but her mother Pelageya is walking beside her, hurrying her on. They are hastening together to the town to find situations.

"Give alms, for Christ's sake!" her mother begs of the people they meet. "Show us the Divine Mercy, kind-hearted gentlefolk!"

"Give the baby here!" a familiar voice answers." "Give the baby here!" the same voice repeats, this time harshly and angrily. "Are you asleep, you wretched girl?"

Varka jumps up, and looking round grasps what is the matter: there is no high road, no Pelageya, no people meeting them, there is only her mistress, who has come to feed the baby, and is standing in the middle of the room. While the stout, broad-shouldered woman nurses the child and soothes it, Varka stands looking at her and waiting till she has done. And outside the windows the air is already turning blue, the shadows and the green patch on the ceiling are visibly growing pale, it will soon be morning.

"Take him," says her mistress, buttoning up her chemise over her bosom; "he is crying. He must be bewitched."

Varka takes the baby, puts him in the cradle and begins rocking it again. The green patch and the shadows gradually disappear, and now there is nothing to force itself on her eyes and cloud her brain. But she is as sleepy as before, fearfully sleepy! Varka lays her head on the edge of the cradle, and rocks her whole body to overcome her sleepiness, but yet her eyes are glued together, and her head is heavy.

"Varka, heat the stove!" she hears the master's voice through the door.

So it is time to get up and set to work. Varka leaves the cradle, and runs to the shed for firewood. She is glad. When one moves and runs about, one is not so sleepy as when one is sitting down. She brings the wood, heats the stove, and feels that her wooden face is getting supple again, and that her thoughts are growing clearer.

"Varka, set the samovar!" shouts her mistress.

Varka splits a piece of wood, but has scarcely time to light the splinters and put them in the samovar, when she hears a fresh order:

"Varka, clean the master's goloshes!"

She sits down on the floor, cleans the goloshes, and thinks how nice it would be to put her head into a big deep golosh, and have a little nap in it. . . . And all at once the golosh grows, swells, fills up the whole room. Varka drops the brush, but at once shakes her head, opens her eyes wide, and tries to look at things so that they may not grow big and move before her eyes.

"Varka, wash the steps outside; I am ashamed for the customers to see them!"

Varka washes the steps, sweeps and dusts the rooms, then heats another stove and runs to the shop. There is a great deal of work: she hasn't one minute free.

But nothing is so hard as standing in the same place at the kitchen table peeling potatoes. Her head droops over the table, the potatoes dance before her eyes, the knife tumbles out of her hand while her fat, angry mistress is moving about near her with her sleeves tucked up, talking so loud that it makes a ringing in Varka's ears. It is agonising, too, to wait at dinner, to wash, to sew, there are minutes when she longs to flop on to the floor regardless of everything, and to sleep.

The day passes. Seeing the windows getting dark, Varka presses her temples that feel as though they were made of wood, and smiles, though she does not know why. The dusk of evening caresses her eyes that will hardly keep open, and promises her sound sleep soon. In the evening visitors come.

"Varka, set the samovar!" shouts her mistress.

The samovar is a little one, and before the visitors have drunk all the tea they want, she has to heat it five times. After tea Varka stands for a whole hour on the same spot, looking at the visitors, and waiting for orders.

"Varka, run and buy three bottles of beer!"

She starts off, and tries to run as quickly as she can, to drive away sleep.

"Varka, fetch some vodka! Varka, where's the corkscrew? Varka, clean a herring!"

But now, at last, the visitors have gone; the lights are put out, the master and mistress go to bed.

"Varka, rock the baby!" she hears the last order.

The cricket churrs in the stove; the green patch on the ceiling and the shadows from the trousers and the baby-clothes force themselves on Varka's half-opened eyes again, wink at her and cloud her mind.

"Hush-a-bye, my baby wee," she murmurs, "and I will sing a song to thee."

And the baby screams, and is worn out with screaming. Again Varka sees the muddy high road, the people with wallets, her mother Pelageya, her father Yefim. She understands everything, she recognises everyone, but through her half sleep she cannot understand the force which binds her, hand and foot, weighs upon her, and prevents her from living. She looks round, searches for that force that she may escape from it, but she cannot find it. At last, tired to death, she does her very utmost, strains her eyes, looks up at the flickering green patch, and listening to the screaming, finds the foe who will not let her live.

That foe is the baby.

She laughs. It seems strange to her that she has failed to grasp such a simple thing before. The green patch, the shadows, and the cricket seem to laugh and wonder too.

The hallucination takes possession of Varka. She gets up from her stool, and with a broad smile on her face and wide unblinking eyes, she walks up and down the room. She feels pleased and tickled at the thought that she will be rid directly of the baby that binds her hand and foot. . . . Kill the baby and then sleep, sleep, sleep. . . .

Laughing and winking and shaking her fingers at the green patch, Varka steals up to the cradle and bends over the baby. When she has strangled him, she quickly lies down on the floor, laughs with delight that she can sleep, and in a minute is sleeping as sound as the dead.

Charles Dickens

Oliver Twist
1837

This scene from one of Dickens's most popular novels seems like a dream. Oliver Twist believes in his vision, and Dickens suggests consciousness remains while we dream: "There is a kind of sleep that steals upon us sometimes, which, while it holds the body prisoner, does not free the mind from a sense of things about it, and enable it to ramble at its pleasure."

The little room in which he was accustomed to sit, when busy at his books, was on the ground-floor, at the back of the house. It was quite a cottage-room, with a lattice-window: around which were clusters of jessamine and honeysuckle, that crept over the casement, and filled the place with their delicious perfume. It looked into a garden, whence a wicket-gate opened into a small paddock; all beyond, was fine meadow-land and wood. There was no other dwelling near, in that direction; and the prospect it commanded was very extensive.

One beautiful evening, when the first shades of twilight were beginning to settle upon the earth, Oliver sat at this window, intent upon his books. He had been poring over them for some time; and, as the day had been uncommonly sultry, and he had exerted himself a great deal, it is no disparagement to the authors, whoever they may have been, to say, that gradually and by slow degrees, he fell asleep.

There is a kind of sleep that steals upon us sometimes, which, while it holds the body prisoner, does not free the mind from a sense of things about it, and enable it to ramble at its pleasure. So far as an overpowering heaviness, a prostration of strength, and an utter inability to control our thoughts or power of motion, can be called sleep, this is it; and yet, we have a consciousness of all that is going on about us, and, if we dream at such a time, words which are really spoken, or sounds which really exist at the moment, accommodate themselves with surprising readiness to our visions, until reality and imagination become so strangely blended that it is afterwards almost a matter of impossibility to separate the two. Nor is this the most striking phenomenon incidental to such a state. It is an undoubted fact, that although our senses of touch and sight be for the time dead, yet our sleeping thoughts, and the visionary scenes that pass before us, will be influenced and materially influenced, by the *mere silent presence* of some external object; which may not have been near us when we closed our eyes: and of whose vicinity we have had no waking consciousness.

Oliver knew, perfectly well, that he was in his own little room; that his books were lying on the table before him; that the sweet air was stirring among the creeping plants outside. And yet he was asleep. Suddenly, the scene changed; the air became close and confined; and he thought, with a glow of terror, that he was in the Jew's house again. There sat the hideous old man, in his accustomed corner, pointing at him, and whispering to another man, with his face averted, who sat beside him.

"Hush, my dear!" he thought he heard the Jew say; "it is he, sure enough. Come away."

"He!" the other man seemed to answer; "could I mistake him, think you? If a crowd of ghosts were to put themselves into his exact shape, and he stood amongst them, there is something that would tell me how to point him out. If you buried him fifty feet deep, and took me across his grave, I fancy I should know, if there wasn't a mark above it, that he lay buried there?"

The man seemed to say this, with such dreadful hatred, that Oliver awoke with the fear, and started up.

Good Heaven! what was that, which sent the blood tingling to his heart, and deprived him of his voice, and of power to move! There—there—at the window—close before him—so close, that he could have almost touched him before he started back: with his eyes peering into the room, and meeting his: there stood the Jew! And beside him, white with rage or fear, or both, were the scowling features of the man who had accosted him in the inn-yard.

It was but an instant, a glance, a flash, before his eyes; and they were gone. But they had recognised him, and he them; and their look was as firmly impressed upon his memory, as if it had been deeply carved in stone, and set before him from his birth. He stood transfixed for a moment; then, leaping from the window into the garden, called loudly for help.

Fyodor Dostoyevsky

Crime and Punishment
1866

Dostoyevsky's novel tells the story of a student who commits two murders to prove that murder will not touch his conscience. In Part 1, Chapter 5, tormented even before the murders, he dreams. In Part 2, Chapter 2, without having confessed or expressed remorse for the murders he has committed, he is tortured by his dreams.

(Part 1, Chapter 5)

In a morbid condition of the brain, dreams often have a singular actuality, vividness, and extraordinary semblance of reality. At times monstrous images are created, but the setting and the whole picture are so truth-like and filled with details so delicate, so unexpectedly, but so artistically consistent, that the dreamer, were he an artist like Pushkin or Turgenev even, could never have invented them in the waking state. Such sick dreams always remain long in the memory and make a powerful impression on the overwrought and deranged nervous system.

Raskolnikov had a fearful dream. He dreamt he was back in his childhood in the little town of his birth. He was a child about seven years old, walking into the country with his father on the evening of a holiday. It was a grey and heavy day, the country was exactly as he remembered it; indeed he recalled it far more vividly in his dream than he had done in memory. The little town stood on a level flat as bare as the hand, not even a willow near it; only in the far distance, a copse lay, a dark blur on the very edge of the horizon. A few paces beyond the last market garden stood a tavern, a big tavern, which had always aroused in him a feeling of aversion, even of fear, when he walked by it with his father. There was always a crowd there, always shouting, laughter and abuse, hideous hoarse singing and often fighting. Drunken and horrible-looking figures were hanging about the tavern. He used to cling close to his father, trembling all over when he met them. Near the tavern the road became a dusty track, the dust of which was always black. It was a winding road, and about a hundred paces further on, it turned to the right to the graveyard. In the middle of the graveyard stood a stone church with a green cupola where he used to go to mass two or three times a year with his father and mother, when a service was held in memory of his grandmother, who had long been dead, and whom he had never seen. On these occasions they used to take on a white dish tied up in a table napkin a special sort of rice pudding with raisins stuck in it in the shape of a cross. He loved that church, the old-fashioned, unadorned ikons and the old priest with the shaking head. Near his grandmother's grave, which was marked by a stone, was the little grave of his younger brother who had died at six months old. He did not remember him at all, but he had been told about his little brother, and whenever he visited the graveyard he used religiously and reverently to cross himself and to bow down and kiss the little grave. And now he dreamt that he was walking with his father past the tavern on the way to the graveyard; he was holding his father's hand and looking with dread at the tavern. A peculiar circumstance attracted his attention: there seemed to be some kind of festivity going on, there were crowds of gaily dressed townspeople, peasant women, their husbands, and riff-raff of all sorts, all singing and all more or less drunk. Near the entrance of the tavern stood a cart, but a strange cart. It was one of those big carts usually drawn by heavy cart-horses and laden with casks of wine or other heavy goods. He always liked looking at those great cart-horses, with their long manes, thick legs, and slow even pace, drawing along a perfect mountain with no appearance of effort, as though it were easier going with a load than without it. But now, strange to say, in the shafts of such a cart he saw a thin little sorrel beast, one of those peasants' nags which he had often seen straining their utmost under a heavy load of wood or hay, especially when the wheels were stuck in the mud or in a rut. And the peasants would beat them so cruelly, sometimes even about the nose and eyes, and he felt so sorry, so sorry for them that he almost cried, and his mother always used to take him away from the window. All of a sudden there was a great uproar of shouting, singing and the balalaïka, and from the tavern a number of big and very drunken peasants came out, wearing red and blue shirts and coats thrown over their shoulders.

"Get in, get in!" shouted one of them, a young thick-necked peasant with a fleshy face red as a carrot. "I'll take you all, get in!"

But at once there was an outbreak of laughter and exclamations in the crowd.

"Take us all with a beast like that!"

"Why, Mikolka, are you crazy to put a nag like that in such a cart?"

"And this mare is twenty if she is a day, mates!"

"Get in, I'll take you all," Mikolka shouted again, leaping first into the cart, seizing the reins and standing straight up in front. "The bay has gone with Matvey," he shouted from the cart—"and this brute, mates, is just breaking my heart, I feel as if I could kill her. She's just eating her head off. Get in, I tell you! I'll make her gallop! She'll gallop!" and he picked up the whip, preparing himself with relish to flog the little mare.

"Get in! Come along!" The crowd laughed. "D'you hear, she'll gallop!"

"Gallop indeed! She has not had a gallop in her for the last ten years!"

"She'll jog along!"

"Don't you mind her, mates, bring a whip each of you, get ready!"

"All right! Give it to her!"

They all clambered into Mikolka's cart, laughing and making jokes. Six men got in and there was still room for more. They hauled in a fat, rosy-cheeked woman. She was dressed in red cotton, in a pointed, beaded headdress and thick leather shoes; she was cracking nuts and laughing. The crowd round them was laughing too and indeed, how could they help laughing? That wretched nag was to drag all the cartload of them at a gallop! Two young fellows in the cart were just getting whips ready to help Mikolka. With the cry of "now," the mare tugged with all her might, but far from galloping, could scarcely move forward; she struggled with her legs, gasping and shrinking from the blows of the three whips which were showered upon her like hail. The laughter in the cart and in the crowd was redoubled, but Mikolka flew into a rage and furiously thrashed the mare, as though he supposed she really could gallop.

"Let me get in, too, mates," shouted a young man in the crowd whose appetite was aroused.

"Get in, all get in," cried Mikolka, "she will draw you all. I'll beat her to death!" And he thrashed and thrashed at the mare, beside himself with fury.

"Father, father," he cried, "father, what are they doing? Father, they are beating the poor horse!"

"Come along, come along!" said his father. "They are drunken and foolish, they are in fun; come away, don't look!" and he tried to draw him away, but he tore himself away from his hand, and, beside himself with horror, ran to the horse. The poor beast was in a bad way. She was gasping, standing still, then tugging again and almost falling.

"Beat her to death," cried Mikolka, "it's come to that. I'll do for her!"

"What are you about, are you a Christian, you devil?" shouted an old man in the crowd.

"Did anyone ever see the like? A wretched nag like that pulling such a cartload," said another.

"You'll kill her," shouted the third.

"Don't meddle! It's my property, I'll do what I choose. Get in, more of you! Get in, all of you! I will have her go at a gallop! . . ."

All at once laughter broke into a roar and covered everything: the mare, roused by the shower of blows, began feebly kicking. Even the old man could not help smiling. To think of a wretched little beast like that trying to kick!

Two lads in the crowd snatched up whips and ran to the mare to beat her about the ribs. One ran each side.

"Hit her in the face, in the eyes, in the eyes," cried Mikolka.

"Give us a song, mates," shouted someone in the cart and everyone in the cart joined in a riotous song, jingling a tambourine and whistling. The woman went on cracking nuts and laughing.

. . . He ran beside the mare, ran in front of her, saw her being whipped across the eyes, right in the eyes! He was crying, he felt choking, his tears were streaming. One of the men gave him a cut with the whip across the face, he did not feel it. Wringing his hands and screaming, he rushed up to the grey-headed old man with the grey beard, who was shaking his head in disapproval. One woman seized him by the hand and would have taken him away, but he tore himself from her and ran back to the mare. She was almost at the last gasp, but began kicking once more.

"I'll teach you to kick," Mikolka shouted ferociously. He threw down the whip, bent forward and picked up from the bottom of the cart a long, thick shaft, he took hold of one end with both hands and with an effort brandished it over the mare.

"He'll crush her," was shouted round him. "He'll kill her!"

"It's my property," shouted Mikolka and brought the shaft down with a swinging blow. There was a sound of a heavy thud.

"Thrash her, thrash her! Why have you stopped?" shouted voices in the crowd.

And Mikolka swung the shaft a second time and it fell a second time on the spine of the luckless mare. She sank back on her haunches, but lurched forward and tugged forward with all her force, tugged first on one side and then on the other, trying to move the cart. But the six whips were attacking her in all directions, and the shaft was raised again and fell upon her a third time, then a fourth, with heavy measured blows. Mikolka was in a fury that he could not kill her at one blow.

"She's a tough one," was shouted in the crowd.

"She'll fall in a minute, mates, there will soon be an end of her," said an admiring spectator in the crowd.

"Fetch an axe to her! Finish her off," shouted a third.

"I'll show you! Stand off," Mikolka screamed frantically; he threw down the shaft, stooped down in the cart and picked up an iron crowbar. "Look out," he shouted, and with all his might he dealt a stunning blow at the poor mare. The blow fell; the mare staggered, sank back, tried to pull, but the bar fell again with a swinging blow on her back and she fell on the ground like a log.

"Finish her off," shouted Mikolka and he leapt beside himself, out of the cart. Several young men, also flushed with drink, seized anything they could come across—whips, sticks, poles, and ran to the dying mare. Mikolka stood on one side and began dealing random blows with the crowbar. The mare stretched out her head, drew a long breath and died.

"You butchered her," someone shouted in the crowd.

"Why wouldn't she gallop then?"

"My property!" shouted Mikolka, with bloodshot eyes, brandishing the bar in his hands. He stood as though regretting that he had nothing more to beat.

"No mistake about it, you are not a Christian," many voices were shouting in the crowd.

But the poor boy, beside himself, made his way, screaming, through the crowd to the sorrel nag, put his arms round her bleeding dead head and kissed it, kissed the eyes and kissed the lips. . . . Then he jumped up and flew in a frenzy with his little fists out at Mikolka. At that instant his father, who had been running after him, snatched him up and carried him out of the crowd.

"Come along, come! Let us go home," he said to him.

"Father! Why did they . . . kill . . . the poor horse!" he sobbed, but his voice broke and the words came in shrieks from his panting chest.

"They are drunk. . . . They are brutal . . . it's not our business!" said his father. He put his arms round his father but he felt choked, choked. He tried to draw a breath, to cry out—and woke up.

He waked up, gasping for breath, his hair soaked with perspiration, and stood up in terror.

"Thank God, that was only a dream," he said, sitting down under a tree and drawing deep breaths. "But what is it? Is it some fever coming on? Such a hideous dream!"

He felt utterly broken: darkness and confusion were in his soul. He rested his elbows on his knees and leaned his head on his hands.

"Good God!" he cried, "can it be, can it be, that I shall really take an axe, that I shall strike her on the head, split her skull open . . . that I shall tread in the sticky warm blood, break the lock, steal and tremble; hide, all spattered in the blood . . . with the axe. . . . Good God, can it be?"

He was shaking like a leaf as he said this.

"But why am I going on like this?" he continued, sitting up again, as it were in profound amazement. "I knew that I could never bring myself to it, so what have I been torturing myself for till now? Yesterday, yesterday, when I went to make that . . . *experiment,* yesterday I realised completely that I could never bear to do it. . . . Why am I going over it again, then? Why am I hesitating? As I came down the stairs yesterday, I said myself that it was base, loathsome, vile, vile . . . the very thought of it made me feel sick and filled me with horror. No, I couldn't do it, I couldn't do it! Granted, granted that there is no flaw in all that reasoning, that all that I have concluded this last month is clear as day, true as arithmetic. . . . My God! Anyway I couldn't bring myself to it! I couldn't do it, I couldn't do it! Why, why then am I still . . . ?"

He rose to his feet, looked round in wonder as though surprised at finding himself in this place, and went towards the bridge. He was pale, his eyes glowed, he was exhausted in every limb, but he seemed suddenly to breathe more easily. He felt he had cast off that fearful burden that had so long been weighing upon him, and all at once there was a sense of relief and peace in his soul. "Lord," he prayed, "show me my path—I renounce that accursed . . . dream of mine."

Crossing the bridge, he gazed quietly and calmly at the Neva, at the glowing red sun setting in the glowing sky. In spite of his weakness he was not conscious of fatigue. It was as though an abscess that had been forming for a month past in his heart had suddenly broken. Freedom, freedom! He was free from that spell, that sorcery, that obsession!

* * *

(Part 2, Chapter 2)

He lost consciousness; it seemed strange to him that he didn't remember how he got into the street. It was late evening. The twilight had fallen and the full moon was shining more and more brightly; but there was a peculiar breathlessness in the air. There were crowds of people in the street; workmen and business people were making their way home; other people had come out for a walk; there was a smell of mortar, dust and stagnant water. Raskolnikov walked along, mournful and anxious; he was distinctly aware of having come out with a purpose, of having to do something in a hurry, but what it was he had forgotten. Suddenly he stood still and saw a man standing on the other side of the street, beckoning to him. He crossed over to him, but at once the man turned and walked away with his head hanging, as though he had made no sign to him. "Stay, did he really beckon?" Raskolnikov wondered, but he tried to overtake him. When he was within ten paces he recognised him and was frightened; it was the same man with stooping shoulders in the long coat. Raskolnikov followed him at a distance; his heart was beating; they went down a turning; the man still did not look round. "Does he know I am following him?" thought Raskolnikov. The man went into the gateway of a big house. Raskolnikov hastened to the gate and looked in to see whether he would look round and sign to him. In the court-yard the man did turn round and again seemed to beckon him. Raskolnikov at once followed him into the yard, but the man was gone. He must have gone up the first staircase. Raskolnikov rushed after him. He heard slow measured steps two flights above. The staircase seemed strangely familiar. He reached the window on the first floor; the moon shone through the panes with a melancholy and mysterious light; then he reached the second floor. Bah! this is the flat where the painters were at work . . . but how was it he did not recognise it at once? The steps of the man above had died away. "So he must have stopped or hidden somewhere." He reached the third storey, should he go on? There was a stillness that was dreadful. . . . But he went on. The sound of his own footsteps scared and frightened him. How dark it was! The man must be hiding in some corner here. Ah! the flat was standing wide open, he hesitated and went in. It was very dark and empty in the passage, as though everything had been removed; he crept on tiptoe into the parlour which was flooded with moonlight. Everything there was as before, the chairs, the looking-glass, the yellow sofa and the pictures in the frames. A huge, round, copper-red moon looked in at the windows. "It's the moon that makes it so still, weaving some mystery," thought Raskolnikov. He stood and waited, waited a long while, and the more silent the moonlight, the more violently his heart beat, till it was painful. And still the same hush. Suddenly he heard a momentary sharp crack like the snapping of a splinter and all was still again. A fly flew up suddenly and struck the window pane with a plaintive buzz. At that moment he noticed in the corner between the window and the little cupboard something like a cloak hanging on the wall. "Why is that cloak here?" he thought, "it wasn't there before. . . ." He went up to it quietly and felt that there was someone hiding behind it. He cautiously moved the cloak and saw, sitting on a chair in the corner, the old woman bent double so that he couldn't see her face; but it was she. He stood over her. "She is afraid," he thought. He stealthily took the axe from the noose and struck her one blow, then another on the skull. But strange to say she did not stir, as though she were made of wood.

He was frightened, bent down nearer and tried to look at her; but she, too, bent her head lower. He bent right down to the ground and peeped up into her face from below, he peeped and turned cold with horror: the old woman was sitting and laughing, shaking with noiseless laughter, doing her utmost that he should not hear it. Suddenly he fancied that the door from the bedroom was opened a little and that there was laughter and whispering within. He was overcome with frenzy and he began hitting the old woman on the head with all his force, but at every blow of the axe the laughter and whispering from the bedroom grew louder and the old woman was simply shaking with mirth. He was rushing away, but the passage was full of people, the doors of the flats stood open and on the landing, on the stairs and everywhere below there were people, rows of heads, all looking, but huddled together in silence and expectation. Something gripped his heart, his legs were rooted to the spot, they would not move. . . . He tried to scream and woke up.

He drew a deep breath—but his dream seemed strangely to persist: his door was flung open and a man whom he had never seen stood in the doorway watching him intently.

Nikolai Gogol

"The Portrait"
1835

The Ukrainian author wrote in Russian and followed, somewhat, in Alexander Pushkin's footsteps. This excerpt from a long eerie story is about the artist Chartkov, whose own work is trite compared to "the portrait" he studies.

[. . .] he approached the portrait, in order to observe those wondrous eyes, and perceived, with terror, that they were gazing at him. This was no copy from Nature; it was life, the strange life which might have lighted up the face of a dead man, risen from the grave. Whether it was the effect of the moonlight, which brought with it fantastic thoughts, and transformed things into strange likenesses, opposed to those of matter-of-fact day, or from some other cause, but it suddenly became terrible to him, he knew not why, to sit alone in the room. He drew back from the portrait, turned aside, and tried not to look at it; but his eye involuntarily, of its own accord, kept glancing sideways towards it. Finally, he became afraid to walk about the room. It seemed as though some one were on the point of stepping up behind him; and every time he turned, he glanced timidly back. He had never been a coward; but his imagination and nerves were sensitive, and that evening he could not explain his involuntary fear. He seated himself in one corner, but even then it seemed to him that some one was peeping over his shoulder into his face. Even Nikita's snores, resounding from the ante-room, did not chase away his fear. At length he rose from the seat, without raising his eyes, went behind a screen, and lay down on his bed. Through the cracks of the screen he saw his room lit up by the moon, and the portrait hanging stiffly on the wall. The eyes were fixed upon him in a yet more terrible and significant manner, and it seemed as if they would not look at anything but himself. Overpowered with a feeling of oppression, he decided to rise from his bed, seized a sheet, and, approaching the portrait, covered it up completely.

Having done this, he lay done more at ease on his bed, and began to meditate upon the poverty and pitiful lot of the artist, and the thorny path lying before him in the world. But meanwhile his eye glanced involuntarily through the joint of the screen at the portrait muffled in the sheet. The light of the moon heightened the whiteness of the sheet, and it seemed to him as though those terrible eyes shone through the cloth. With terror he fixed his eyes more steadfastly on the spot, as if wishing to convince himself that it was all nonsense. But at length he saw—saw clearly; there was no longer a sheet—the portrait was quite uncovered, and was gazing beyond everything around it, straight at him; gazing as it seemed fairly into his heart. His heart grew cold. He watched anxiously; the old man moved, and suddenly, supporting himself on the frame with both arms, raised himself by his hands, and, putting forth both feet, leapt out of the frame. Through the crack of the screen, the empty frame alone was now visible. Footsteps resounded through the room, and approached nearer and nearer to the screen. The poor artist's heart began beating fast. He expected every moment, his breath failing for fear, that the old man would look round the screen at him. And lo! he did look from behind the screen, with the very same bronzed face, and with his big eyes roving about.

Chartkov tried to scream, and felt that his voice was gone; he tried to move; his limbs refused their office. With open mouth, and failing breath, he gazed at the tall phantom, draped in some kind of a flowing

Asiatic robe, and waited for what it would do. The old man sat down almost on his very feet, and then pulled out something from among the folds of his wide garment. It was a purse. The old man untied it, took it by the end, and shook it. Heavy rolls of coin fell out with a dull thud upon the floor. Each was wrapped in blue paper, and on each was marked, "1000 ducats." The old man protruded his long, bony hand from his wide sleeves, and began to undo the rolls. The gold glittered. Great as was the artist's unreasoning fear, he concentrated all his attention upon the gold, gazing motionless, as it made its appearance in the bony hands, gleamed, rang lightly or dully, and was wrapped up again. Then he perceived one packet which had rolled farther than the rest, to the very leg of his bedstead, near his pillow. He grasped it almost convulsively, and glanced in fear at the old man to see whether he noticed it.

But the old man appeared very much occupied: he collected all his rolls, replaced them in the purse, and went outside the screen without looking at him. Chartkov's heart beat wildly as he heard the rustle of the retreating footsteps sounding through the room. He clasped the roll of coin more closely in his hand, quivering in every limb. Suddenly he heard the footsteps approaching the screen again. Apparently the old man had recollected that one roll was missing. Lo! again he looked round the screen at him. The artist in despair grasped the roll with all his strength, tried with all his power to make a movement, shrieked—and awoke.

He was bathed in a cold perspiration; his heart beat as hard as it was possible for it to beat; his chest was oppressed, as though his last breath was about to issue from it. "Was it a dream?" he said, seizing his head with both hands. But the terrible reality of the apparition did not resemble a dream. As he woke, he saw the old man step into the frame: the skirts of the flowing garment even fluttered, and his hand felt plainly that a moment before it had held something heavy. The moonlight lit up the room, bringing out from the dark corners here a canvas, there the model of a hand: a drapery thrown over a chair; trousers and dirty boots. Then he perceived that he was not lying in his bed, but standing upright in front of the portrait. How he had come there, he could not in the least comprehend. Still more surprised was he to find the portrait uncovered, and with actually no sheet over it. Motionless with terror, he gazed at it, and perceived that the living, human eyes were fastened upon him. A cold perspiration broke out upon his forehead. He wanted to move away, but felt that his feet had in some way become rooted to the earth. And he felt that this was not a dream. The old man's features moved, and his lips began to project towards him, as though he wanted to suck him in. With a yell of despair he jumped back—and awoke.

"Was it a dream?" With his heart throbbing to bursting, he felt about him with both hands. Yes, he was lying in bed, and in precisely the position in which he had fallen asleep. Before him stood the screen. The moonlight flooded the room. Through the crack of the screen, the portrait was visible, covered with the sheet, as it should be, just as he had covered it. And so that, too, was a dream? But his clenched fist still felt as though something had been held in it. The throbbing of his heart was violent, almost terrible; the weight upon his breast intolerable. He fixed his eyes upon the crack, and stared steadfastly at the sheet. And lo! he saw plainly the sheet begin to open, as though hands were pushing from underneath, and trying to throw it off. "Lord God, what is it!" he shrieked, crossing himself in despair—and awoke.

And was this, too, a dream? He sprang from his bed, half-mad, and could not comprehend what had happened to him. Was it the oppression of a nightmare, the raving of fever, or an actual apparition? Striving to calm, as far as possible, his mental tumult, and stay the wildly rushing blood, which beat with straining pulses in every vein, he went to the window and opened it. The cool breeze revived him. The moonlight lay on the roofs and the white walls of the houses, though small clouds passed frequently across the sky. All was still: from time to time there struck the ear the distant rumble of a carriage. He put his head out of the window, and gazed for some time. Already the signs of approaching dawn were spreading over the sky. At last he felt drowsy, shut to the window, stepped back, lay down in bed, and quickly fell, like one exhausted, into a deep sleep.

He awoke late, and with the disagreeable feeling of a man who has been half-suffocated with coal-gas: his head ached painfully. The room was dim: an unpleasant moisture pervaded the air, and penetrated the cracks of his windows. Dissatisfied and depressed as a wet cock, he seated himself on his dilapidated divan, not knowing what to do, what to set about, and at length remembered the whole of his dream. As he recalled it, the dream presented itself to his mind as so oppressively real that he even began to wonder whether it were a dream, whether there were not something more here, whether it were not really an apparition. Removing the sheet, he looked at the terrible portrait by the light of day. The eyes were really striking in their liveliness, but he found nothing particularly

terrible about them, though an indescribably unpleasant feeling
lingered in his mind. Nevertheless, he could not quite convince
himself that it was a dream. It struck him that there must have been
some terrible fragment of reality in the vision. It seemed as though
there were something in the old man's very glance and expression
which said that he had been with him that night: his hand still felt
the weight which had so recently lain in it as if some one had but
just snatched it from him. It seemed to him that, if he had only
grasped the roll more firmly, it would have remained in his hand,
even after his awakening.

Victor Hugo

Les Misérables
1862

*Victor Hugo's immense novel expands in many directions as he tells
the story of the downtrodden citizens of Paris in the 1810s and 1820s.
This episode, "Chapter 4—Forms Assumed by Suffering During
Sleep," features the ex-convict Jean Valjean, the most important of
many important characters.*

Three o'clock in the morning had just struck, and he had been
walking thus for five hours, almost uninterruptedly, when he at length
allowed himself to drop into his chair.

There he fell asleep and had a dream.

This dream, like the majority of dreams, bore no relation to the
situation, except by its painful and heart-rending character, but it
made an impression on him. This nightmare struck him so forcibly
that he wrote it down later on. It is one of the papers in his own
handwriting which he has bequeathed to us. We think that we have
here reproduced the thing in strict accordance with the text.

Of whatever nature this dream may be, the history of this night
would be incomplete if we were to omit it: it is the gloomy adventure
of an ailing soul.

Here it is. On the envelope we find this line inscribed, "The
Dream I had that Night."

"I was in a plain; a vast, gloomy plain, where there was no grass.
It did not seem to me to be daylight nor yet night.

"I was walking with my brother, the brother of my childish years, the brother of whom, I must say, I never think, and whom I now hardly remember.

"We were conversing and we met some passers-by. We were talking of a neighbor of ours in former days, who had always worked with her window open from the time when she came to live on the street. As we talked we felt cold because of that open window.

"There were no trees in the plain. We saw a man passing close to us. He was entirely nude, of the hue of ashes, and mounted on a horse which was earth color. The man had no hair; we could see his skull and the veins on it. In his hand he held a switch which was as supple as a vine-shoot and as heavy as iron. This horseman passed and said nothing to us.

"My brother said to me, 'Let us take to the hollow road.'

"There existed a hollow way wherein one saw neither a single shrub nor a spear of moss. Everything was dirt-colored, even the sky. After proceeding a few paces, I received no reply when I spoke: I perceived that my brother was no longer with me.

"I entered a village which I espied. I reflected that it must be Romainville. (Why Romainville?)

"The first street that I entered was deserted. I entered a second street. Behind the angle formed by the two streets, a man was standing erect against the wall. I said to this man:—

"'What country is this? Where am I?' The man made no reply. I saw the door of a house open, and I entered.

"The first chamber was deserted. I entered the second. Behind the door of this chamber a man was standing erect against the wall. I inquired of this man, 'Whose house is this? Where am I?' The man replied not.

"The house had a garden. I quitted the house and entered the garden. The garden was deserted. Behind the first tree I found a man standing upright. I said to this man, 'What garden is this? Where am I?' The man did not answer.

"I strolled into the village, and perceived that it was a town. All the streets were deserted, all the doors were open. Not a single living being was passing in the streets, walking through the chambers or strolling in the gardens. But behind each angle of the walls, behind each door, behind each tree, stood a silent man. Only one was to be seen at a time. These men watched me pass.

"I left the town and began to ramble about the fields.

"After the lapse of some time I turned back and saw a great crowd coming up behind me. I recognized all the men whom I had seen in that town. They had strange heads. They did not seem to be in a hurry, yet they walked faster than I did. They made no noise as they walked. In an instant this crowd had overtaken and surrounded me. The faces of these men were earthen in hue.

"Then the first one whom I had seen and questioned on entering the town said to me:—

"'Whither are you going! Do you not know that you have been dead this long time?'

"I opened my mouth to reply, and I perceived that there was no one near me."

He woke. He was icy cold. A wind which was chill like the breeze of dawn was rattling the leaves of the window, which had been left open on their hinges. The fire was out. The candle was nearing its end. It was still black night.

He rose, he went to the window. There were no stars in the sky even yet.

From his window the yard of the house and the street were visible. A sharp, harsh noise, which made him drop his eyes, resounded from the earth.

Below him he perceived two red stars, whose rays lengthened and shortened in a singular manner through the darkness.

As his thoughts were still half immersed in the mists of sleep, "Hold!" said he, "there are no stars in the sky. They are on earth now."

But this confusion vanished; a second sound similar to the first roused him thoroughly; he looked and recognized the fact that these two stars were the lanterns of a carriage. By the light which they cast he was able to distinguish the form of this vehicle. It was a tilbury harnessed to a small white horse. The noise which he had heard was the trampling of the horse's hoofs on the pavement.

Franz Kafka

"A Country Doctor"
1919

As well as any writer in world literature, Kafka narrates completely within a dreamer's point of view. This story is complete.

I was in a most awkward predicament: I needed to leave at once on an urgent journey; a seriously ill patient was waiting for me in a village ten miles away; a heavy snowstorm filled the wide interval between him and me; I had a carriage, light, with large wheels, perfectly suited to our country roads; wrapped in my fur coat, my instrument bag in my hand, I was already standing in the yard ready to go; but I lacked a horse, a horse. The previous night my own horse had died as a result of overwork in this glacial winter; my maid was now running all over the village trying to borrow a horse; but it was hopeless, I knew, and with more and more snow piling up on me, becoming more and more immobile, I stood there aimlessly. The maid showed up at the gate alone, swinging her lantern; naturally, who would lend his horse for such a ride?

I walked across the yard once again; I could see no possibility; distracted, tormented, I kicked at the ramshackle door of the pigpen, which hadn't been used for years. It opened and swung back and forth on its hinges. Warmth and the smell like that of horses came out of it. A murky stable lantern was swinging by a rope inside. A man, crouching in the low shed, showed his candid, blue-eyed face. "Shall I hitch up?" he asked, creeping out on all fours. I could think of nothing to say, and only stooped down to see what else was in the pen.

The maid stood next to me. "People don't know what they've got available in their own house," she said, and we both laughed.

"Hey there, Brother! Hey there, Sister!" called the groom, and two horses, powerful animals with strong flanks, their legs drawn up tight to their bodies, lowering their well-formed heads like camels, slid out of the door one after the other solely by twisting their bodies to and fro, and occupied the doorway completely with not an inch to spare. But immediately they stood up on tall legs, their bodies steaming with dense vapor.

"Help him," I said, and the willing maid ran to hand the groom the carriage harness.

But the moment she reached him, the groom embraces her and shoves his face against hers. She yells out and escapes over to me; two rows of teeth have left their red marks on the girl's cheek. "You beast," I shout furiously, "would you like to feel my whip?" But I instantly recall that he's a stranger, that I don't know where he has come from, and that he's volunteering to help me when all the rest are failing me.

As if he knew my thoughts, he isn't vexed by my threat, but still busy with the horses, merely turns once to face me. "Get in," he then says, and truly: everything is in readiness.

I observe that I have never before handled such a beautiful team, and I get in cheerfully. "I'll do the driving, you don't know the way," I say.

"Sure," he says, "I'm not going along at all, I'm staying with Rosa."

"No!" yells Rosa and with a true foreboding that her fate is inevitable, she runs into the house; I hear the door chain rattle as she draws it tight; I hear the lock snap shut; I watch as, in addition, she turns off all the lights, first in the vestibule and then racing through the rooms, so she won't be found. "You're coming along," I say to the groom, "or I'm giving up the trip, no matter how urgent it is. I have no wish to hand the maid over to you as fare for the ride."

"Giddy-up!" he says and claps his hands; the carriage is swept away like a piece of wood in a current; I can still hear the door of my house cracking and splintering as the groom assaults it, then my eyes and ears are filled with a rustling wind that penetrates all my senses uniformly. But even that lasts only a moment, because, as if my patient's farmyard opened up directly in front of the gate of my own yard, I am already there; the horses are standing calmly; the snowfall has ended; moonlight all around; the parents of the patient rush out of the house; his sister after them; they practically lift me out of the carriage; I can't make out any of their confused talk; in the sickroom the air is barely breathable; the stove, which hadn't been tended to, is smoking. I intend to open the window; but first I want to see the patient.

Then, with no fever, not cold, not warm, with expressionless eyes, without a shirt, the boy raises himself up under the feather bed, embraces my neck and whispers in my ear: "Doctor, let me die." I look around; no one has heard; his parents are standing in silence, bending forward in expectation of my medical opinion; the sister has brought a chair for my bag. I open the bag and look through my instruments; the boy continues to grope toward me from his bed in order to remind me of his request; I take hold of some tweezers, examine them in the candlelight and put them down again.

"Yes," I think blasphemously, "in such cases, the gods come to your aid; they send the missing horse; because of the urgency, they add a second one; and in their bounty they then grant you the groom—" It is only then that I think of Rosa again; what am I to do, how can I rescue her, how can I pull her out from under that groom when I am ten miles away from her and unmanageable horses are harnessed to my carriage? Those horses, which somehow have now loosened the reins and in some unknown way have opened the windows from outside! Each one has thrust his head in through a window and, heedless of the family's outcry, is scrutinizing the patient. "I'll ride right back," I think, as if the horses are inviting me to go, but I allow the sister, who believes I am numb from the heat, to take off my fur coat. A glass of rum is prepared for me, the old man pats me on the shoulder; the surrender of this treasure of his justifies that familiarity. I shake my head; I would grow ill within the old man's circumscribed way of thinking; for that reason alone, I refuse to drink.

The mother stands by the bed and entices me over; I obey and, while a horse neighs loudly at the ceiling, I place my head on the chest of the boy, who shivers at the touch of my wet beard. What I know is confirmed: the boy is healthy, so that the best thing would be to shove him out of bed. But I'm not out to improve the world, and I let him lie there. I'm an employee of the district government and I do my duty to the hilt, to the point where it's almost too much. Though badly paid, I'm generous and helpful to the poor. I still must take care of Rosa, then the boy may be right and I, too, shall die. What am I doing here in this endless winter? My horse is dead, and there's no one in the village who'll lend me his. I have to find my team in the pigpen; if, by chance, they weren't horses, I'd have to drive them with sows. That's the way it is. And I nod at the family. They know nothing about it, and if they knew, they wouldn't believe it. Writing prescriptions is easy, but, otherwise, communicating with people is hard. Well, this seems to be the end of my call here, once again I've been annoyed for nothing; I'm used to that, with the help of my night bell the whole district tortures me; but having to give up Rosa, too, this time, that beautiful girl who has lived in my house for years, and whom I scarcely noticed—that sacrifice is too great, and I must somehow square it temporarily in my own mind through sophistries if I'm not to make an all-out attack on this family, because, even with the best will in the world, they can't give me back Rosa.

But as I am closing my bag and signaling to have my coat brought over, as the family stands there together, the father sniffing at the glass of rum in his hand, the mother, whom I have most likely disappointed—what do the people expect of me?—biting her lips tearfully, and the sister waving a blood-soaked towel, I am somehow ready to admit on certain conditions that the boy is perhaps ill after all.

I go over to him, he smiles at me as I approach as if I were bringing him, say, the most invigorating soap—oh, now both horses are neighing; the noise, ordained by some lofty powers, is probably meant to facilitate my examination—and I find: yes, the boy is ill. On his right side, around the hip, a wound as large as the palm of one's hand has opened up. Pink, in many shades, dark as it gets deeper, becoming light at the edges, softly granular, with irregular accumulations of blood, wide open as the surface of the entrance to a mine. That's how it looks from some distance. But, close up, a complication can be seen, as well. Who can look at it without giving a low whistle? Worms as long and thick as my little finger, naturally rose-colored and in addition spattered with blood, firmly attached to the inside of the wound, with white heads and many legs, are writhing upward into the light. Poor boy, there's no hope for you. I have discovered your great wound; you will be destroyed by this flower on your side.

The family is happy; it sees me active; the sister tells it to the mother, the mother to the father, the father to a few guests who are entering the open door through the moonlight on tiptoe, balancing with outstretched arms. "Will you save me?" the boy whispers with a sob, completely dazzled by the life in his wound. That's how the people are in my area. Always asking the doctor for the impossible. They've lost their old faith; the priest sits home and picks his vestments to pieces, one after the other; but the doctor is supposed to accomplish everything with his gentle, surgical hands. Well, have it any way you like: I didn't offer my services; if you misuse me for religious purposes, I'll go along with that, too; what better can I ask for, an old country doctor, robbed of my maid! And they come, the family and the village elders, and they undress me; a school choir led by their teacher is standing in front of the house and singing an extremely simple setting of these words:

> Undress him, then he will cure,
> And if he doesn't cure, then kill him!
> It's only a doctor, it's only a doctor.

Then I'm undressed and, my fingers in my beard, I look at the people calmly with head bowed. I am completely composed and superior to them all, and remain so, too, even though it doesn't help me, because now they take me by the head and feet and carry me into the bed. They lay me against the wall, on the side where the wound is. Then they all leave the room; the door is closed; the singing dies away; clouds pass in front of the moon; the bedclothes lie warmly on top of me, the horses' heads in the window openings waver like shadows. "Do you know," I hear, spoken into my ear, "I don't have much confidence in you. You just drifted in here from some-where, you didn't come on your own two feet. Instead of helping, you're just crowding me out of my deathbed. I'd like most of all to scratch your eyes out."

"Right," I say, "it's a disgrace. But I'm a doctor, you see. What should I do? Believe me, it's not easy for me, either."

"Am I supposed to be contented with that excuse? Oh, I guess I must, I'm always forced to be contented. I came into the world with a fine wound; that was my entire portion in life."

"My young friend," I say, "your mistake is this: you don't have the big picture. I, who have already been in all sickrooms, far and wide, tell you: your wound isn't that bad. Brought on by two hatchet blows at an acute angle. Many people offer their sides and scarcely hear the hatchet in the forest, let alone having it come closer to them."

"Is it really so, or are you fooling me in my fever?"

"It's really so, take a government doctor's word of honor into the next world with you." And he took it, and fell silent. But now it was time to think about how to save myself. The horses still stood faithfully in their places. Clothing, fur coat and bag were quickly seized and bundled together; I didn't want to waste time getting dressed; if the horses made the same good time as on the way over, I would, so to speak, be jumping out of this bed into mine. Obediently a horse withdrew from the window; I threw the bundle into the carriage; the fur coat flew too far, it just barely caught on to a hook with one sleeve. Good enough. I leaped onto the horse. The reins loosely trailing along, one horse just barely attached to the other, the carriage mean-dering behind, the fur coat bringing up the rear in the snow. "Giddy-up, and look lively," I said, but the ride wasn't lively; as slowly as old we proceeded across the snowy waste; for a long time there resounded behind us the new, but incorrect, song of the children:

> Rejoice, O patients,
> The doctor has been put in bed alongside you!

Traveling this way, I'll never arrive home; my flourishing practice is lost; a successor is robbing me, but it will do him no good, because he can't replace me; in my house the loathsome groom is rampaging; Rosa is his victim; I don't want to think of all the consequences. Naked, exposed to the frost of this most unhappy era, with an earthly carriage and unearthly horses, I, an old man, roam about aimlessly. My fur coat I hanging in back of the carriage, but I can't reach it, and no one among the sprightly rabble of my patients lifts a finger to help. Betrayed! Betrayed! Having obeyed the false ringing of the night bell just once—the mistake can never be rectified.

Guy de Maupassant

"The Horla"
1887

Maupassant was the most productive and exemplary short story author in France in the second half of the nineteenth century. This famous and terrifying story in diary format is about a dream or hallucinatory vision named by the ill narrator as the mysterious "Horla": "I go to bed, and I wait for sleep as a man might wait for the executioner. . . . I do not feel this perfidious sleep coming over me as I used to, but a sleep which is close to me and watching me, which is going to seize me by the head, to close my eyes and annihilate me."

[. . .]

May 16. I am ill, decidedly! I was so well last month! I am feverish, horribly feverish, or rather I am in a state of feverish enervation, which makes my mind suffer as much as my body. I have without ceasing the horrible sensation of some danger threatening me, the apprehension of some coming misfortune or of approaching death, a presentiment which is no doubt, an attack of some illness still unnamed, which germinates in the flesh and in the blood.

May 18. I have just come from consulting my medical man, for I can no longer get any sleep. He found that my pulse was high, my eyes dilated, my nerves highly strung, but no alarming symptoms. I must have a course of shower baths and of bromide of potassium.

May 25. No change! My state is really very peculiar. As the evening comes on, an incomprehensible feeling of disquietude seizes me, just as if night concealed some terrible menace toward me. I dine quickly, and then try to read, but I do not understand the words, and can scarcely distinguish the letters. Then I walk up and down my drawing-room, oppressed by a feeling of confused and irresistible fear, a fear of sleep and a fear of my bed.

About ten o'clock I go up to my room. As soon as I have entered I lock and bolt the door. I am frightened—of what? Up till the present time I have been frightened of nothing. I open my cupboards, and look under my bed; I listen—I listen—to what? How strange it is that a simple feeling of discomfort, of impeded or heightened circulation, perhaps the irritation of a nervous center, a slight congestion, a small disturbance in the imperfect and delicate functions of our living machinery, can turn the most light-hearted of men into a melancholy one, and make a coward of the bravest? Then, I go to bed, and I wait for sleep as a man might wait for the executioner. I wait for its coming with dread, and my heart beats and my legs tremble, while my whole body shivers beneath the warmth of the bedclothes, until the moment when I suddenly fall asleep, as a man throws himself into a pool of stagnant water in order to drown. I do not feel this perfidious sleep coming over me as I used to, but a sleep which is close to me and watching me, which is going to seize me by the head, to close my eyes and annihilate me.

I sleep—a long time—two or three hours perhaps—then a dream—no—a nightmare lays hold on me. I feel that I am in bed and asleep—I feel it and I know it—and I feel also that somebody is coming close to me, is looking at me, touching me, is getting on to my bed, is kneeling on my chest, is taking my neck between his hands and squeezing it—squeezing it with all his might in order to strangle me.

I struggle, bound by that terrible powerlessness which paralyzes us in our dreams; I try to cry out—but I cannot; I want to move—I cannot; I try, with the most violent efforts and out of breath, to turn over and throw off this being which is crushing and suffocating me—I cannot!

And then suddenly I wake up, shaken and bathed in perspiration; I light a candle and find that I am alone, and after that crisis, which occurs every night, I at length fall asleep and slumber tranquilly till morning.

[. . .]

July 4. I am decidedly taken again; for my old nightmares have returned. Last night I felt somebody leaning on me who was sucking my life from between my lips with his mouth. Yes, he was sucking it out of my neck like a leech would have done. Then he got up, satiated, and I woke up, so beaten, crushed, and annihilated that I could not move. If this continues for a few days, I shall certainly go away again.

July 5. Have I lost my reason? What has happened? What I saw last night is so strange that my head wanders when I think of it!

As I do now every evening, I had locked my door; then, being thirsty, I drank half a glass of water, and I accidentally noticed that the water-bottle was full up to the cut-glass stopper.

Then I went to bed and fell into one of my terrible sleeps, from which I was aroused in about two hours by a still more terrible shock.

Picture to yourself a sleeping man who is being murdered, who wakes up with a knife in his chest, a gurgling in his throat, is covered with blood, can no longer breathe, is going to die and does not understand anything at all about it—there you have it.

Having recovered my senses, I was thirsty again, so I lighted a candle and went to the table on which my water-bottle was. I lifted it up and tilted it over my glass, but nothing came out. It was empty! It was completely empty! At first I could not understand it at all; then suddenly I was seized by such a terrible feeling that I had to sit down, or rather fall into a chair! Then I sprang up with a bound to look about me; then I sat down again, overcome by astonishment and fear, in front of the transparent crystal bottle! I looked at it with fixed eyes, trying to solve the puzzle, and my hands trembled! Somebody had drunk the water, but who? I? I without any doubt. It could surely only be I? In that case I was a somnambulist—was living, without knowing it, that double, mysterious life which makes us doubt whether there are not two beings in us—whether a strange, unknowable, and invisible being does not, during our moments of mental and physical torpor, animate the inert body, forcing it to a more willing obedience than it yields to ourselves.

Oh! Who will understand my horrible agony? Who will understand the emotion of a man sound in mind, wide-awake, full of sense, who looks in horror at the disappearance of a little water while he was asleep, through the glass of a water-bottle! And I remained sitting until it was daylight, without venturing to go to bed again.

July 6. I am going mad. Again all the contents of my water-bottle have been drunk during the night; or rather I have drunk it!

But is it I? Is it I? Who could it be? Who? Oh! God! Am I going mad? Who will save me?

July 10. I have just been through some surprising ordeals. Undoubtedly I must be mad! And yet! On July 6, before going to bed, I put some wine, milk, water, bread, and strawberries on my table. Somebody drank—I drank—all the water and a little of the milk, but neither the wine, nor the bread, nor the strawberries were touched.

On the seventh of July I renewed the same experiment, with the same results, and on July 8 I left out the water and the milk and nothing was touched.

Lastly, on July 9 I put only water and milk on my table, taking care to wrap up the bottles in white muslin and to tie down the stoppers. Then I rubbed my lips, my beard, and my hands with pencil lead, and went to bed.

Deep slumber seized me, soon followed by a terrible awakening. I had not moved, and my sheets were not marked. I rushed to the table. The muslin round the bottles remained intact; I undid the string, trembling with fear. All the water had been drunk, and so had the milk! Ah! Great God! I must start for Paris immediately.

July 12. Paris. I must have lost my head during the last few days! I must be the plaything of my enervated imagination, unless I am really a somnambulist, or I have been brought under the power of one of those influences—hypnotic suggestion, for example—which are known to exist, but have hitherto been inexplicable. In any case, my mental state bordered on madness, and twenty-four hours of Paris sufficed to restore me to my equilibrium.

Yesterday after doing some business and paying some visits, which instilled fresh and invigorating mental air into me, I wound up my evening at the Théâtre Français. A drama by Alexander Dumas the Younger was being acted, and his brilliant and powerful play completed my cure. Certainly solitude is dangerous for active minds. We need men who can think and can talk, around us. When we are alone for a long time, we people space with phantoms.

I returned along the boulevards to my hotel in excellent spirits. Amid the jostling of the crowd I thought, not without irony, of my terrors and surmises of the previous week, because I believed, yes, I believed, that an invisible being lived beneath my roof. How weak our mind is; how quickly it is terrified and unbalanced as soon as we are confronted with a small, incomprehensible fact. Instead of dismissing the problem with: "We do not understand because we cannot find the cause," we immediately imagine terrible mysteries and supernatural powers.

[. . .]

August 17. Oh! What a night! what a night! And yet it seems to me that I ought to rejoice. I read until one o'clock in the morning!

Herestauss, Doctor of Philosophy and Theogony, wrote the history and the manifestation of all those invisible beings which hover around man, or of whom he dreams. He describes their origin, their domains, their power; but none of them resembles the one which haunts me. One might say that man, ever since he has thought, has had a foreboding and a fear of a new being, stronger than himself, his successor in this world, and that, feeling him near, and not being able to foretell the nature of the unseen one, he has, in his terror, created the whole race of hidden beings, vague phantoms born of fear.

Having, therefore, read until one o'clock in the morning, I went and sat down at the open window, in order to cool my forehead and my thoughts in the calm night air. It was very pleasant and warm! How I should have enjoyed such a night formerly!

There was no moon, but the stars darted out their rays in the dark heavens. Who inhabits those worlds? What forms, what living beings, what animals are there yonder? Do those who are thinkers in those distant worlds know more than we do? What can they do more than we? What do they see which we do not? Will not one of them, some day or other, traversing space, appear on our earth to conquer it, just as formerly the Norsemen crossed the sea in order to subjugate nations feebler than themselves?

We are so weak, so powerless, so ignorant, so small—we who live on this particle of mud which revolves in liquid air.

I fell asleep, dreaming thus in the cool night air, and then, having slept for about three quarters of an hour, I opened my eyes without moving, awakened by an indescribably confused and strange sensation. At first I saw nothing, and then suddenly it appeared to me as if a page of the book, which had remained open on my table, turned over of its own accord. Not a breath of air had come in at my window, and I was surprised and waited. In about four minutes, I saw, I saw—yes, I saw with my own eyes— another page lift itself up and fall down on the others, as if a finger had turned it over. My armchair was empty, appeared empty, but I knew that He was there, He, and sitting in my place, and that He was reading. With a furious bound, the bound of an enraged wild beast that wishes to disembowel its tamer, I crossed my room to seize him, to strangle him, to kill him! But before I could reach it, my chair fell over as if somebody had run away from me. My table rocked, my lamp fell and went out, and my window closed as if some thief had been surprised and had fled out into the night, shutting it behind him.

So He had run away; He had been afraid; He, afraid of me!

So tomorrow, or later—some day or other, I should be able to hold him in my clutches and crush him against the ground! Do not dogs occasionally bite and strangle their masters? [. . .]

Alexander Pushkin

"The Coffin-Maker"
1831

Pushkin (1799–1837) is usually regarded as the father of Russian literature. He harvested the everyday language of the people to write his poems and stories. This comic tale, slightly abridged, is an example of his elegance and humor.

The last of the effects of the coffin-maker, Adrian Prokhorov, were placed upon the hearse, and a couple of sorry-looking jades dragged themselves along for the fourth time from Basmannaia to Nikitskaia, whither the coffin-maker was removing with all his household. After locking up the shop, he posted upon the door a placard announcing that the house was to be let or sold, and then made his way on foot to his new abode. On approaching the little yellow house, which had so long captivated his imagination, and which at last he had bought for a considerable sum, the old coffin-maker was astonished to find that his heart did not rejoice. When he crossed the unfamiliar threshold and found his new home in the greatest confusion, he sighed for his old hovel, where for eighteen years the strictest order had prevailed. [. . .]

[Prokhorov and his daughters are invited to a party the next day at their new neighbor the shoemaker's, to which other local artisans have also been invited.]

"To the health of my amiable guests!" exclaimed the host, uncorking a second bottle; and the guests thanked him by draining their glasses once more.

Then followed a succession of toasts. The health of each individual guest was drunk; they drank to the health of Moscow and to quite a dozen little German towns; they drank to the health of all corporations in general and of each in particular; they drank to the health of the masters and foremen. Adrian drank with enthusiasm and became so merry, that he proposed a facetious toast to himself. Suddenly one of the guests, a fat baker, raised his glass and exclaimed:

"To the health of those for whom we work, our customers!"

This proposal, like all the others, was joyously and unanimously received. The guests began to salute each other; the tailor bowed to the shoemaker, the shoemaker to the tailor, the baker to both, the whole company to the baker, and so on. In the midst of these mutual congratulations, Yourko [a watchman] exclaimed, turning to his neighbour:

"Come, little father! Drink to the health of your corpses!"

Everybody laughed, but the coffin-maker considered himself insulted, and frowned. Nobody noticed it, the guests continued to drink, and the bell had already rung for vespers when they rose from the table.

The guests dispersed at a late hour, the greater part of them in a very merry mood. The fat baker and the bookbinder, whose face seemed as if bound in red morocco, linked their arms in those of Yourko and conducted him back to his little watch-house, thus observing the proverb: "One good turn deserves another."

The coffin-maker returned home drunk and angry.

"Why is it," he exclaimed aloud, "why is it that my trade is not as honest as any other? Is a coffin-maker brother to the hangman? Why did those heathens laugh? Is a coffin-maker a buffoon? I wanted to invite them to my new dwelling and give them a feast, but now I'll do nothing of the kind. Instead of inviting them, I will invite those for whom I work: the orthodox dead."

"What is the matter, little father?" said the servant, who was engaged at that moment in taking off his boots: "why do you talk such nonsense? Make the sign of the cross! Invite the dead to your new house! What folly!"

"Yes, by the Lord! I will invite them," continued Adrian, "and that, too, for tomorrow! . . . Do me the favour, my benefactors, to come and feast with me tomorrow evening; I will regale you with what God has sent me."

With these words the coffin-maker turned into bed and soon began to snore.

It was still dark when Adrian was awakened out of his sleep. Trukhina, the shopkeeper's wife, had died during the course of that very night, and a special messenger was sent off on horseback by her bailiff to carry the news to Adrian. The coffin-maker gave him ten copecks to buy brandy with, dressed himself as hastily as possible, took a droshky and set out for Rasgouliai. Before the door of the house in which the deceased lay, the police had already taken their stand, and the trades-people were passing backwards and forwards, like ravens that smell a dead body. The deceased lay upon a table, yellow as wax, but not yet disfigured by decomposition. Around her stood her relatives, neigh-bours and domestic servants. All the windows were open; tapers were burning; and the priests were reading the prayers for the dead. Adrian went up to the nephew of Trukhina, a young shopman in a fashionable surtout, and informed him that the coffin, wax candles, pall, and the other funeral accessories would be immediately delivered with all possible exactitude. The heir thanked him in an absent-minded manner, saying that he would not bargain about the price, but would rely upon him acting in everything according to his conscience. The coffin-maker, in accordance with his usual custom, vowed that he would not charge him too much, exchanged significant glances with the bailiff, and then departed to commence operations.

The whole day was spent in passing to and fro between Rasgouliai and the Nikitskaia Gate. Towards evening everything was finished, and he returned home on foot, after having dismissed his driver. It was a moonlight night. The coffin-maker reached the Nikitskaia Gate in safety. Near the Church of the Ascension he was hailed by our acquaintance Yourko, who, recognizing the coffin-maker, wished him good-night. It was late. The coffin-maker was just approaching his house, when suddenly he fancied he saw some one approach his gate, open the wicket, and disappear within.

"What does that mean?" thought Adrian. "Who can be wanting me again? Can it be a thief come to rob me? Or have my foolish girls got lovers coming after them? It means no good, I fear!"

And the coffin-maker thought of calling his friend Yourko to his assistance. But at that moment, another person approached the wicket and was about to enter, but seeing the master of the house hastening towards him, he stopped and took off his three-cornered hat. His face seemed familiar to Adrian, but in his hurry he had not been able to examine it closely.

"You are favouring me with a visit," said Adrian, out of breath. "Walk in, I beg of you."

"Don't stand on ceremony, little father," replied the other, in a hollow voice; "you go first, and show your guests the way."

Adrian had no time to spend upon ceremony. The wicket was open; he ascended the steps followed by the other. Adrian thought he could hear people walking about in his rooms.

"What the devil does all this mean!" he thought to himself, and he hastened to enter. But the sight that met his eyes caused his legs to give way beneath him.

The room was full of corpses. The moon, shining through the windows, lit up their yellow and blue faces, sunken mouths, dim, half-closed eyes, and protruding noses. Adrian, with horror, recognized in them people that he himself had buried, and in the guest who entered with him, the brigadier who had been buried during the pouring rain. They all, men and women, surrounded the coffin-maker, with bowings and salutations, except one poor fellow lately buried gratis, who, conscious and ashamed of his rags, did not venture to approach, but meekly kept aloof in a corner. All the others were decently dressed: the female corpses in caps and ribbons, the officials in uniforms, but with their beards unshaven, the tradesmen in their holiday caftans.

"You see, Prokhorov," said the brigadier in the name of all the honourable company, "we have all risen in response to your invitation. Only those have stopped at home who were unable to come, who have crumbled to pieces and have nothing left but fleshless bones. But even of these there was one who hadn't the patience to remain behind—so much did he want to come and see you. . . ."

At this moment a little skeleton pushed his way through the crowd and approached Adrian. His fleshless face smiled affably at the coffin-maker. Shreds of green and red cloth and rotten linen hung on him here and there as on a pole, and the bones of his feet rattled inside his big jack-boots, like pestles in mortars.

"You do not recognize me, Prokhorov," said the skeleton. "Don't you remember the retired sergeant of the Guards, Peter Petrovich Kourilkin, the same to whom, in the year 1799, you sold your first coffin, and that, too, of deal instead of oak?"

With these words the corpse stretched out his bony arms towards him; but Adrian, collecting all his strength, shrieked and pushed him from him. Peter Petrovich staggered, fell, and crumbled all to pieces. Among the corpses arose a murmur of indignation; all stood up for the honour of their companion, and they overwhelmed Adrian with such threats and imprecations, that the poor host, deafened by their shrieks and almost crushed to death, lost his presence of mind, fell upon the bones of the retired sergeant of the Guards, and swooned away.

For some time the sun had been shining upon the bed on which lay the coffin-maker. At last he opened his eyes and saw before him the servant attending to the tea-urn. With horror, Adrian recalled all the incidents of the previous day. Trukhina, the brigadier, and the sergeant, Kourilkin, rose vaguely before his imagination. He waited in silence for the servant to open the conversation and inform him of the events of the night.

"How you have slept, little father Adrian Prokhorovich!" said Aksinia, handing him his dressing-gown. "Your neighbour, the tailor, has been here, and the watchman also called to inform you that today is his name-day; but you were so sound asleep, that we did not wish to wake you."

"Did anyone come for me from the late Trukhina?"

"The late? Is she dead, then?"

"What a fool you are! Didn't you yourself help me yesterday to prepare the things for her funeral?"

"Have you taken leave of your senses, little father, or have you not yet recovered from the effects of yesterday's drinking-bout? What funeral was there yesterday? You spent the whole day feasting at the German's, and then came home drunk and threw yourself upon the bed, and have slept till this hour, when the bells have already rung for mass."

"Really!" said the coffin-maker, greatly relieved.

"Yes, indeed," replied the servant.

"Well, since that is the case, make the tea as quickly as possible and call my daughters."

Harriet Beecher Stowe

Uncle Tom's Cabin
1852

A prototype of villainy, the slave driver Simon Legree only finds consciousness of his criminality while asleep. Stowe's antislavery novel was so influential that President Abraham Lincoln told her it had helped start the Civil War (1861–65).

While this conversation was passing in the chamber, Legree, overcome with his carouse, had sunk to sleep in the room below. Legree was not an habitual drunkard. His coarse, strong nature craved, and could endure, a continual stimulation, that would have utterly wrecked and crazed a finer one. But a deep, underlying spirit of cautiousness prevented his often yielding to appetite in such measure as to lose control of himself.

This night, however, in his feverish efforts to banish from his mind those fearful elements of woe and remorse which woke within him, he had indulged more than common; so that, when he had discharged his sable attendants, he fell heavily on a settle in the room, and was sound asleep.

O! how dares the bad soul to enter the shadowy world of sleep?—that land whose dim outlines lie so fearfully near to the mystic scene of retribution! Legree dreamed. In his heavy and feverish sleep, a veiled form stood beside him, and laid a cold, soft hand upon him. He thought he knew who it was; and shuddered, with creeping horror, though the face was veiled. Then he thought he felt *that hair* twining round his fingers; and then, that it slid smoothly round his neck, and tightened and tightened, and he could not draw his breath; and then he thought voices *whispered* to him,—whispers that chilled him with horror. Then it seemed to him he was on the edge of a frightful abyss, holding on and struggling in mortal fear, while dark hands stretched up, and were pulling him over; and Cassy came behind him laughing, and pushed him. And then rose up that solemn veiled figure, and drew aside the veil. It was his mother; and she turned away from him, and he fell down, down, down, amid a confused noise of shrieks, and groans, and shouts of demon laughter,—and Legree awoke.

Calmly the rosy hue of dawn was stealing into the room. The morning star stood, with its solemn, holy eye of light, looking down on the man of sin, from out the brightening sky. O, with what freshness, what solemnity and beauty, is each new day born; as if to say to insensate man, "Behold! thou hast one more chance! *Strive* for immortal glory!" There is no speech nor language where this voice is not heard; but the bold, bad man heard it not. He woke with an oath and a curse. What to him was the gold and purple, the daily miracle of morning! What to him the sanctity of the star which the Son of God has hallowed as his own emblem? Brute-like, he saw without perceiving; and, stumbling forward, poured out a tumbler of brandy, and drank half of it.

"I've had a h——l of a night!" he said to Cassy, who just then entered from an opposite door.

"You'll get plenty of the same sort, by and by," said she, dryly.

"What do you mean, you minx?"

"You'll find out, one of these days," returned Cassy, in the same tone.

Leo Tolstoy

Anna Karenina
1877

After a famous epigraph and introductory paragraph, Tolstoy begins the novel's narration with Anna Karenina's brother Stiva Oblonsky. Despite his family being in domestic crisis as a result of the exposure of his affair, Oblonsky awakens happily as he remembers his dream.

(Part 1, Chapter 1)

Three days after the quarrel, Prince Stepan Arkadyevich Oblonsky— Stiva, as he was called in the fashionable world—woke up at his usual hour, that is, at eight o'clock in the morning, not in his wife's bed-room, but on the leather-covered sofa in his study. He turned over his stout, well-cared-for person on the springy sofa, as though he would sink into a long sleep again; he vigorously embraced the pillow on the other side and buried his face in it; but all at once he jumped up, sat up on the sofa, and opened his eyes.

"Yes, yes, how was it now?" he thought, going over his dream. "Now, how was it? To be sure! Alabin was giving a dinner at Darmstadt; no, not Darmstadt, but something American. Yes, but then, Darmstadt was in America. Yes, Alabin was giving a dinner on glass tables, and the tables sang, Il mio tesoro—not Il mio tesoro though, but something better, and there were some sort of little decanters on the table, and they were women, too," he remembered.

Stepan Arkadyevich's eyes twinkled gaily, and he pondered with a smile. "Yes, it was nice, very nice. There was a great deal more that was delightful, only there's no putting it into words, or even expressing it in one's thoughts awake." And noticing a gleam of light peeping in beside one of the serge curtains, he cheerfully dropped his feet over the edge of the sofa, and felt about with them for his slippers, a present on his last birthday, worked for him by his wife on gold-colored morocco. And, as he had done every day for the last nine years, he stretched out his hand, without getting up, towards the place where his dressing-gown always hung in his bedroom. And thereupon he suddenly remembered that he was not sleeping in his wife's room, but in his study, and why: the smile vanished from his face, he knitted his brows.

"Ah, ah, ah! Oo! . . ." he muttered, recalling everything that had happened. And again every detail of his quarrel with his wife was present to his imagination, all the hopelessness of his position, and worst of all, his own fault.

"Yes, she won't forgive me, and she can't forgive me. And the most awful thing about it is that it's all my fault—all my fault, though I'm not to blame. That's the point of the whole situation," he reflected. "Oh, oh, oh!" he kept repeating in despair, as he remembered the acutely painful sensations caused him by this quarrel.

* * *

Anna Karenina, fatefully pregnant, relates a frightening dream that terrifies her lover, the steady, composed Captain Vronsky, who, unbeknownst to Anna, has had a similar dream.

(Part 4, Chapter 3)

"[. . .] Tell me what you've been doing? What is the matter? What has been wrong with you, and what did the doctor say?"

She looked at him with mocking amusement. Evidently she had hit on other absurd and grotesque aspects in her husband and was awaiting the moment to give expression to them.

But he went on:

"I imagine that it's not illness, but your condition. When will it be?"

The ironical light died away in her eyes, but a different smile, a consciousness of something, he did not know what, and of quiet melancholy, came over her face.

"Soon, soon. You say that our position is miserable, that we must put an end to it. If you knew how terrible it is to me, what I would give to be able to love you freely and boldly! I should not torture myself and torture you with my jealousy. . . . And it will come soon but not as we expect."

And at the thought of how it would come, she seemed so pitiable to herself that tears came into her eyes, and she could not go on. She laid her hand on his sleeve, dazzling and white with its rings in the lamplight.

"It won't come as we suppose. I didn't mean to say this to you, but you've made me. Soon, soon, all will be over, and we shall all, all be at peace, and suffer no more."

"I don't understand," he said, understanding her.

"You asked when? Soon. And I shan't live through it. Don't interrupt me!" and she made haste to speak. "I know it; I know for certain. I shall die; and I'm very glad I shall die, and release myself and you."

Tears dropped from her eyes; he bent down over her hand and began kissing it, trying to hide his emotion, which, he knew, had no sort of grounds, though he could not control it.

"Yes, it's better so," she said, tightly gripping his hand. "That's the only way, the only way left us."

He had recovered himself, and lifted his head.

"How absurd! What absurd nonsense you are talking!"

"No, it's the truth."

"What, what's the truth?"

"That I shall die. I have had a dream."

"A dream?" repeated Vronsky, and instantly he recalled the peasant of his dream.

"Yes, a dream," she said. "It's a long while since I dreamed it. I dreamed that I ran into my bedroom, that I had to get something there, to find out something; you know how it is in dreams," she said, her eyes wide with horror; "and in the bedroom, in the corner, stood something."

"Oh, what nonsense! How can you believe . . ."

But she would not let him interrupt her. What she was saying was too important to her.

"And the something turned round, and I saw it was a peasant with a disheveled beard, little, and dreadful looking. I wanted to run away, but he bent down over a sack, and was fumbling there with his hands . . ."

She showed how he had moved his hands. There was terror in her face. And Vronsky, remembering his dream, felt the same terror filling his soul.

"He was fumbling and kept talking quickly, quickly in French, you know: *Il faut le battre, le fer, le brayer, le petrir.*[11] . . . And in my horror I tried to wake up, and woke up . . . but woke up in the

---

11 French for "You have to hammer iron, pound it, crush it."

dream. And I began asking myself what it meant. And Korney said to me: 'In childbirth you'll die, ma'am, you'll die. . . .' And I woke up."

"What nonsense, what nonsense!" said Vronsky; but he felt himself that there was no conviction in his voice.

"But don't let's talk of it. Ring the bell, I'll have tea. And stay a little now; it's not long I shall . . ."

But all at once she stopped. The expression of her face instantaneously changed. Horror and excitement were suddenly replaced by a look of soft, solemn, blissful attention. He could not comprehend the meaning of the change. She was listening to the stirring of the new life within her.

II. Mythology, History, and Religion

The Bible

Joseph, the Dream-Interpreter (The Book of Genesis,
Chapters 37–46)
Sixth century BCE

*The most famous dreamer in Western religion and literature is Joseph, the
favored son of Jacob (also known as Israel), in the first book of the Bible.
The turning points of his life are determined by his ability to interpret
dreams.*

And Jacob dwelt in the land wherein his father was a stranger, in the
land of Canaan. [. . .] Joseph, being seventeen years old, was feeding
the flock with his brethren; and the lad was with the sons of Bilhah,
and with the sons of Zilpah, his father's wives: and Joseph brought
unto his father their evil report. Now Israel loved Joseph more than
all his children, because he was the son of his old age: and he made
him a coat of many colours. And when his brethren saw that their
father loved him more than all his brethren, they hated him, and
could not speak peaceably unto him.

And Joseph dreamed a dream, and he told it his brethren: and they
hated him yet the more. And he said unto them, Hear, I pray you,
this dream which I have dreamed: For, behold, we were binding
sheaves in the field, and, lo, my sheaf arose, and also stood upright;
and, behold, your sheaves stood round about, and made obeisance
to my sheaf.

And his brethren said to him, Shalt thou indeed reign over us? Or
shalt thou indeed have dominion over us? And they hated him yet
the more for his dreams, and for his words.

And he dreamed yet another dream, and told it his brethren, and
said, Behold, I have dreamed a dream more; and, behold, the sun
and the moon and the eleven stars made obeisance to me.

And he told it to his father, and to his brethren: and his father rebuked him, and said unto him, What is this dream that thou hast dreamed? Shall I and thy mother and thy brethren indeed come to bow down ourselves to thee to the earth? And his brethren envied him; but his father observed the saying.

And his brethren went to feed their father's flock in Shechem. And Israel said unto Joseph, Do not thy brethren feed the flock in Shechem? come, and I will send thee unto them. And he said to him, Here am I. And he said to him, Go, I pray thee, see whether it be well with thy brethren, and well with the flocks; and bring me word again. So he sent him out of the vale of Hebron, and he came to Shechem. And a certain man found him, and, behold, he was wandering in the field: and the man asked him, saying, What seekest thou? And he said, I seek my brethren: tell me, I pray thee, where they feed their flocks. And the man said, They are departed hence; for I heard them say, Let us go to Dothan. And Joseph went after his brethren, and found them in Dothan. And when they saw him afar off, even before he came near unto them, they conspired against him to slay him.

And they said one to another, Behold, this dreamer cometh. Come now therefore, and let us slay him, and cast him into some pit, and we will say, Some evil beast hath devoured him: and we shall see what will become of his dreams.

And Reuben heard it, and he delivered him out of their hands; and said, Let us not kill him. And Reuben said unto them, Shed no blood, but cast him into this pit that is in the wilderness, and lay no hand upon him; that he might rid him out of their hands, to deliver him to his father again.

And it came to pass, when Joseph was come unto his brethren, that they stript Joseph out of his coat, his coat of many colours that was on him; and they took him, and cast him into a pit: and the pit was empty, there was no water in it. And they sat down to eat bread: and they lifted up their eyes and looked, and, behold, a company of Ishmeelites came from Gilead with their camels bearing spicery and balm and myrrh, going to carry it down to Egypt.

And Judah said unto his brethren, What profit is it if we slay our brother, and conceal his blood? Come, and let us sell him to the Ishmeelites, and let not our hand be upon him; for he is our brother and our flesh. And his brethren were content.

Then there passed by Midianites merchantmen; and they drew and lifted up Joseph out of the pit, and sold Joseph to the Ishmeelites for twenty pieces of silver: and they brought Joseph into Egypt.

And Reuben returned unto the pit; and, behold, Joseph was not in the pit; and he rent his clothes. And he returned unto his brethren, and said, The child is not; and I, whither shall I go?

And they took Joseph's coat, and killed a kid of the goats, and dipped the coat in the blood; and they sent the coat of many colours, and they brought it to their father; and said, This have we found: know now whether it be thy son's coat or no.

And he knew it, and said, It is my son's coat; an evil beast hath devoured him; Joseph is without doubt rent in pieces. And Jacob rent his clothes, and put sackcloth upon his loins, and mourned for his son many days. And all his sons and all his daughters rose up to comfort him; but he refused to be comforted; and he said, For I will go down into the grave unto my son mourning. Thus his father wept for him. And the Midianites sold him into Egypt unto Potiphar, an officer of Pharaoh's, and captain of the guard.

[. . .]

And Joseph was brought down to Egypt; and Potiphar, an officer of Pharaoh, captain of the guard, an Egyptian, bought him of the hands of the Ishmeelites, which had brought him down thither. And the Lord was with Joseph, and he was a prosperous man; and he was in the house of his master the Egyptian. And his master saw that the Lord was with him, and that the Lord made all that he did to prosper in his hand. And Joseph found grace in his sight, and he served him: and he made him overseer over his house, and all that he had he put into his hand. And it came to pass from the time that he had made him overseer in his house, and over all that he had, that the Lord blessed the Egyptian's house for Joseph's sake; and the blessing of the Lord was upon all that he had in the house, and in the field. And he left all that he had in Joseph's hand; and he knew not ought he had, save the bread which he did eat. And Joseph was a good person, and well favoured. And it came to pass after these things, that his master's wife cast her eyes upon Joseph; and she said, Lie with me. But he refused, and said unto his master's wife, Behold, my master wotteth not what is with me in the house, and he hath committed all that he hath to my hand; There is none greater in this house than I; neither hath he kept back any thing from me but thee, because thou art his wife: how then can I do this great wickedness, and sin against God? And it came to pass, as she spake to Joseph day by day, that he hearkened not unto her, to lie by her, or to be with her. And it came to pass about this time, that Joseph went into the house to do his business; and there was none of the men of the house there within. And she caught him by his garment, saying, Lie with me: and he left his garment in her hand, and fled, and got him out.

And it came to pass, when she saw that he had left his garment in her hand, and was fled forth, That she called unto the men of her house, and spake unto them, saying, See, he hath brought in an Hebrew unto us to mock us; he came in unto me to lie with me, and I cried with a loud voice: And it came to pass, when he heard that I lifted up my voice and cried, that he left his garment with me, and fled, and got him out. And she laid up his garment by her, until his lord came home. And she spake unto him according to these words, saying, The Hebrew servant, which thou hast brought unto us, came in unto me to mock me: And it came to pass, as I lifted up my voice and cried, that he left his garment with me, and fled out.

And it came to pass, when his master heard the words of his wife, which she spake unto him, saying, After this manner did thy servant to me; that his wrath was kindled. And Joseph's master took him, and put him into the prison, a place where the king's prisoners were bound: and he was there in the prison. But the Lord was with Joseph, and shewed him mercy, and gave him favour in the sight of the keeper of the prison. And the keeper of the prison committed to Joseph's hand all the prisoners that were in the prison; and whatsoever they did there, he was the doer of it. The keeper of the prison looked not to any thing that was under his hand; because the Lord was with him, and that which he did made it to prosper.

And it came to pass after these things, that the butler of the king of Egypt and his baker had offended their lord the king of Egypt. And Pharaoh was wroth against two of his officers, against the chief of the butlers, and against the chief of the bakers. And he put them in ward in the house of the captain of the guard, into the prison, the place where Joseph was bound. And the captain of the guard charged Joseph with them, and he served them: and they continued a season in ward. And they dreamed a dream both of them, each man his dream in one night, each man according to the interpretation of his dream, the butler and the baker of the king of Egypt, which were bound in the prison. And Joseph came in unto them in the morning, and looked upon them, and, behold, they were sad. And he asked Pharaoh's officers that were with him in the ward of his lord's house, saying, Wherefore look ye so sadly to day? And they said unto him, We have dreamed a dream, and there is no interpreter of it. And Joseph said unto them, Do not interpretations belong to God? tell me them, I pray you.

And the chief butler told his dream to Joseph, and said to him, In my dream, behold, a vine was before me; And in the vine were three branches: and it was as though it budded, and her blossoms shot forth; and the clusters thereof brought forth ripe grapes: And Pharaoh's cup was in my hand: and I took the grapes, and pressed them into Pharaoh's cup, and I gave the cup into Pharaoh's hand. And Joseph said unto him, This is the interpretation of it: The three branches are three days: Yet within three days shall Pharaoh lift up thine head, and restore thee unto thy place: and thou shalt deliver Pharaoh's cup into his hand, after the former manner when thou wast his butler. But think on me when it shall be well with thee, and shew kindness, I pray thee, unto me, and make mention of me unto Pharaoh, and bring me out of this house: For indeed I was stolen away out of the land of the Hebrews: and here also have I done nothing that they should put me into the dungeon.

When the chief baker saw that the interpretation was good, he said unto Joseph, I also was in my dream, and, behold, I had three white baskets on my head: And in the uppermost basket there was of all manner of bakemeats for Pharaoh; and the birds did eat them out of the basket upon my head. And Joseph answered and said, This is the interpretation thereof: The three baskets are three days: Yet within three days shall Pharaoh lift up thy head from off thee, and shall hang thee on a tree; and the birds shall eat thy flesh from off thee.

And it came to pass the third day, which was Pharaoh's birthday, that he made a feast unto all his servants: and he lifted up the head of the chief butler and of the chief baker among his servants. And he restored the chief butler unto his butlership again; and he gave the cup into Pharaoh's hand: But he hanged the chief baker: as Joseph had interpreted to them. Yet did not the chief butler remember Joseph, but forgat him.

And it came to pass at the end of two full years, that Pharaoh dreamed: and, behold, he stood by the river. And, behold, there came up out of the river seven well favoured kine and fat-fleshed; and they fed in a meadow. And, behold, seven other kine came up after them out of the river, ill favoured and lean-fleshed; and stood by the other kine upon the brink of the river. And the ill favoured and lean-fleshed kine did eat up the seven well favoured and fat kine. So Pharaoh awoke. And he slept and dreamed the second time: and, behold, seven ears of corn came up upon one stalk, rank and good. And, behold, seven thin ears and blasted with the east wind sprung up after them. And the seven thin ears devoured the seven rank and full ears. And Pharaoh awoke, and, behold, it was a dream. And it came to pass in the morning that his spirit was troubled; and he sent and called for all the magicians of Egypt, and all the wise men thereof: and Pharaoh told them his dream; but there was none that could interpret them unto Pharaoh.

Then spake the chief butler unto Pharaoh, saying, I do remember my faults this day: Pharaoh was wroth with his servants, and put me in ward in the captain of the guard's house, both me and the chief baker: And we dreamed a dream in one night, I and he; we dreamed each man according to the interpretation of his dream. And there was there with us a young man, an Hebrew, servant to the captain of the guard; and we told him, and he interpreted to us our dreams; to each man according to his dream he did interpret. And it came to pass, as he interpreted to us, so it was; me he restored unto mine office, and him he hanged.

Then Pharaoh sent and called Joseph, and they brought him hastily out of the dungeon: and he shaved himself, and changed his raiment, and came in unto Pharaoh. And Pharaoh said unto Joseph, I have dreamed a dream, and there is none that can interpret it: and I have heard say of thee, that thou canst understand a dream to interpret it. And Joseph answered Pharaoh, saying, It is not in me: God shall give Pharaoh an answer of peace. And Pharaoh said unto Joseph, In my dream, behold, I stood upon the bank of the river: And, behold, there came up out of the river seven kine, fat-fleshed and well favoured; and they fed in a meadow: And, behold, seven other kine came up after them, poor and very ill favoured and lean-fleshed, such as I never saw in all the land of Egypt for badness: And the lean and the ill favoured kine did eat up the first seven fat kine: And when they had eaten them up, it could not be known that they had eaten them; but they were still ill favoured, as at the beginning. So I awoke. And I saw in my dream, and, behold, seven ears came up in one stalk, full and good: And, behold, seven ears, withered, thin, and blasted with the east wind, sprung up after them: And the thin ears devoured the seven good ears: and I told this unto the magicians; but there was none that could declare it to me.

And Joseph said unto Pharaoh, The dream of Pharaoh is one: God hath shewed Pharaoh what he is about to do. The seven good kine are seven years; and the seven good ears are seven years: the dream is one. And the seven thin and ill favoured kine that came up after them are seven years; and the seven empty ears blasted with the east wind shall be seven years of famine. This is the thing which I have spoken unto Pharaoh: What God is about to do he sheweth unto Pharaoh. Behold, there come seven years of great plenty throughout all the land of Egypt: And there shall arise after them seven years of famine; and all the plenty shall be forgotten in the land of Egypt; and the famine shall consume the land; And the plenty shall not be known in the land by reason of that famine following; for it shall be very grievous. And for that the dream was doubled unto Pharaoh twice; it is because the thing is established by God, and God will shortly bring it to pass. Now therefore let Pharaoh look out a man discreet and wise, and set him over the land of Egypt. Let Pharaoh do this, and let him appoint officers over the land, and take up the fifth part of the land of Egypt in the seven plenteous years. And let them gather all the food of those good years that come, and lay up corn under the hand of Pharaoh, and let them keep food in the cities. And that food shall be for store to the land against the seven years of famine, which shall be in the land of Egypt; that the land perish not through the famine.

And the thing was good in the eyes of Pharaoh, and in the eyes of all his servants. And Pharaoh said unto his servants, Can we find such a one as this is, a man in whom the Spirit of God is? And Pharaoh said unto Joseph, Forasmuch as God hath shewed thee all this, there is none so discreet and wise as thou art: Thou shalt be over my house, and according unto thy word shall all my people be ruled: only in the throne will I be greater than thou. And Pharaoh said unto Joseph, See, I have set thee over all the land of Egypt. And Pharaoh took off his ring from his hand, and put it upon Joseph's hand, and arrayed him in vestures of fine linen, and put a gold chain about his neck; And he made him to ride in the second chariot which he had; and they cried before him, Bow the knee: and he made him ruler over all the land of Egypt. And Pharaoh said unto Joseph, I am Pharaoh, and without thee shall no man lift up his hand or foot in all the land of Egypt. And Pharaoh called Joseph's name Zaphnath-paaneah; and he gave him to wife Asenath the daughter of Poti-pherah priest of On. And Joseph went out over all the land of Egypt.

And Joseph was thirty years old when he stood before Pharaoh king of Egypt. And Joseph went out from the presence of Pharaoh, and went throughout all the land of Egypt. And in the seven plenteous years the earth brought forth by handfuls. And he gathered up all the food of the seven years, which were in the land of Egypt, and laid up the food in the cities: the food of the field, which was round about every city, laid he up in the same. And Joseph gathered corn as the sand of the sea, very much, until he left numbering; for it was without number.

And unto Joseph were born two sons before the years of famine came, which Asenath the daughter of Poti-pherah priest of On bare unto him. And Joseph called the name of the firstborn Manasseh: For God, said he, hath made me forget all my toil, and all my father's house. And the name of the second called he Ephraim: For God hath caused me to be fruitful in the land of my affliction.

And the seven years of plenteousness, that was in the land of Egypt, were ended. And the seven years of dearth began to come, according as Joseph had said: and the dearth was in all lands; but in all the land of Egypt there was bread. And when all the land of Egypt was famished, the people cried to Pharaoh for bread: and Pharaoh said unto all the Egyptians, Go unto Joseph; what he saith to you, do. And the famine was over all the face of the earth: and Joseph opened all the storehouses, and sold unto the Egyptians; and the famine waxed sore in the land of Egypt. And all countries came into Egypt to Joseph for to buy corn; because that the famine was so sore in all lands.

Now when Jacob saw that there was corn in Egypt, Jacob said unto his sons, Why do ye look one upon another? And he said, Behold, I have heard that there is corn in Egypt: get you down thither, and buy for us from thence; that we may live, and not die.

And Joseph's ten brethren went down to buy corn in Egypt. But Benjamin, Joseph's brother, Jacob sent not with his brethren; for he said, Lest peradventure mischief befall him. And the sons of Israel came to buy corn among those that came: for the famine was in the land of Canaan.

And Joseph was the governor over the land, and he it was that sold to all the people of the land: and Joseph's brethren came, and bowed down themselves before him with their faces to the earth.

And Joseph saw his brethren, and he knew them, but made himself strange unto them, and spake roughly unto them; and he said unto them, Whence come ye? And they said, From the land of Canaan to buy food.

And Joseph knew his brethren, but they knew not him. And Joseph remembered the dreams which he dreamed of them, and said unto them, Ye are spies; to see the nakedness of the land ye are come.

And they said unto him, Nay, my lord, but to buy food are thy servants come. We are all one man's sons; we are true men, thy servants are no spies.

And he said unto them, Nay, but to see the nakedness of the land ye are come.

And they said, Thy servants are twelve brethren, the sons of one man in the land of Canaan; and, behold, the youngest is this day with our father, and one is not.

And Joseph said unto them, That is it that I spake unto you, saying, Ye are spies: Hereby ye shall be proved: By the life of Pharaoh ye shall not go forth hence, except your youngest brother come hither. Send one of you, and let him fetch your brother, and ye shall be kept in prison, that your words may be proved, whether there be any truth in you: or else by the life of Pharaoh surely ye are spies.

And he put them all together into ward three days.

And Joseph said unto them the third day, This do, and live; for I fear God: If ye be true men, let one of your brethren be bound in the house of your prison: go ye, carry corn for the famine of your houses: But bring your youngest brother unto me; so shall your words be verified, and ye shall not die. And they did so.

And they said one to another, We are verily guilty concerning our brother, in that we saw the anguish of his soul, when he besought us, and we would not hear; therefore is this distress come upon us.

And Reuben answered them, saying, Spake I not unto you, saying, Do not sin against the child; and ye would not hear? therefore, behold, also his blood is required.

And they knew not that Joseph understood them; for he spake unto them by an interpreter. And he turned himself about from them, and wept; and returned to them again, and communed with them, and took from them Simeon, and bound him before their eyes. Then Joseph commanded to fill their sacks with corn, and to restore every man's money into his sack, and to give them provision for the way: and thus did he unto them.

And they laded their asses with the corn, and departed thence.

And as one of them opened his sack to give his ass provender in the inn, he espied his money; for, behold, it was in his sack's mouth. And he said unto his brethren, My money is restored; and, lo, it is even in my sack: and their heart failed them, and they were afraid, saying one to another, What is this that God hath done unto us?

And they came unto Jacob their father unto the land of Canaan, and told him all that befell unto them; saying, The man, who is the lord of the land, spake roughly to us, and took us for spies of the country. And we said unto him, We are true men; we are no spies: We be twelve brethren, sons of our father; one is not, and the youngest is this day with our father in the land of Canaan. And the man, the lord of the country, said unto us, Hereby shall I know that ye are true men; leave one of your brethren here with me, and take food for the famine of your households, and be gone: And bring your youngest brother unto me: then shall I know that ye are no spies, but that ye are true men: so will I deliver you your brother, and ye shall traffick in the land.

And it came to pass as they emptied their sacks, that, behold, every man's bundle of money was in his sack: and when both they and their father saw the bundles of money, they were afraid.

And Jacob their father said unto them, Me have ye bereaved of my children: Joseph is not, and Simeon is not, and ye will take Benjamin away: all these things are against me.

And Reuben spake unto his father, saying, Slay my two sons, if I bring him not to thee: deliver him into my hand, and I will bring him to thee again.

And he said, My son shall not go down with you; for his brother is dead, and he is left alone: if mischief befall him by the way in the which ye go, then shall ye bring down my gray hairs with sorrow to the grave.

And the famine was sore in the land.

And it came to pass, when they had eaten up the corn which they had brought out of Egypt, their father said unto them, Go again, buy us a little food.

And Judah spake unto him, saying, The man did solemnly protest unto us, saying, Ye shall not see my face, except your brother be with you. If thou wilt send our brother with us, we will go down and buy thee food: But if thou wilt not send him, we will not go down: for the man said unto us, Ye shall not see my face, except your brother be with you.

And Israel said, Wherefore dealt ye so ill with me, as to tell the man whether ye had yet a brother?

And they said, The man asked us straitly of our state, and of our kindred, saying, Is your father yet alive? have ye another brother? and we told him according to the tenor of these words: could we certainly know that he would say, Bring your brother down?

And Judah said unto Israel his father, Send the lad with me, and we will arise and go; that we may live, and not die, both we, and thou, and also our little ones. I will be surety for him; of my hand shalt thou require him: if I bring him not unto thee, and set him before thee, then let me bear the blame for ever: For except we had lingered, surely now we had returned this second time.

And their father Israel said unto them, If it must be so now, do this; take of the best fruits in the land in your vessels, and carry down the man a present, a little balm, and a little honey, spices, and myrrh, nuts, and almonds: And take double money in your hand; and the money that was brought again in the mouth of your sacks, carry it again in your hand; peradventure it was an oversight: Take also your brother, and arise, go again unto the man: And God Almighty give you mercy before the man, that he may send away your other brother, and Benjamin. If I be bereaved of my children, I am bereaved.

And the men took that present, and they took double money in their hand, and Benjamin; and rose up, and went down to Egypt, and stood before Joseph.

And when Joseph saw Benjamin with them, he said to the ruler of his house, Bring these men home, and slay, and make ready; for these men shall dine with me at noon.

And the man did as Joseph bade; and the man brought the men into Joseph's house.

And the men were afraid, because they were brought into Joseph's house; and they said, Because of the money that was returned in our sacks at the first time are we brought in; that he may seek occasion against us, and fall upon us, and take us for bondmen, and our asses.

And they came near to the steward of Joseph's house, and they communed with him at the door of the house, and said, O sir, we came indeed down at the first time to buy food: and it came to pass, when we came to the inn, that we opened our sacks, and, behold, every man's money was in the mouth of his sack, our money in full weight: and we have brought it again in our hand. And other money have we brought down in our hands to buy food: we cannot tell who put our money in our sacks.

And he said, Peace be to you, fear not: your God, and the God of your father, hath given you treasure in your sacks: I had your money. And he brought Simeon out unto them.

And the man brought the men into Joseph's house, and gave them water, and they washed their feet; and he gave their asses provender. And they made ready the present against Joseph came at noon: for they heard that they should eat bread there. And when Joseph came home, they brought him the present which was in their hand into the house, and bowed themselves to him to the earth.

And he asked them of their welfare, and said, Is your father well, the old man of whom ye spake? Is he yet alive?

And they answered, Thy servant our father is in good health, he is yet alive. And they bowed down their heads, and made obeisance.

And he lifted up his eyes, and saw his brother Benjamin, his mother's son, and said, Is this your younger brother, of whom ye spake unto me? And he said, God be gracious unto thee, my son.

And Joseph made haste; for his bowels did yearn upon his brother: and he sought where to weep; and he entered into his chamber, and wept there. And he washed his face, and went out, and refrained himself, and said, Set on bread.

And they set on for him by himself, and for them by themselves, and for the Egyptians, which did eat with him, by themselves: because the Egyptians might not eat bread with the Hebrews; for that is an abomination unto the Egyptians. And they sat before him, the first-born according to his birthright, and the youngest according to his youth: and the men marvelled one at another. And he took and sent messes unto them from before him: but Benjamin's mess was five times so much as any of theirs. And they drank, and were merry with him.

And he commanded the steward of his house, saying, Fill the men's sacks with food, as much as they can carry, and put every man's money in his sack's mouth. And put my cup, the silver cup, in the sack's mouth of the youngest, and his corn money. And he did according to the word that Joseph had spoken.

As soon as the morning was light, the men were sent away, they and their asses.

And when they were gone out of the city, and not yet far off, Joseph said unto his steward, Up, follow after the men; and when thou dost overtake them, say unto them, Wherefore have ye rewarded evil for good? Is not this it in which my lord drinketh, and whereby indeed he divineth? ye have done evil in so doing. And he overtook them, and he spake unto them these same words.

And they said unto him, Wherefore saith my lord these words? God forbid that thy servants should do according to this thing: Behold, the money, which we found in our sacks' mouths, we brought again unto thee out of the land of Canaan: how then should we steal out of thy lord's house silver or gold? With whomsoever of thy servants it be found, both let him die, and we also will be my lord's bondmen.

And he said, Now also let it be according unto your words; he with whom it is found shall be my servant; and ye shall be blameless.

Then they speedily took down every man his sack to the ground, and opened every man his sack. And he searched, and began at the eldest, and left at the youngest: and the cup was found in Benjamin's sack.

Then they rent their clothes, and laded every man his ass, and returned to the city. And Judah and his brethren came to Joseph's house; for he was yet there: and they fell before him on the ground.

And Joseph said unto them, What deed is this that ye have done? wot ye not that such a man as I can certainly divine?

And Judah said, What shall we say unto my lord? what shall we speak? or how shall we clear ourselves? God hath found out the iniquity of thy servants: behold, we are my lord's servants, both we, and he also with whom the cup is found.

And he said, God forbid that I should do so: but the man in whose hand the cup is found, he shall be my servant; and as for you, get you up in peace unto your father.

Then Judah came near unto him, and said, Oh my lord, let thy servant, I pray thee, speak a word in my lord's ears, and let not thine anger burn against thy servant: for thou art even as Pharaoh. My lord asked his servants, saying, Have ye a father, or a brother? And we said unto my lord, We have a father, an old man, and a child of his old age, a little one; and his brother is dead, and he alone is left of his mother, and his father loveth him. And thou saidst unto thy servants, Bring him down unto me, that I may set mine eyes upon him. And we said unto my lord, The lad cannot leave his father: for if he should leave his father, his father would die. And thou saidst unto thy servants, Except your youngest brother come down with you, ye shall see my face no more. And it came to pass when we came up unto thy servant my father, we told him the words of my lord. And our father said, Go again, and buy us a little food. And we said, We cannot go down: if our youngest brother be with us, then will we go down: for we may not see the man's face, except our youngest brother be with us. And thy servant my father said unto us, Ye know that my wife bare me two sons: And the one went out from me, and I said, Surely he is torn in pieces; and I saw him not since: And if ye take this also from me, and mischief befall him, ye shall bring down my gray hairs with sorrow to the grave. Now therefore when I come to thy servant my father, and the lad be not with us; seeing that his life is bound up in the lad's life; it shall come to pass, when he seeth that the lad is not with us, that he will die: and thy servants shall bring down the gray hairs of thy servant our father with sorrow to the grave. For thy servant became surety for the lad unto my father, saying, If I bring him not unto thee, then I shall bear the blame to my father for ever. Now therefore, I pray thee, let thy servant abide instead of the lad a bondman to my lord; and let the lad go up with his brethren. For how shall I go up to my father, and the lad be not with me? lest peradventure I see the evil that shall come on my father.

Then Joseph could not refrain himself before all them that stood by him; and he cried, Cause every man to go out from me. And there stood no man with him, while Joseph made himself known unto his brethren.

And he wept aloud: and the Egyptians and the house of Pharaoh heard.

And Joseph said unto his brethren, I am Joseph; doth my father yet live? And his brethren could not answer him; for they were troubled at his presence.

And Joseph said unto his brethren, Come near to me, I pray you. And they came near. And he said, I am Joseph your brother, whom ye sold into Egypt. Now therefore be not grieved, nor angry with yourselves, that ye sold me hither: for God did send me before you to preserve life. For these two years hath the famine been in the land: and yet there are five years, in the which there shall neither be earing nor harvest. And God sent me before you to preserve you a posterity in the earth, and to save your lives by a great deliverance. So now it was not you that sent me hither, but God: and he hath made me a father to Pharaoh, and lord of all his house, and a ruler throughout all the land of Egypt. Haste ye, and go up to my father, and say unto him, Thus saith thy son Joseph, God hath made me lord of all Egypt: come down unto me, tarry not: And thou shalt dwell in the land of Goshen, and thou shalt be near unto me, thou, and thy children, and thy children's children, and thy flocks, and thy herds, and all that thou hast: And there will I nourish thee; for yet there are five years of famine; lest thou, and thy household, and all that thou hast, come to poverty. And, behold, your eyes see, and the eyes of my brother Benjamin, that it is my mouth that speaketh unto you. And ye shall tell my father of all my glory in Egypt, and of all that ye have seen; and ye shall haste and bring down my father hither.

And he fell upon his brother Benjamin's neck, and wept; and Benjamin wept upon his neck. he kissed all his brethren, and wept upon them: and after that his brethren talked with him.

And the fame thereof was heard in Pharaoh's house, saying, Joseph's brethren are come: and it pleased Pharaoh well, and his servants. And Pharaoh said unto Joseph, Say unto thy brethren, This do ye; lade your beasts, and go, get you unto the land of Canaan; and take your father and your households, and come unto me: and I will give you the good of the land of Egypt, and ye shall eat the fat of the land. Now thou art commanded, this do ye; take you wagons out of the land of Egypt for your little ones, and for your wives, and bring your father, and come. Also regard not your stuff; for the good of all the land of Egypt is yours.

And the children of Israel did so: and Joseph gave them wagons, according to the commandment of Pharaoh, and gave them provision for the way. To all of them he gave each man changes of raiment; but to Benjamin he gave three hundred pieces of silver, and five changes of raiment. And to his father he sent after this manner; ten asses laden with the good things of Egypt, and ten she asses laden with corn and bread and meat for his father by the way.

So he sent his brethren away, and they departed: and he said unto them, See that ye fall not out by the way.

And they went up out of Egypt, and came into the land of Canaan unto Jacob their father, and told him, saying, Joseph is yet alive, and he is governor over all the land of Egypt. And Jacob's heart fainted, for he believed them not.

And they told him all the words of Joseph, which he had said unto them: and when he saw the wagons which Joseph had sent to carry him, the spirit of Jacob their father revived: And Israel said, It is enough; Joseph my son is yet alive: I will go and see him before I die.

And Israel took his journey with all that he had, and came to Beer-sheba, and offered sacrifices unto the God of his father Isaac.

And God spake unto Israel in the visions of the night, and said, Jacob, Jacob. And he said, Here am I.

And he said, I am God, the God of thy father: fear not to go down into Egypt; for I will there make of thee a great nation: I will go down with thee into Egypt; and I will also surely bring thee up again: and Joseph shall put his hand upon thine eyes.

The Bible

Daniel as Interpreter of King Nebuchadnezzar's Dream
(The Book of Daniel, Chapter 2)
Second century BCE

The prisoner Daniel must not only interpret but describe a dream, the details of which King Nebuchadnezzar has completely forgotten.

And in the second year of the reign of Nebuchadnezzar Nebuchadnezzar dreamed dreams, wherewith his spirit was troubled, and his sleep brake from him.

Then the king commanded to call the magicians, and the astrologers, and the sorcerers, and the Chaldeans, for to shew the king his dreams. So they came and stood before the king. And the king said unto them, I have dreamed a dream, and my spirit was troubled to know the dream.

Then spake the Chaldeans to the king in Syriack, O king, live for ever: tell thy servants the dream, and we will shew the interpretation.

The king answered and said to the Chaldeans, The thing is gone from me: if ye will not make known unto me the dream, with the interpretation thereof, ye shall be cut in pieces, and your houses shall be made a dunghill. But if ye shew the dream, and the interpretation thereof, ye shall receive of me gifts and rewards and great honour: therefore shew me the dream, and the interpretation thereof.

They answered again and said, Let the king tell his servants the dream, and we will shew the interpretation of it.

The king answered and said, I know of certainty that ye would gain the time, because ye see the thing is gone from me. But if ye will not make known unto me the dream, there is but one decree for you: for ye have prepared lying and corrupt words to speak before me, till the time be changed: therefore tell me the dream, and I shall know that ye can shew me the interpretation thereof.

The Chaldeans answered before the king, and said, There is not a man upon the earth that can shew the king's matter: therefore there is no king, lord, nor ruler, that asked such things at any magician, or astrologer, or Chaldean. And it is a rare thing that the king requireth, and there is none other that can shew it before the king, except the gods, whose dwelling is not with flesh.

For this cause the king was angry and very furious, and commanded to destroy all the wise men of Babylon. And the decree went forth that the wise men should be slain; and they sought Daniel and his fellows to be slain.

Then Daniel answered with counsel and wisdom to Arioch the captain of the king's guard, which was gone forth to slay the wise men of Babylon: He answered and said to Arioch the king's captain, Why is the decree so hasty from the king? Then Arioch made the thing known to Daniel. Then Daniel went in, and desired of the king that he would give him time, and that he would shew the king the interpretation. Then Daniel went to his house, and made the thing known to Hananiah, Mishael, and Azariah, his companions: That they would desire mercies of the God of heaven concerning this secret; that Daniel and his fellows should not perish with the rest of the wise men of Babylon.

Then was the secret revealed unto Daniel in a night vision. Then Daniel blessed the God of heaven. Daniel answered and said, Blessed be the name of God for ever and ever: for wisdom and might are his: And he changeth the times and the seasons: he removeth kings, and setteth up kings: he giveth wisdom unto the wise, and knowledge to them that know understanding: He revealeth the deep and secret things: he knoweth what is in the darkness, and the light dwelleth with him. I thank thee, and praise thee, O thou God of my fathers, who hast given me wisdom and might, and hast made known unto me now what we desired of thee: for thou hast now made known unto us the king's matter.

Therefore Daniel went in unto Arioch, whom the king had ordained to destroy the wise men of Babylon: he went and said thus unto him; Destroy not the wise men of Babylon: bring me in before the king, and I will shew unto the king the interpretation.

Then Arioch brought in Daniel before the king in haste and said thus unto him, I have found a man of the captives of Judah, that will make known unto the king the interpretation.

The king answered and said to Daniel, whose name was Belteshazzar, Art thou able to make known unto me the dream which I have seen, and the interpretation thereof?

Daniel answered in the presence of the king, and said,

The secret which the king hath demanded cannot the wise men, the astrologers, the magicians, the soothsayers, shew unto the king; but there is a God in heaven that revealeth secrets, and maketh known to the king Nebuchadnezzar what shall be in the latter days. Thy dream, and the visions of thy head upon thy bed, are these; as for thee, O king, thy thoughts came into thy mind upon thy bed, what should come to pass hereafter: and he that revealeth secrets maketh known to thee what shall come to pass. But as for me, this secret is not revealed to me for any wisdom that I have more than any living, but for their sakes that shall make known the interpretation to the king, and that thou mightest know the thoughts of thy heart.

Thou, O king, sawest, and behold a great image. This great image, whose brightness was excellent, stood before thee; and the form thereof was terrible. This image's head was of fine gold, his breast and his arms of silver, his belly and his thighs of brass, his legs of iron, his feet part of iron and part of clay. Thou sawest till that a stone was cut out without hands, which smote the image upon his feet that were of iron and clay, and brake them to pieces. Then was the iron, the clay, the brass, the silver, and the gold, broken to pieces together, and became like the chaff of the summer threshing floors; and the wind carried them away, that no place was found for them: and the stone that smote the image became a great mountain, and filled the whole earth. This is the dream; and we will tell the interpretation thereof before the king.

Thou, O king, art a king of kings: for the God of heaven hath given thee a kingdom, power, and strength, and glory. And wheresoever the children of men dwell, the beasts of the field and the fowls of the heaven hath he given into thine hand, and hath made thee ruler over them all. Thou art this head of gold. And after thee shall arise another kingdom inferior to thee, and another third kingdom of brass, which shall bear rule over all the earth. And the fourth kingdom shall be strong as iron: forasmuch as iron breaketh in pieces and subdueth all things: and as iron that breaketh all these, shall it break in pieces and bruise. And whereas thou sawest the feet and toes, part of potters' clay, and part of iron, the kingdom shall be divided; but there shall be in it of the strength of the iron, forasmuch as thou sawest the iron mixed with miry clay. And as the toes of the feet were part of iron, and part of clay, so the kingdom shall be partly strong, and partly broken. And whereas thou sawest iron mixed with miry clay, they shall mingle themselves with the seed of men: but they shall not cleave one to another, even as iron is not mixed with clay. And in the days of these kings shall the God of heaven set up a kingdom, which shall never be destroyed: and the kingdom shall not be left to other people, but it shall break in pieces and consume all these kingdoms, and it shall stand for ever. Forasmuch as thou sawest that the stone was cut out of the mountain without hands, and that it brake in pieces the iron, the brass, the clay, the silver, and the gold; the great God hath made known to the king what shall come to pass hereafter: and the dream is certain, and the interpretation thereof sure.

Then the king Nebuchadnezzar fell upon his face, and worshipped Daniel, and commanded that they should offer an oblation and sweet odours unto him. The king answered unto Daniel, and said, Of a truth it is, that your God is a God of gods, and a Lord of kings, and a revealer of secrets, seeing thou couldest reveal this secret.

Then the king made Daniel a great man, and gave him many great gifts, and made him ruler over the whole province of Babylon, and chief of the governors over all the wise men of Babylon.

Then Daniel requested of the king, and he set Shadrach, Meshach, and Abed-nego, over the affairs of the province of Babylon: but Daniel sat in the gate of the king.

The Bible

Dreams in the Life of Jesus (The Book of Matthew)
c. 80–90 C.E.

Dreams weigh heavily in the life of Jesus, from his heralding to Pilate's persecution of him. These passages are from Chapters 1–2 and 27.

Now the birth of Jesus Christ was on this wise: When as his mother Mary was espoused to Joseph, before they came together, she was found with child of the Holy Ghost. Then Joseph her husband, being a just man, and not willing to make her a publick example, was minded to put her away privily. But while he thought on these things, behold, the angel of the Lord appeared unto him in a dream, saying, Joseph, thou son of David, fear not to take unto thee Mary thy wife: for that which is conceived in her is of the Holy Ghost. And she shall bring forth a son, and thou shalt call his name Jesus: for he shall save his people from their sins.

Now all this was done, that it might be fulfilled which was spoken of the Lord by the prophet, saying, Behold, a virgin shall be with child, and shall bring forth a son, and they shall call his name Emmanuel, which being interpreted is, God with us.

Then Joseph being raised from sleep did as the angel of the Lord had bidden him, and took unto him his wife: And knew her not till she had brought forth her firstborn son: and he called his name Jesus.

Now when Jesus was born in Bethlehem of Judaea in the days of Herod the king, behold, there came wise men from the east to Jerusalem, Saying, Where is he that is born King of the Jews? For we have seen his star in the east, and are come to worship him.

When Herod the king had heard these things, he was troubled, and all Jerusalem with him. And when he had gathered all the chief priests and scribes of the people together, he demanded of them where Christ should be born.

And they said unto him, In Bethlehem of Judaea: for thus it is written by the prophet, And thou Bethlehem, in the land of Juda, art not the least among the princes of Juda: for out of thee shall come a Governor, that shall rule my people Israel.

Then Herod, when he had privily called the wise men, enquired of them diligently what time the star appeared.

And he sent them to Bethlehem, and said, Go and search diligently for the young child; and when ye have found him, bring me word again, that I may come and worship him also.

When they had heard the king, they departed; and, lo, the star, which they saw in the east, went before them, till it came and stood over where the young child was. When they saw the star, they rejoiced with exceeding great joy.

And when they were come into the house, they saw the young child with Mary his mother, and fell down, and worshipped him: and when they had opened their treasures, they presented unto him gifts; gold, and frankincense and myrrh. And being warned of God in a dream that they should not return to Herod, they departed into their own country another way.

And when they were departed, behold, the angel of the Lord appeareth to Joseph in a dream, saying, Arise, and take the young child and his mother, and flee into Egypt, and be thou there until I bring thee word: for Herod will seek the young child to destroy him.

When he arose, he took the young child and his mother by night, and departed into Egypt: And was there until the death of Herod: that it might be fulfilled which was spoken of the Lord by the prophet, saying, Out of Egypt have I called my son.

Then Herod, when he saw that he was mocked of the wise men, was exceeding wroth, and sent forth, and slew all the children that

were in Bethlehem, and in all the coasts thereof, from two years old
and under, according to the time which he had diligently enquired
of the wise men.

Then was fulfilled that which was spoken by Jeremy the prophet,
saying, In Rama was there a voice heard, lamentation, and weeping,
and great mourning, Rachel weeping for her children, and would
not be comforted, because they are not.

But when Herod was dead, behold, an angel of the Lord appeareth
in a dream to Joseph in Egypt, Saying, Arise, and take the young
child and his mother, and go into the land of Israel: for they are dead
which sought the young child's life.

And he arose, and took the young child and his mother, and came
into the land of Israel.

But when he heard that Archelaus did reign in Judaea in the room
of his father Herod, he was afraid to go thither: notwithstanding,
being warned of God in a dream, he turned aside into the parts of
Galilee: And he came and dwelt in a city called Nazareth: that it
might be fulfilled which was spoken by the prophets, He shall be
called a Nazarene.

[. . .]

(Ch. 27) {*Thirty-three years later.*}

And Jesus stood before the governor: and the governor asked
him, saying, Art thou the King of the Jews? And Jesus said unto him,
Thou sayest.

And when he was accused of the chief priests and elders, he
answered nothing.

Then said Pilate unto him, Hearest thou not how many things
they witness against thee?

And he answered him to never a word; insomuch that the governor
marvelled greatly.

Now at that feast the governor was wont to release unto the people
a prisoner, whom they would. And they had then a notable prisoner,
called Barabbas. Therefore when they were gathered together, Pilate
said unto them, Whom will ye that I release unto you? Barabbas, or
Jesus which is called Christ? For he knew that for envy they had
delivered him.

When he was set down on the judgment seat, his wife sent unto
him, saying, Have thou nothing to do with that just man: for I have
suffered many things this day in a dream because of him. But the
chief priests and elders persuaded the multitude that they should ask
Barabbas, and destroy Jesus.

Euripides

Hecuba
c. 424 BCE

In this play by Euripides, the Trojan Queen Hecuba's nightmare at the conclusion of the Trojan War is indeed a premonition, and though her prayer is moving, it falls on deaf ears.

HECUBA: Guide these aged steps, my servants, forth before the house; guide and support your fellow-slave, your queen of yore, ye maids of Troy. Take hold upon my aged hand, support me, guide me, lift me up; and I will lean upon your bended arm as on a staff and quicken my halting footsteps onwards.

O dazzling light of Zeus! O gloom of night! why am I thus scared by fearful visions of the night? O Earth, dread queen, mother of dreams that flit on sable wings! I am seeking to avert the vision of the night, the sight of horror which I saw so clearly in my dreams touching my son, who is safe in Thrace, and Polyxena, my daughter dear. Ye gods of this land! preserve my son, the last and only anchor of my house, now settled in Thrace, the land of snow, safe in the keeping of his father's friend. Some fresh disaster is in store, a new strain of sorrow will be added to our woe. Such ceaseless thrills of terror never wrung my heart before. Oh! where, ye Trojan maidens, can I find inspired Helenus or Cassandra, that they may read me my dream? For I saw a dappled deer mangled by a wolf's bloody fangs, torn from my knees by force, piteously. And this too filled me with fright; over the summit of his tomb appeared Achilles' phantom, and for his prize he would have one of the luckless maids of Troy. Therefore, I implore you, powers divine, avert this horror from my daughter, from my child.

Herodotus

Histories (The Dream of Croesus)
c. 430 BCE

Herodotus's Histories *are a product of his travels around the regions surrounding the Mediterranean Sea in the fifth century BCE. He gathered information and illuminating stories about various cultures and legendary peoples. In this passage, King Croesus of Sardis queries his visitor Solon: " 'Stranger of Athens, we have heard much of thy wisdom and of thy travels through many lands, from love of knowledge and a wish to see the world. I am curious therefore to inquire of thee, whom, of all the men that thou hast seen, thou deemest the most happy?' This he asked because he thought himself the happiest of mortals: but Solon answered him without flattery, according to his true sentiments. . . ." Thus Solon's explanation below. Later, after a nightmare foreseeing his favored son's death, Croesus acts to prevent it. But what parent has ever been able to protect their children from harm eternally?*

[Solon] "[. . .] A long life gives one to witness much, and experience much oneself, that one would not choose. Seventy years I regard as the limit of the life of man. In these seventy years are contained, without reckoning intercalary months, twenty-five thousand and two hundred days. Add an intercalary month to every other year, that the seasons may come round at the right time, and there will be, besides the seventy years, thirty-five such months, making an addition of one thousand and fifty days. The whole number of the days contained in the seventy years will thus be twenty-six thousand two hundred and fifty, whereof not one but will produce events unlike the rest. Hence man is wholly accident. For thyself, oh! Croesus, I see that thou art wonderfully rich, and art the lord of many nations; but with respect to that whereon thou questionest me, I have no answer to give, until I hear that thou hast closed thy life happily. For assuredly he who possesses great store of riches is no nearer happiness than he who has what suffices for his daily needs unless it so hap that luck attend upon him, and so he continue in the enjoyment of all his good things to the end of life. For many of the wealthiest men have been unfavoured of fortune, and many whose means were moderate have had excellent luck. Men of the former class excel those of the latter but in two respects; these last excel the former in many. The wealthy man is better able to content his desires, and to bear up against a sudden buffet of calamity. The other has less ability to withstand these evils (from which, however, his good luck keeps him clear), but he enjoys all these following blessings: he is whole of limb, a stranger to disease, free from misfortune, happy in his children, and comely to look upon. If, in addition to all this, he end his life well, he is of a truth the man of whom thou art in search, the man who may rightly be termed happy. Call him, however, until he die, not happy but fortunate.

"Scarcely, indeed, can any man unite all these advantages: as there is no country which contains within it all that it needs, but each, while it possesses some things, lacks others, and the best country is that which contains the most; so no single human being is complete in every respect—something is always lacking. He who unites the greatest number of advantages, and retaining them to the day of his death, then dies peaceably, that man alone, sire, is, in my judgment, entitled to bear the name of 'happy.' But in every matter it behoves us to mark well the end: for oftentimes God gives men a gleam of happiness, and then plunges them into ruin."

Such was the speech which Solon addressed to Croesus, a speech which brought him neither largess nor honour. The king saw him depart with much indifference, since he thought that a man must be an arrant fool who made no account of present good, but bade men always wait and mark the end.

After Solon had gone away a dreadful vengeance, sent of God, came upon Croesus, to punish him, it is likely, for deeming himself the happiest of men. First he had a dream in the night, which foreshowed him truly the evils that were about to befall him in the person of his son. For Croesus had two sons, one blasted by a natural defect, being deaf and dumb; the other, distinguished far above all his co-mates in every pursuit. The name of the last was Atys. It was this son concerning whom he dreamt a dream, that he would die by the blow of an iron weapon. When he woke, he considered earnestly with himself, and, greatly alarmed at the dream, instantly made his son take a wife, and whereas in former years the youth had been wont to command the Lydian forces in the field, he now would not suffer him to accompany them. All the spears and javelins, and weapons used in the wars, he removed out of the male apartments, and laid them in heaps in the chambers of the women, fearing lest perhaps one of the weapons that hung against the wall might fall and strike him.

Now it chanced that while he was making arrangements for the wedding, there came to Sardis a man under a misfortune, who had upon him the stain of blood. He was by race a Phrygian, and belonged to the family of the king. Presenting himself at the palace of Croesus, he prayed to be admitted to purification according to the customs of the country. Now the Lydian method of purifying is very nearly the same as the Greek. Croesus granted the request, and went through all the customary rites, after which he asked the suppliant of his birth and country, addressing him as follows: "Who art thou, stranger, and from what part of Phrygia fleddest thou to take refuge at my hearth? And whom, moreover, what man or what woman, hast thou slain?"

"Oh! king," replied the Phrygian, "I am the son of Gordias, son of Midas. I am named Adrastus. The man I unintentionally slew was my own brother. For this my father drove me from the land, and I lost all. Then fled I here to thee."

"Thou art the offspring," Croesus rejoined, "of a house friendly to mine, and thou art come to friends. Thou shalt want for nothing so long as thou abidest in my dominions. Bear thy misfortune as easily as thou mayest, so will it go best with thee." Thenceforth Adrastus lived in the palace of the king.

It chanced that at this very same time there was in the Mysian Olympus a huge monster of a boar, which went forth often from this mountain-country, and wasted the corn-fields of the Mysians. Many a time had the Mysians collected to hunt the beast, but instead of doing him any hurt, they came off always with some loss to themselves. At length they sent ambassadors to Croesus, who delivered their message to him in these words: "Oh! king, a mighty monster of a boar has appeared in our parts, and destroys the labour of our hands. We do our best to take him, but in vain. Now therefore we beseech thee to let thy son accompany us back, with some chosen youths and hounds, that we may rid our country of the animal." Such was the tenor of their prayer.

But Croesus bethought him of his dream, and answered, "Say no more of my son going with you; that may not be in any wise. He is but just joined in wedlock, and is busy enough with that. I will grant you a picked band of Lydians, and all my huntsmen and hounds; and I will charge those whom I send to use all zeal in aiding you to rid your country of the brute."

With this reply the Mysians were content; but the king's son, hearing what the prayer of the Mysians was, came suddenly in, and on the refusal of Croesus to let him go with them, thus addressed his father: "Formerly, my father, it was deemed the noblest and most suitable thing for me to frequent the wars and hunting-parties, and win myself glory in them; but now thou keepest me away from both, although thou hast never beheld in me either cowardice or lack of spirit. What face meanwhile must I wear as I walk to the forum or return from it? What must the citizens, what must my young bride think of me? What sort of man will she suppose her husband to be? Either, therefore, let me go to the chase of this boar, or give me a reason why it is best for me to do according to thy wishes."

Then Croesus answered, "My son, it is not because I have seen in thee either cowardice or aught else which has displeased me that I keep thee back; but because a vision which came before me in a dream as I slept, warned me that thou wert doomed to die young, pierced by an iron weapon. It was this which first led me to hasten on thy wedding, and now it hinders me from sending thee upon this enterprise. Fain would I keep watch over thee, if by any means I may cheat fate of thee during my own lifetime. For thou art the one and only son that I possess; the other, whose hearing is destroyed, I regard as if he were not."

"Ah! father," returned the youth, "I blame thee not for keeping watch over me after a dream so terrible; but if thou mistakest, if thou dost not apprehend the dream aright, 'tis no blame for me to show thee wherein thou errest. Now the dream, thou saidst thyself, foretold that I should die stricken by an iron weapon. But what hands has a boar to strike with? What iron weapon does he wield? Yet this is what thou fearest for me. Had the dream said that I should die pierced by a tusk, then thou hadst done well to keep me away; but it said a weapon. Now here we do not combat men, but a wild animal. I pray thee, therefore, let me go with them."

"There thou hast me, my son," said Croesus, "thy interpretation is better than mine. I yield to it, and change my mind, and consent to let thee go."

Then the king sent for Adrastus, the Phrygian, and said to him, "Adrastus, when thou wert smitten with the rod of affliction—no reproach, my friend—I purified thee, and have taken thee to live with me in my palace, and have been at every charge. Now, therefore, it behoves thee to requite the good offices which thou hast received at my hands by consenting to go with my son on this hunting party, and to watch over him, if perchance you should be attacked upon the road by some band of daring robbers. Even apart from this, it were right for thee to go where thou mayest make thyself famous by noble deeds. They are the heritage of thy family, and thou too art so stalwart and strong."

Adrastus answered, "Except for thy request. Oh! king, I would rather have kept away from this hunt; for methinks it ill beseems a man under a misfortune such as mine to consort with his happier compeers; and besides, I have no heart to it. On many grounds I had stayed behind; but, as thou urgest it, and I am bound to pleasure thee (for truly it does behove me to requite thy good offices), I am content to do as thou wishest. For thy son, whom thou givest into my charge, be sure thou shalt receive him back safe and sound, so far as depends upon a guardian's carefulness."

Thus assured, Croesus let them depart, accompanied by a band of picked youths, and well provided with dogs of chase. When they reached Olympus, they scattered in quest of the animal; he was soon found, and the hunters, drawing round him in a circle, hurled their weapons at him. Then the stranger, the man who had been purified of blood, whose name was Adrastus, he also hurled his spear at the boar, but missed his aim, and struck Atys. Thus was the son of Croesus slain by the point of an iron weapon, and the warning of the vision was fulfilled. Then one ran to Sardis to bear the tidings to the king, and he came and informed him of the combat and of the fate that had befallen his son.

If it was a heavy blow to the father to learn that his child was dead, it yet more strongly affected him to think that the very man whom he himself once purified had done the deed. In the violence of his grief he called aloud on Jupiter Catharsius to be a witness of what he had suffered at the stranger's hands. Afterwards he invoked the same god as Jupiter Ephistius and Hetaereus—using the one term because he had unwittingly harboured in his house the man who had now slain his son; and the other, because the stranger, who had been sent as his child's guardian, had turned out his most cruel enemy.

Presently the Lydians arrived, bearing the body of the youth, and behind them followed the homicide. He took his stand in front of the corpse, and, stretching forth his hands to Croesus, delivered himself into his power with earnest entreaties that he would sacrifice him upon the body of his son—"his former misfortune was burthen enough; now that he had added to it a second, and had brought ruin on the man who purified him, he could not bear to live."

Then Croesus, when he heard these words, was moved with pity towards Adrastus, notwithstanding the bitterness of his own calamity; and so he answered, "Enough, my friend; I have all the revenge that I require, since thou givest sentence of death against thyself. But in sooth it is not thou who hast injured me, except so far as thou hast unwittingly dealt the blow. Some god is the author of my misfortune, and I was forewarned of it a long time ago." Croesus after this buried the body of his son, with such honours as befitted the occasion. Adrastus, son of Gordias, son of Midas, the destroyer of his brother in time past, the destroyer now of his purifier, regarding himself as the most unfortunate wretch whom he had ever known, so soon as all was quiet about the place, slew himself upon the tomb. Croesus, bereft of his son, gave himself up to mourning for two full years.

Homer

The Iliad (The Dream of Agamemnon)
c. 800–700 BCE

*In the ancient Greek tale of the Trojan War by the anonymous poet
we refer to as Homer, Zeus, the king of the gods, commands a dream
to deceive Agamemnon, the leader of the Greek armies. So vivid and
persuasive is the dream that Agamemnon is prompted to immediate—but
foolish—action.*

(Book 2)

Now all the other gods and men, lords of chariots, slumbered the
whole night through, but Zeus was not holden of sweet sleep, for he
was pondering in his heart how he might do honour to Achilles and
lay many low beside the ships of the Achaeans. And this plan seemed
to his mind the best, to send to Agamemnon, son of Atreus, a baneful
dream. So he spake, and addressed him with winged words: "Up, go,
thou baneful Dream, unto the swift ships of the Achaeans, and
when thou art come to the hut of Agamemnon, son of Atreus, tell
him all my word truly, even as I charge thee. Bid him arm the long-
haired Achaeans with all speed, since now he may take the broad-wayed
city of the Trojans. For the immortals, that have homes upon Olympus,
are no longer divided in counsel, since Hera hath bent the minds of
all by her supplication, and over the Trojans hang woes."

So spake he, and the Dream went his way, when he had heard
this saying. Forthwith he came to the swift ships of the Achaeans,
and went his way to Agamemnon, son of Atreus, and found him
sleeping in his hut, and over him was shed ambrosial slumber. So he
took his stand above his head, in the likeness of the son of Neleus,
even Nestor, whom above all the elders Agamemnon held in honour;
likening himself to him, the Dream from heaven spake, saying: "Thou
sleepest, son of wise-hearted Atreus, the tamer of horses. To sleep
the whole night through beseemeth not a man that is a counsellor,
to whom a host is entrusted, and upon whom rest so many cares.
But now, hearken thou quickly unto me, for I am a messenger to
thee from Zeus, who, far away though he be, hath exceeding care
for thee and pity. He biddeth thee arm the long-haired Achaeans
with all speed, since now thou mayest take the broad-wayed city of
the Trojans. For the immortals that have homes upon Olympus are
no longer divided in counsel, since Hera hath bent the minds of all

by her supplication, and over the Trojans hang woes by the will of Zeus. But do thou keep this in thy heart, nor let forgetfulness lay hold of thee, when so honey-hearted sleep shall let thee go."

So spoke the Dream, and departed, and left him there, pondering in his heart on things that were not to be brought to pass. For in sooth he deemed that he should take the city of Priam that very day, fool that he was! seeing he knew not what deeds Zeus was purposing, who was yet to bring woes and groanings on Trojans alike and Danaans throughout the course of stubborn fights. Then he awoke from sleep, and the divine voice was ringing in his ears. He sat upright and did on his soft tunic, fair and glistering, and about him cast his great cloak, and beneath his shining feet he bound his fair sandals, and about his shoulders flung his silver-studded sword; and he grasped the sceptre of his fathers, imperishable ever, and therewith took his way along the ships of the brazen-coated Achaeans.

Now the goddess Dawn went up to high Olympus, to announce the light to Zeus and the other immortals, but Agamemnon bade the clear-voiced heralds summon to the place of gathering the long-haired Achaeans. And they made summons, and the men gathered full quickly. But the king first made the council of the great-souled elders to sit down beside the ship of Nestor, the king Pylos-born. And when he had called them together, he contrived a cunning plan, and said: "Hearken, my friends, a Dream from heaven came to me in my sleep through the ambrosial night, and most like was it to goodly Nestor, in form and in stature and in build. It took its stand above my head, and spake to me, saying: 'Thou sleepest, son of wise-hearted Atreus, the tamer of horses. To sleep the whole night through beseemeth not a man that is a counsellor, to whom a host is entrusted, and upon whom rest so many cares. But now, hearken thou quickly unto me, for I am a messenger to thee from Zeus, who, far away though he be, hath exceeding care for thee and pity. He biddeth thee arm the long-haired Achaeans with all speed, since now thou mayest take the broad-wayed city of the Trojans. For the immortals that have homes upon Olympus are no longer divided in counsel, since Hera hath bent the minds of all by her supplication, and over the Trojans hang woes by the will of Zeus. But do thou keep this in thy heart.' So spake he, and was flown away, and sweet sleep let me go. Nay, come now, if in any wise we may, let us arm the sons of the Achaeans; but first will I make trial of them in speech, as is right, and will bid them flee with their benched ships; but do you from this side and from that bespeak them, and strive to hold them back."

So saying, he sate him down, and among them uprose Nestor, that was king of sandy Pylos. He with good intent addressed their gathering and spake among them: "My friends, leaders and rulers of the Argives, were it any other of the Achaeans that told us this dream we might deem it a false thing, and turn away therefrom the more; but now hath he seen it who declares himself to be far the mightiest of the Achaeans. Nay, come then, if in any wise we may arm the sons of the Achaeans."

He spake, and led the way forth from the council, and the other sceptred kings rose up thereat and obeyed the shepherd of the host; and the people the while were hastening on. Even as the tribes of thronging bees go forth from some hollow rock, ever coming on afresh, and in clusters over the flowers of spring fly in throngs, some here, some there; even so from the ships and huts before the low sea-beach marched forth in companies their many tribes to the place of gathering.

★ ★ ★

The Dream of Achilles

In the second to last book of The Iliad, *Achilles dreams of his slain beloved, the warrior Patroclus, who asks Achilles to retrieve his body from the battlefield. Patroclus also foretells Achilles' end. Most heartbreakingly, Achilles reaches out for a final embrace.*

(Book 23)

But when they had put from them the desire of food and drink, they went each man to his hut to take his rest; but the son of Peleus [Achilles] upon the shore of the loud-resounding sea lay groaning heavily amid the host of the Myrmidons, in an open space where the waves splashed upon the shore. And when sleep seized him, loosening the cares of his heart, being shed in sweetness round about him—for sore weary were his glorious limbs with speeding after Hector unto windy Ilios—then there came to him the spirit of hapless Patroclus, in all things like his very self, in stature and fair eyes and in voice, and in like raiment was he clad withal; and he stood above Achilles' head and spake to him, saying: "Thou sleepest, and hast forgotten me, Achilles. Not in my life wast thou unmindful of me, but now in my death! Bury me with all speed, that I pass within the gates of Hades. Afar do the spirits keep me aloof, the phantoms of men that have done with toils, neither suffer they me to join myself to them beyond the River, but vainly I wander through the wide-gated house of Hades. And give me thy hand, I pitifully entreat thee, for never more again shall I come back from out of Hades, when once ye have given me my due of fire. Never more in life shall we sit apart from our dear comrades and take counsel together, but for me hath loathly fate opened its maw, the fate that was appointed me even from my birth. Aye, and thou thyself also, Achilles like to the gods, art doomed to be brought low beneath the wall of the wealthy Trojans. And another thing will I speak, and charge thee, if so be thou wilt hearken. Lay not my bones apart from thine, Achilles, but let them lie together, even as we were reared in your house, when Menoetius brought me, being yet a little lad, from Opoeis to your country, by reason of grievous man-slaying, on the day when I slew Amphidamus' son in my folly, though I willed it not, in wrath over the dice. Then the knight Peleus received me into his house and reared me with kindly care and named me thy squire; even so let one coffer enfold our bones, a golden coffer with handles twain, the which thy queenly mother gave thee."

Then in answer spake to him Achilles, swift of foot: "Wherefore, O head beloved, art thou come hither, and thus givest me charge about each thing? Nay, verily I will fulfill thee all, and will hearken even as thou biddest. But, I pray thee, draw thou nigher; though it be but for a little space let us clasp our arms one about the other, and take our fill of dire lamenting." So saying he reached forth with his hands, yet clasped him not; but the spirit like a vapour was gone beneath the earth, gibbering faintly. And seized with amazement Achilles sprang up, and smote his hands together, and spake a word of wailing: "Look you now, even in the house of Hades is the spirit and phantom somewhat, albeit the mind be not anywise therein; for the whole night long hath the spirit of hapless Patroclus stood over me, weeping and wailing, and gave me charge concerning each thing, and was wondrously like his very self." So spake he, and in them all aroused the desire of lament, and rosy-fingered Dawn shone forth upon them while yet they wailed around the piteous corpse.

Homer

The Odyssey (Penelope's Dream)
c. 800–700 BCE

Odysseus, who left twenty years before to fight in the Trojan War, returns to his home in Ithaca, disguised as a beggar. Penelope, his extraordinarily patient wife, has been awaiting him. In Book 19, she recounts to the "stranger," whom, it seems, she unconsciously recognizes, her very telling dream, which has its own interpretation built in. Odysseus elaborates upon her interpretation, which will indeed come true.

And when she had washed him, and anointed him richly with oil, Odysseus again drew his chair nearer to the fire to warm himself, and hid the scar with his rags. Then wise Penelope was the first to speak, saying: "Stranger, this little thing further will I ask thee myself, for it will soon be the hour for pleasant rest, for him at least on whom sweet sleep may come despite his care. But to me has a god given sorrow that is beyond all measure, for day by day I find my joy in mourning and lamenting, while looking to my household tasks and those of my women in the house, but when night comes and sleep lays hold of all, I lie upon my bed, and sharp cares, crowding close about my throbbing heart, disquiet me, as I mourn. Even as when the daughter of Pandareus, the nightingale of the greenwood, sings sweetly, when spring is newly come, as she sits perched amid the thick leafage of the trees, and with many trilling notes pours forth her rich voice in wailing for her child, dear Itylus, whom she had one day slain with the sword unwittingly, Itylus, the son of king Zethus; even so my heart sways to and fro in doubt, whether to abide with my son and keep all things safe, my possessions, my slaves, and my great, high-roofed house, respecting the bed of my husband and the voice of the people, or to go now with him whosoever is best of the Achaeans, who woos me in the halls and offers bride-gifts past counting. Furthermore my son, so long as he was a child and slack of wit, would not suffer me to marry and leave the house of my husband; but now that he is grown and has reached the bounds of manhood, lo, he even prays me to go back again from these halls, being vexed for his substance that the Achaeans devour to his cost. But come now, hear this dream of mine, and interpret it for me. Twenty geese I have in the house that come forth from the water and eat wheat, and my heart warms with joy as I watch them. But forth from the mountain there came a great eagle with crooked beak and broke all their necks and killed them; and they lay strewn in a heap in the halls, while he was borne aloft to the bright sky. Now for my part I wept and wailed, in a dream though it was, and round me thronged the fair-tressed Achaean women, as I grieved piteously because the eagle had slain my geese. Then back he came and perched upon a projecting roof-beam, and with the voice of a mortal man checked my weeping, and said: 'Be of good cheer, daughter of far-famed Icarius; this is no dream, but a true vision of good which shall verily find fulfillment. The geese are the wooers, and I, that before was the eagle, am now again come back as thy husband, who will let loose a cruel doom upon all the wooers.' So he spoke, and sweet sleep released me, and looking about I saw the geese in the halls, feeding on wheat beside the trough, where they had before been wont to feed."

Then Odysseus of many wiles answered her and said: "Lady, in no wise is it possible to wrest this dream aside and give it another meaning, since verily Odysseus himself has shewn thee how he will bring it to pass. For the wooers' destruction is plain to see, for one and all; not one of them shall escape death and the fates."

Then wise Penelope answered him again: "Stranger, dreams verily are baffling and unclear of meaning, and in no wise do they find fulfillment in all things for men. For two are the gates of shadowy dreams, and one is fashioned of horn and one of ivory. Those dreams that pass through the gate of sawn ivory deceive men, bringing words that find no fulfillment. But those that come forth through the gate of polished horn bring true issues to pass, when any mortal sees them. But in my case it was not from thence, methinks, that my strange dream came. Ah, truly it would then have been welcome to me and to my son. But another thing will I tell thee, and do thou lay it to heart. Even now is coming on this morn of evil name which is to cut me off from the house of Odysseus; for now I shall appoint for a contest those axes which he was wont to set up in line in his halls, like props of a ship that is building, twelve in all, and he would stand afar off and shoot an arrow through them. Now then I shall set this contest before the wooers: whosoever shall most easily string the bow in his hands, and shoot an arrow through all twelve axes, with him will I go and forsake this house of my wedded life, a house most fair and filled with livelihood, which, methinks, I shall ever remember even in my dreams."

Then Odysseus of many wiles answered her, and said: "Honored wife of Odysseus, son of Laertes, no longer now do thou put off this contest in thy halls; for, I tell thee, Odysseus of many wiles will be here, ere these men, handling this polished bow, shall have strung it, and shot an arrow through the iron."

Then wise Penelope answered him: "If thou couldest but wish, stranger, to sit here in my halls and give me joy, sleep should never be shed over my eyelids. But it is in no wise possible that men should forever be sleepless, for the immortals have appointed a proper time for each thing upon the earth, the giver of grain. But I verily will go to my upper chamber and lay me on my bed, which has become for me a bed of wailings, ever bedewed with my tears, since the day when Odysseus went to see evil Ilios, that should never be named. There will I lay me down, but do thou lie down here in the hall, when thou hast strewn bedding on the floor; or let the maids set a bedstead for thee." So saying, she went up to her bright upper chamber, not alone, for with her went her handmaids as well. And when she had gone up to her upper chamber with her handmaids, she then bewailed Odysseus, her dear husband, until flashing-eyed Athena cast sweet sleep upon her eyelids.

Ovid

Metamorphoses
c. 8 CE

From his elaboration of Sleep's chamber to Sleep's son Morpheus appearing to the sailor Ceyx's wife Halcyone to announce Ceyx's death, the Latin poet Ovid (43 BCE–17 CE) soars with invention in this tale of metamorphosis. Because transformation is Ovid's theme, the husband and wife are fittingly metamorphosed and reunited.

Meanwhile, Halcyone, all unaware of his sad wreck, counts off the passing nights and hastens to prepare for him his clothes that he may wear as soon as he returns to her; and she is choosing what to wear herself, and vainly promises his safe return—all this indeed, while she in hallowed prayer is giving frankincense to please the gods: and first of loving adorations, she paid at the shrine of Juno. There she prayed for Ceyx—after he had suffered death, that he might journey safely and return and might love her above all other women, this one last prayer alone was granted to her but Juno could not long accept as hers these supplications on behalf of one then dead; and that she might persuade Halcyone to turn her death-polluted hands away from hallowed altars, Juno said in haste, "O, Iris, best of all my messengers, go quickly to the dreadful court of Sleep, and in my name command him to despatch a dream in the shape of Ceyx, who is dead, and tell Halcyone the woeful truth." So she commanded.—Iris instantly assumed a garment of a thousand tints; and as she marked the high skies with her arch, went swiftly thence as ordered, to the place where Sleep was then concealed beneath a rock.

Near the Cimmerian Land there is a cave, with a long entrance, in a hallowed mountain, the home of slothful Sleep. To that dark cave the Sun, when rising or in middle skies, or setting, never can approach with light. There dense fogs, mingled with the dark, exhale darkness from the black soil—and all that place is shadowed in a deep mysterious gloom. No wakeful bird with visage crested high calls forth the morning's beauty in clear notes; nor do the watchful dogs, more watchful geese, nor wild beasts, cattle, nor the waving trees, make sound or whisper; and the human voice is never heard there—silent Rest is there. But, from the bottom of a rock beneath, Lethean waters of a stream ooze forth, sounds of a rivulet, which trickle with soft murmuring amid the pebbles and invite soft sleep. Before the cavern doors most fertile poppies and a wealth of herbs bloom in abundance, from the juice of which the humid night-hours gather sleep and spread it over darkened Earth. No door is in that cavern-home and not a hinge's noise nor guarding porter's voice disturbs the calm. But in the middle is a resting-couch, raised high on night-black ebony and soft with feathered cushions, all jet black, concealed by a rich coverlet as dark as night, on which the god of sleep, dissolved in sloth lies with unmoving limbs. Around him there in all directions, unsubstantial dreams recline in imitation of all shapes—as many as the uncounted ears of corn at harvest—as the myriad leaves of trees—or tiny sand grains spread upon the shore.

As soon as Iris entered that dread gloom, she pushed aside the visions in her way with her fair glowing hands; and instantly, that sacred cavern of the god of Sleep was all illuminated with the glow and splendor of her garment.—Out of himself the god with difficulty lifted up his languid eyes. From this small sign of life relapsing many times to languid sloth, while nodding, with his chin he struck his breast again and again. At last he roused himself from gloom and slumber; and, while raised upon his elbow, he enquired of Iris why she came to him.—He knew her by her name. She answered him, "O, Sleep, divine repose of all things! Gentlest of the deities! Peace to the troubled mind, from which you drive the cares of life, restorer of men's strength when wearied with the toils of day, command a vision that shall seem the actual form of royal Ceyx to visit Trachin famed for Hercules and tell Halcyone his death by shipwreck. It is Juno's wish." Iris departed after this was said. For she no longer could endure the effect of slumber-vapor; and as soon as she knew sleep was creeping over her tired limbs she flew from there—and she departed by the rainbow, over which she came before.

Out of the multitude—his thousand sons—the god of sleep raised Morpheus by his power. Most skillful of his sons, who had the art of imitating any human shape; and dexterously could imitate in men the gait and countenance, and every mode of speaking. He could simulate the dress and customary words of any man he chose to represent—but he could not assume the form of anything but man. Such was his art. Another of Sleep's sons could imitate all kinds of animals; such as a wild beast or a flying bird, or even a serpent with its twisted shape; and that son, by the gods above was called Icelos— but the inhabitants of earth called him Phobetor—and a third son, named Phantasos, cleverly could change himself into the forms of earth that have no life; into a statue, water, or a tree. It was the habit of these three to show themselves at night to kings and generals; and other sons would frequently appear among the people of the common class. All such the aged god of Sleep passed by. Selecting only Morpheus from among the many brothers to accomplish this, and execute what Iris had desired. And after all that work, he dropped his head, and sank again in languid drowsiness, shrinking to sloth within his lofty couch.

Morpheus at once flew through the night of darkness, on his wings that make no sound, and in brief space of intervening time, arrived at the Haemonian city walls; and there he laid aside his wings, and took the face and form of Ceyx. In that form as one deprived of life, devoid of clothes, wan and ghastly, he stood beside the bed of the sad wife. The hero's beard seemed dripping, sea water streamed down from his drenching hair. Then leaning on the bed, while dropping tears were running down his cheeks, he said these words: "Most wretched wife, can you still recognize your own loved Ceyx, or have my looks changed: so much with death you can not?—Look at me, and you will be assured I am your own: but here instead of your dear husband, you will find only his ghost. Your faithful prayers did not avail, Halcyone, and I have perished. Give up all deluding hopes of my return. The stormy Southwind caught my ship while sailing the Aegean sea; and there, tossed by the mighty wind, my ship was dashed to pieces. While I vainly called upon your name, the angry waters closed above my drowning head and it is no uncertain messenger that tells you this and nothing from vague rumors has been told. But it is I myself, come from the wreck, now telling you my fate. Come then, arise, shed tears, and put on mourning; do not send me un-lamented, down to Tartarus." And Morpheus added to these words a voice which she would certainly believe was her beloved husband's; and he seemed to be shedding fond human tears; and even his hands were moved in gestures that Ceyx often used. Halcyone shed tears and groaned aloud, and, as she moved her arms and caught at his dear body, she embraced the vacant air she cried out loudly, "Stay, oh stay with me! Why do you hurry from me? We will go together!" Agitated by her own excited voice; and by what seemed to be her own dear husband, she awoke from sleep. And first looked all about her to persuade herself that he whom she had lately seen must yet be with her, for she had aroused the servants who in haste brought lights desired.

When she could find him nowhere, in despair she struck her face and tore her garment from her breast and beat her breast with mourning hands. She did not wait to loosen her long hair; but tore it with her hands and to her nurse, who asked the cause of her wild grief, she cried: "Alas, Halcyone is no more! no more! with her own Ceyx she is dead! is dead! Away with words of comfort, he is lost by shipwreck! I have seen him, and I knew him surely—as a ghost he came to me; and when desirous to detain him, I stretched forth my arms to him, his ghost left me—it vanished from me; but it surely was the ghost of my dead husband. If you ask description of it, I must truly say he did not have his well known features—he was not so cheerful as he was in life! Alas, I saw him pale and naked, with his hair still dripping—his ghost from the waves stood on this very spot": and while she moaned she sought his footprints on the floor. "Alas, this was my fear, and this is what my mind shuddered to think of, when I begged that you would not desert me for the wind's control. But how I wish, since you were sailing forth to perish, that you had but taken me with you. If I had gone with you, it would have been advantage to me, for I should have shared the whole course of my life with you and you would not have met a separate death. I linger here but I have met my death, I toss on waves, and drift upon the sea. My heart would be more cruel than the waves, if it should ask me to endure this life—if I should struggle to survive such grief. I will not strive nor leave you so forlorn, at least I'll follow you to death. If not the urn at least the lettered stone shall keep us still together. If your bones are not united with my bones, 'tis sure our names must be united." Overcome with grief, she could not say another word—but she continued wailing, and her groans were heaved up from her sorrow-stricken breast.

At early dawn, she went from her abode down to the seashore, where most wretchedly, she stood upon the spot from which he sailed, and sadly said; "He lingered here while he was loosening the cables, and he kissed me on this seashore when he left me here." And while she called to recollection all that she had seen when standing there, and while she looked far out on flowing waves from there, she noticed floating on the distant sea—what shall I say? At first even she could not be sure of what she saw. But presently although still distant—it was certainly a floating corpse. She could not see what man he might be, but because it seemed to her it surely was a shipwrecked body, she was moved as at an omen and began to weep; and, moaning as she stood there, said:—"Ah wretched one, whoever it may be, ah, wretched is the wife whom you have left!" As driven by the waves the body came still nearer to her, she was less and less the mistress of herself, the more she looked upon it; and, when it was close enough for her to see its features, she beheld her husband. "It is he," she cried and then she tore her face, her hair, her royal robe and then, extending both her trembling hands towards Ceyx, "So dearest one! So do you come to me again?" She cried, "O luckless mate."

A breakwater, made by the craft of man, adjoins the sea and breaks the shoreward rush of waves. To this she leaped—it seemed impossible—and then, while beating the light air with wings that instant formed upon her, she flew on, a mourning bird, and skimmed above the waves. And while she lightly flew across the sea her clacking mouth with its long slender bill, full of complaining, uttered moaning sounds: but when she touched the still and pallid form, embracing his dear limbs with her new wings, she gave cold kisses with her hardened bill. All those who saw it doubted whether Ceyx could feel her kisses; and it seemed to them the moving waves had raised his countenance. But he was truly conscious of her grief; and through the pity of the gods above, at last they both were changed to flying birds, together in their fate. Their love lived on, nor in these birds were marriage bonds dissolved, and they soon coupled and were parent birds. Each winter during seven full days of calm Halcyone broods on her floating nest—her nest that sails upon a halcyon sea: the passage of the deep is free from storms, throughout those seven full days; and Aeolus restraining harmful winds, within their cave, for his descendants' sake gives halcyon seas.

Sophocles

Oedipus the King
c. 429 BCE

Iocasta speaks great sense, refuting her husband Oedipus's nightmare-induced fear of his fate: to marry his mother. This, however, he has already done—for Iocasta is his mother. This most disturbing of all Greek myths—and Iocasta's statement—led to Sigmund Freud's most famous literary and psychological analysis, the Oedipus Complex.

IOCASTA: What should a mortal man fear, for whom the decrees of Fortune are supreme, and who has clear foresight of nothing? It is best to live at random, as one may. But fear not that you will wed your mother. Many men before now have slept with their mothers in dreams. But he to whom these things are as though nothing bears his life most easily.

III. Philosophy and Psychology

Anonymous

The Questions of King Milinda
c. 100 BCE–200 CE

This ancient text, composed over centuries, is a series of challenging dialogues between an inquisitive king and the Buddhist philosopher Nâgasena about human experience. This is "Dilemma the 75ᵗʰ: Dreams."

"Venerable Nâgasena, men and women in this world see dreams pleasant and evil, things they have seen before and things they have not, things they have done before and things they have not, dreams peaceful and terrible, dreams of matters near to them and distant from them, full of many shapes and innumerable colours. What is this that men call a dream, and who is it who dreams it?"

"It is a suggestion, O king, coming across the path of the mind which is what is called a dream. And there are six kinds of people who see dreams—the man who is of a windy humour, or of a bilious one, or of a phlegmatic one, the man who dreams dreams by the influence of a god, the man who does so by the influence of his own habits, and the man who does so in the way of prognostication. And of these, O king, only the last kind of dreams is true; all the rest are false."

"Venerable Nâgasena, when a man dreams a dream that is a prognostication, how is it? Does his own mind set out itself to seek the omen, or does the prognostication come of its own accord into the path of his mind, or does some one else come and tell him of it?"

"His own mind does not itself seek the omen, neither does any one else come and tell him of it. The prognostication comes of its own accord into his mind. It is like the case of a looking-glass, which does not go anywhere to seek for the reflection; neither does any one else come and put the reflection on to the looking-glass. But the object reflected comes from somewhere or other across the sphere over which the reflecting power of the looking-glass extends."

"Venerable Nâgasena, does the same mind which sees the dream also know: 'Such and such a result, auspicious or terrible, will follow?'"

"No, that is not so, O king. After the omen has occurred he tells others, and then they explain the meaning of it."

"Come, now, Nâgasena, give me a simile to explain this."

"It is like the marks, O king, and pimples, and cutaneous eruptions which arise on a man's body to his profit or loss, to his fame or dishonour, to his praise or blame, to his happiness or woe. Do in that case the pimples come because they know: 'Such and such is the event which we shall bring about?'"

"Certainly not, Sir. But according to the place on which the pimples have arisen, the fortune-tellers, making their observations, give decision, saying: 'Such and such will be the result.'"

"Well, in the same way, O king, it is not the same mind which dreams the dream which also knows: 'Such and such a result, conspicuous or terrible, will follow.' But after the omen has occurred he tells others, and they then explain the meaning of it."

"Venerable Nâgasena, when a man dreams a dream, is he awake or asleep?"

"Neither the one, O king; nor yet the other. But when his sleep has become light, and he is not yet fully conscious, in that interval it is that dreams are dreamt. When a man is in deep sleep, O king, his mind has returned home (has entered again into the Bhavanga), and a mind thus shut in does not act, and a mind hindered in its action knows not the evil and the good, and he who knows not has no dreams. It is when the mind is active that dreams are dreamt. Just, O king, as in the darkness and gloom, where no light is, no shadow will fall even on the most burnished mirror, so when a man is in deep sleep his mind has returned into itself, and a mind shut in does not act, and a mind inactive knows not the evil and the good, and he who knows not does not dream. For it is when the mind is active that dreams are dreamt. As the mirror, O king, are you to regard the body, as the darkness sleep, as the light the mind. Or again, O king, just as the glory of a sun veiled in fog is imperceptible, as its rays, though they do exist, are unable to pierce through, and as when its rays act not there is no light, so when a man is in deep sleep his mind has returned into itself, and a mind shut in does not act, and a mind inactive knows not the evil and the good, and he who knows not does not dream. For it is when the mind is active that dreams are dreamt. As the sun, O king, are you to regard the body, as the veil of fog sleep, as the rays the mind.

"Under two conditions, O king, is the mind inactive though the body is there—when a man being in deep sleep the mind has returned into itself, and when the man has fallen into a trance. The mind of a man who is awake, O king, is excited, open, clear, untrammelled, and no prognostication occurs to one whose mind is so. Just, O king, as men seeking concealment avoid the man who is open, candid, unoccupied, and unreserved,—just so is it that the divine intention is not manifested to the wakeful man, and the man who is awake therefore sees no dream. Or again, O king, just as the qualities which lead to wisdom are found not in that brother whose mode of livelihood and conduct are wrong, who is the friend of sinners, wicked, insolent, devoid of zeal,—just so is it that the divine intention is not manifested to the wakeful man, and the man who is awake, therefore, sees no dream."

"Venerable Nâgasena, is there a beginning, a middle, and an end in sleep?"

"Yes, O king, there is."

"Which then is the beginning, which the middle, and which the end?"

"The feeling of oppression and inability in the body, O king, of weakness, slackness, inertness—that is the beginning of sleep. The light 'monkey's sleep' in which a man still guards his scattered thoughts—that is the middle of sleep. When the mind has entered into itself—that is the end of sleep. And it is in the middle stage, O king, in the 'monkey's sleep' that dreams are dreamt. Just, O king, as when a man self-restrained with collected thoughts, stedfast in the faith, unshaken in wisdom, plunges deep into the woods far from the sound of strife, and thinks over some subtle matter, he there, tranquil and at peace, will master the meaning of it—just so a man still watchful, not fallen into sleep, but dozing in a 'monkey's sleep,' will dream a dream. As the sound of strife, so, O king, are you to regard wakefulness, and as the lonely wood the 'monkey's sleep.' And as that man avoiding the sound of strife, keeping out of sleep, remaining in the middle stage, will master the meaning of that subtle matter, so the

still watchful man, not fallen into sleep, but dozing in a 'monkey's sleep,'
will dream a dream."

"Very good, Nâgasena! That is so, and I accept it as you say."

Here ends the dilemma as to dreams.

Mary Arnold-Forster

Studies in Dreams
1921

*Arnold-Forster (1861–1951), though not a psychologist or specialist,
proved herself an incisive analyst of lucid dreaming.[12] The author whose
books she dreams of, George Borrow, was a nineteenth-century novelist and travel writer. Arnold-Forster dates her dream June 1913.*

I dreamed that a great prize had been offered in the *Westminster
Gazette* for an essay competition. The subject of the essay was to
be "The Books found in a Guest-chamber on a Week-end Visit."
I was on my way to a country house, and I wondered what books I
should actually find in the bedroom that I should occupy in the
house to which I was going. . . . The big country house that I came
to was like O— and I was taken upstairs on my arrival to a room
which I recognised as one in which I had several times slept on
visits there.

With my thoughts running on the essay I went quickly to the
bookshelf and looked eagerly at its contents. There was a little row
of books. Those that I glanced at first were familiar to me, books
that I had read, novels I think, but I did not look at them much, for
they were of no use for my special purpose, for the essay which was
absorbing my thoughts. I do not even remember what they were;
but I found towards the end of the shelf a single volume entitled
"Candide." Opening it, I found a short preface which stated that this
was a quite newly discovered volume, hitherto unpublished, and of
remarkable interest; a continuation, in fact, of Candide's story. I wondered if this might not serve my turn and provide stuff for the essay.

---

12 See David Robson's informative article about Mary Arnold-Forster: https://
   www.bbc.com/future/article/20150819-a-dream-travellers-guide-to-
   the-sleeping-mind.

I thought that it might, and began to turn over its pages, when my eye fell on the last two volumes standing in the little row. They were dark-blue books, lettered in gold, and their title ran "Mr. Petulengro, Vol. I, and Mr. Petulengro, Vol. II."

"Oh, wonderful and delightful discovery!" I thought; "imagine finding two perfectly new books by Borrow! A new 'Lavengro' and an unread and hitherto unheard-of 'Romany Rye'! How unexpected and how enchanting ! Could it be a mistake?"—and I eagerly opened the two blue volumes. No, the promise held good. Here on the first pages that I looked at were the familiar names, Jasper Petulengro, Mrs. Petulengro, Ursula. . . . Chapter headings, too, there were that seemed familiar, but that yet were all new! . . .

The opening of my essay began to frame itself in my mind. The sentences with which it should begin, and in which I should tell of my discovery to the world, came quite readily, and I repeated them over to myself, though the importance of the fifty-guinea prize faded quite away in comparison with the excitement of the discovery that I had made.

But then—alas! the dark-blue volumes themselves began to fade. I tried hard to keep them, but in vain; and I woke up to find that my favourite row of "bedside books" near at hand contained indeed the familiar slim green volumes which I knew so nearly by heart, but that "Mr. Petulengro, Vol. I, and Mr. Petulengro, Vol. II," had disappeared with my dream.

★ ★ ★

I have been obliged to illustrate these studies of dreaming by notes of my own dreams. This has been unavoidable, because actual experience has been their foundation, and experience is my only qualification for writing on this subject. Where I could obtain records made by friends I have done so, but this has not been often, because few people will make these notes immediately on awaking from sleep, and records made after the lapse of some hours are of comparatively little value. An apology must, however, be made for using my own dreams in this way. We have all suffered at times from having to listen to the recital of dreams, which, though of scanty interest to the hearer, doubtless still possess for the teller some of the humour and the charm that they seemed to have in the night. Somewhat imperfectly remembered, and narrated in the cold light of day, these poor shadows of dreams convey none of their original glamour. No doubt from the earliest ages the same thing has happened; dreams have been dreamed, and have been re-told, and have wearied their hearers. Eighteen hundred years ago Epictetus laid down for his pupils the sound rule, which one amongst them evidently laid to heart and recorded: "Beware that thou never tell thy dreams, for notwithstanding thou mayst take pleasure in reciting the dreams of the night, the company will take little pleasure in hearing them." The moral, though a salutary one, now as it was then, is a discouraging maxim for a writer on dreams; but the reader, on the other hand, who is now duly forewarned, has a clear advantage over an unwilling listener, since it lies entirely within his own choice whether he reads, or whether he skips, the written dream.

Thomas Browne

Religio Medici (A Doctor's Religion)
1643

The seventeenth-century doctor and essayist Sir Thomas Browne's meditation on dreams explains that "wee are somewhat more than our selves in our sleepes" as a result of "the waking of the soule."

Let me not injure the felicity of others, if I say I am as happy as any, *Ruat coelum, Fiat voluntas tua*[13], salveth all; so that whatsoever happens, it is but what our daily prayers desire. In briefe, I am content, and what should providence adde more? Surely this is it wee call Happinesse, and this doe I enjoy, with this I am happy in a dreame, and as content to enjoy a happinesse in a fancy, as others in a more apparent truth and reality. There is surely a neerer apprehension of any thing that delights us in our dreames than in our waked senses; without this I were unhappy, for my awaked judgement discontents mee, ever whispering unto me, that I am from my friend, but my friendly dreames in the night requite me, and make me thinke I am within his armes. I thanke God for my happy dreames, as I doe for my good rest, for there is a satisfaction in them unto reasonable desires, and such as can be content with a fit of happinesse; and surely

---

13 Latin for "Though Heaven fall, Thy will be done."

it is not a melancholy conceite to thinke we are all asleepe in this world, and that the conceits of this life are as meere dreames to those of the next, as the Phantasmes of the night, to the conceite of the day. There is an equall delusion in both, and the one doth but seeme to bee the embleme or picture of the other; wee are somewhat more than our selves in our sleepes, and the slumber of the body seemes to bee but the waking of the soule. It is the ligation of sense, but the liberty of reason, and our awaking conceptions doe not match the fancies of our sleepes. At my Nativity, my ascendant was the watery signe of *Scorpius*, I was borne in the Planetary houre of *Saturne*, and I think I have a piece of that Leaden planet in mee. I am no way facetious, nor disposed for the mirth and galliardize of company, yet in one dreame I can compose a whole Comedy, behold the action, apprehend the jests and laugh my selfe awake at the conceits thereof; were my memory as faithfull as my reason is then fruitfull, I would never study but in my dreames; and this time also would I chuse for my devotions; but our grosser memories have then so little hold of our abstracted understandings, that they forget the story, and can only relate to our awaked soules, a confused and broken tale of that that hath passed. *Aristotle*, who hath written a singular tract of sleepe, hath not me thinkes throughly defined it, nor yet *Galen*, though he seeme to have corrected it; for those *Noctambuloes* and night-walkers, though in their sleepe, doe yet enjoy the action of their senses: wee must therefore say that there is something in us that is not in the jurisdiction of *Morpheus*; and that those abstracted and ecstatick soules doe walke about in their owne corps, as spirits with the bodies they assume, wherein they seeme to heare, see, and feele, though indeed the Organs are destitute of sense, and their natures of those faculties that should informe them. Thus it is observed that men sometimes upon the houre of their departure, doe speake and reason above themselves. For then the soule begins to be freed from the ligaments of the body, begins to reason like her selfe and to discourse in a straine above mortality.

We tearme sleep a death, and yet it is waking that kils us, and destroyes those spirits that are the house of life. Tis indeed a part of life that best expresseth death, for every man truely lives so long as hee acts his nature, or someway makes good the faculties of himselfe: *Themistocles* therefore that slew his Souldier in his sleepe was a mercifull executioner, 'tis a kinde of punishment the mildnesse of no lawes hath invented; I wonder the fancy of *Lucan* and *Seneca* did not discover it. It is that death by which wee may be literally said to die daily, a death which *Adam* died before his mortality; a death whereby wee live a middle and moderating point betweene life and death; in fine, so like death, I dare not trust it without my prayers, and an halfe adiew unto the world, and take my farewell in a Colloquy with God.

> *The night is come like to the day,*
> *Depart not thou great God away.*
> *[. . .]*
> *Sleepe is a death, O make me try,*
> *By sleeping what it is to die.*
> *And as gently lay my head*
> *On my Grave, as now my bed.*
> *How ere I rest, great God let me*
> *Awake againe at last with thee.*
> *And thus assur'd, behold I lie*
> *Securely, or to wake or die.*
> *These are my drowsie dayes, in vaine*
> *I doe now wake to sleepe againe.*
> *O come that houre, when I shall never*
> *Sleepe againe, but wake for ever!*

This is the dormitive I take to bedward, I need no other *Laudanum* than this to make mee sleep; after which I close mine eyes in security, content to take my leave of the Sunne, and sleepe unto the resurrection.

Cicero

On Divination
c. 45 BCE

The Roman philosopher and statesman Marcus Tullius Cicero (106– 43 BCE) lays out his argument, in the form of a dialogue with his brother Quintus, against the divine origin of dreams.

"[. . .] Surely you must assume, either that there is a Divine Power which, in planning for our good, gives us information by means of dreams; or that, because of some natural connexion and association— the Greeks call it συμπάθεια—interpreters of dreams know what sort of a dream is required to fit any situation and what sort of a result will follow any dream; or that neither of these suppositions is true, but that the usual result or consequence of every dream is known by a consistent system of rules based on long-continued observation. In the first place, then, it must be understood that there is no divine power which creates dreams. And indeed it is perfectly clear that none of the visions seen in dreams have their origin in the will of the gods; for the gods, for our sakes, would so interpose that we might be able to foresee the future.

"But how often, pray, do you find anyone who pays any attention to dreams or who understands or remembers them? On the other hand, how many treat them with disdain, and regard a belief in them as the superstition of a weak and effeminate mind! Moreover, why does God, in planning for the good of the human race, convey his warnings by means of dreams which men consider unworthy not only of worrying about, but even of remembering? For it is impossible that God does not know how people generally regard dreams; and to do anything needlessly and without a cause is unworthy of a god and is inconsistent even with the habits of right-thinking men. And hence, if most dreams are unnoticed and disregarded, either God is ignorant of that fact, or he does a vain thing in conveying information by means of dreams; but neither supposition accords with the nature of a god, therefore, it must be admitted that God conveys no information by means of dreams.

"I also ask, if God gives us these visions as forewarnings, why does he not give them to us when we are awake rather than when we are asleep? For, whether our souls in sleep are impelled by some external and foreign force; or whether they are self-moved; or whether there is some other cause why, during sleep, we imagine ourselves seeing or hearing, or doing certain things—whatever the cause, it would apply just as well when we are awake. If the gods did send us warnings in our sleep and for our good they would do the same for us when we are awake, especially since, as Chrysippus says in replying to the Academicians, appearances seen when we are awake are much more distinct and trustworthy than those seen in dreams. It would, there-fore, have been more in keeping with the beneficence of gods, in consulting for our good, to send us clear visions in our waking moments rather than unintelligible ones in our dreams. But since that is not the case, dreams ought not to be held divine. And further, what is the need of a method which, instead of being direct, is so circuitous and roundabout that we have to employ men to interpret our dreams? And if it be true that God consults for our advantage he would say: 'Do this,' 'Don't do that,' and not give us visions when we are awake rather than when we are asleep.

"And further, would anybody dare to say that all dreams are true? 'Some dreams are true,' says Ennius, 'but not necessarily all.' Pray how do you distinguish between the two? What mark have the false and what the true? And if God sends the true, whence come the false? Surely if God sends the false ones too what is more untrustworthy than God? Besides what is more stupid than to excite the souls of mortals with false and lying visions? But if true visions are divine while the false and meaningless ones are from nature, what sort of caprice decided that God made the one and nature made the other, rather than that God made them all, which your school denies, or that nature made them all? Since you deny that God made them all you must admit that nature made them all. [. . .]

"In our consideration of dreams we come now to the remaining point left for discussion, which is your contention that 'by long-continued observation of dreams and by recording the results an art has been evolved.' Really? Then, it is possible, I suppose, to 'observe' dreams? If so, how? For they are of infinite variety and there is no imaginable thing too absurd, too involved, or too abnormal for us to dream about it. How, then, is it possible for us either to remember this countless and ever-changing mass of visions or to observe and record the subsequent results? Astronomers have recorded the movements of the planets and thereby have discovered an orderly course of the stars, not thought of before. But tell me, if you can, what is the orderly course of dreams and what is the harmonious relation between them and subsequent events? And by what means can the true be distinguished from the false, in view of the fact that the same dreams have certain consequences for one person and different consequences for another and seeing also that even for the same individual the same dream is not always followed by the same result? As a rule we do not believe a liar even when he tells the truth, but, to my surprise, if one dream turns out to be true, your Stoics do not withdraw their belief in the prophetic value of that one though it is only one out of many; rather, from the character of the one true dream, they establish the character of countless others that are false.

"Therefore, if God is not the creator of dreams; if there is no connexion between them and the laws of nature; and finally, if, by means of observation no art of divining can be found in them, it follows that absolutely no reliance can be placed in dreams. This becomes especially evident when we consider that those who have the dreams deduce no prophecies from them; that those who interpret them depend upon conjecture and not upon nature; that in the course of the almost countless ages, chance has worked more miracles through all other agencies than through the agency of dreams; and, finally, that nothing is more uncertain than conjecture, which may be led not only into varying, but sometimes even into contradictory, conclusions.

"Then let dreams, as a means of divination, be rejected along with the rest. Speaking frankly, superstition, which is widespread among the nations, has taken advantage of human weakness to cast its spell over the mind of almost every man. This same view was stated in my treatise *On the Nature of the Gods*; and to prove the correctness of that view has been the chief aim of the present discussion. For I thought that I should be rendering a great service both to myself and to my countrymen if I could tear this superstition up by the roots. But I want it distinctly understood that the destruction of superstition does not mean the destruction of religion. For I consider it the part of wisdom to preserve the institutions of our forefathers by retaining their sacred rites and ceremonies. Furthermore, the celestial order and the beauty of the universe compel me to confess that there is some excellent and eternal Being, who deserves the respect and homage of men."

René Descartes

The Meditations
1641

> *The French philosopher throws us off-balance in this meditation in order to make us find our balance, to assure us that even in our dreams there is truth or bases for truth: "How often has it happened to me that in the night I dreamt that I found myself in this particular place, that I was dressed and seated near the fire, whilst in reality I was lying undressed in bed!"*

All that up to the present time I have accepted as most true and certain I have learned either from the senses or through the senses; but it is sometimes proved to me that these senses are deceptive, and it is wiser not to trust entirely to anything by which we have once been deceived.

But it may be that although the senses sometimes deceive us concerning things which are hardly perceptible, or very far away, there are yet many others to be met with as to which we cannot reasonably have any doubt, although we recognise them by their means. For example, there is the fact that I am here, seated by the fire, attired in a dressing gown, having this paper in my hands and other similar matters. And how could I deny that these hands and this body are mine, were it not perhaps that I compare myself to certain persons, devoid of sense, whose cerebella are so troubled and clouded by the violent vapours of black bile, that they constantly assure us that they think they are kings when they are really quite poor, or that they are clothed in purple when they are really without covering, or who imagine that they have an earthenware head or are nothing but pumpkins or are made of glass. But they are mad, and I should not be any the less insane were I to follow examples so extravagant.

At the same time I must remember that I am a man, and that consequently I am in the habit of sleeping, and in my dreams representing to myself the same things or sometimes even less probable things, than do those who are insane in their waking moments. How often has it happened to me that in the night I dreamt that I found myself in this particular place, that I was dressed and seated near the fire, whilst in reality I was lying undressed in bed! At this moment it does indeed seem to me that it is with eyes awake that I am looking at this paper; that this head which I move is not asleep, that it is deliberately and of set purpose that I extend my hand and perceive it; what happens in sleep does not appear so clear nor so distinct as does all this. But in thinking over this I remind myself that on many occasions I have in sleep been deceived by similar illusions, and in dwelling carefully on this reflection I see so manifestly that there are no certain indications by which we may clearly distinguish wakefulness from sleep that I am lost in astonishment. And my astonishment is such that it is almost capable of persuading me that I now dream.

Now let us assume that we are asleep and that all these particulars, e.g. that we open our eyes, shake our head, extend our hands, and so on, are but false delusions; and let us reflect that possibly neither our hands nor our whole body are such as they appear to us to be. At the same time we must at least confess that the things which are represented to us in sleep are like painted representations which can only have been formed as the counterparts of something real and true, and that in this way those general things at least, i.e. eyes, a head, hands, and a whole body are not imaginary things, but things really existent. For, as a matter of fact, painters, even when they study with the greatest skill to represent sirens and satyrs by forms the most strange and extraordinary, cannot give them natures which are entirely new, but merely make a certain medley of the members of different animals; or if their imagination is extravagant enough to invent something so novel that nothing similar has ever before been seen, and that then their work represents a thing purely fictitious and absolutely false, it is certain all the same that the colours of which this is composed are necessarily real. And for the same reason, although these general things, to wit, (a body), eyes, a head, hands, and such like, may be imaginary, we are bound at the same time to confess that there are at least some other objects yet more simple and more universal, which are real and true; and of these just in the same way as with certain real colours, all these images of things which dwell in our thoughts, whether true and real or false and fantastic, are formed.

Sigmund Freud

On Dreams
1911

The great psychoanalyst Sigmund Freud brought the interpretation of dreams into the limelight and into controversy at the beginning of the twentieth century. In this excerpt from Chapter 2, from an uncontroversial interpretation of one of his own minor dreams, he explains the limits of any dream interpretation—privacy and discretion: "Why, then, do not I choose another dream whose analysis would be more suitable for publication, so that I could awaken a fairer conviction of the sense and cohesion of the results disclosed by analysis? The answer is, because every dream which I investigate leads to the same difficulties and places me under the same need of discretion; nor should I forgo this difficulty any the more were I to analyze the dream of some one else. That could only be done when opportunity allowed all concealment to be dropped without injury to those who trusted me."

One day I discovered to my amazement that the popular view grounded in superstition, and not the medical one, comes nearer to the truth about dreams. I arrived at new conclusions about dreams by the use of a new method of psychological investigation, one which had rendered me good service in the investigation of phobias, obsessions, illusions, and the like, and which, under the name "psycho-analysis," had found acceptance by a whole school of investigators. The manifold analogies of dream life with the most diverse conditions of psychical disease in the waking state have been rightly insisted upon by a number of medical observers. It seemed, therefore, a priori, hopeful to apply to the interpretation of dreams methods of investigation, which had been tested in psychopathological processes. Obsessions and those peculiar sensations of haunting dread remain as strange to normal consciousness as do dreams to our waking consciousness; their origin is as unknown to consciousness as is that of dreams. It was practical ends that impelled us, in these diseases, to fathom their origin and formation. Experience had shown us that a cure and a consequent mastery of the obsessing ideas did result when once those thoughts, the connecting links between the morbid ideas and the rest of the psychical content, were revealed which were heretofore veiled from consciousness. The procedure I employed for the interpretation of dreams thus arose from psychotherapy.

This procedure is readily described, although its practice demands instruction and experience. Suppose the patient is suffering from intense morbid dread. He is requested to direct his attention to the idea in question, without, however, as he has so frequently done, meditating upon it. Every impression about it, without any exception, which occurs to him should be imparted to the doctor. The statement, which will be perhaps then made, that he cannot concentrate his attention upon anything at all, is to be countered by assuring him most positively that such a blank state of mind is utterly impossible. As a matter of fact, a great number of impressions will soon occur, with which others will associate themselves. These will be invariably accompanied by the expression of the observer's opinion that they have no meaning or are unimportant. It will be at once noticed that it is this self-criticism, which prevented the patient from imparting the ideas, which had indeed already excluded them from consciousness. If the patient can be induced to abandon this self-criticism and to pursue the trains of thought which are yielded by concentrating the attention, most significant matter will be obtained, matter which will be presently seen to be clearly linked to the morbid idea in question. Its connection with other ideas will be manifest, and later on will permit the replacement of the morbid idea by a fresh one, which is perfectly adapted to psychical continuity.

This is not the place to examine thoroughly the hypothesis upon which this experiment rests, or the deductions which follow from its invariable success. It must suffice to state that we obtain matter enough for the resolution of every morbid idea if we especially direct our attention to the unbidden associations which disturb our thoughts—those which are otherwise put aside by the critic as worthless refuse. If the procedure is exercised on oneself, the best plan of helping the experiment is to write down at once all one's first indistinct fancies.

I will now point out where this method leads when I apply it to the examination of dreams. Any dream could be made use of in this way. From certain motives I, however, choose a dream of my own, which appears confused and meaningless to my memory, and one which has the advantage of brevity. Probably my dream of last night satisfies the requirements. Its content, fixed immediately after awakening, runs as follows:

"Company; at table or table d'hote. . . . Spinach is served. Mrs. E. L., sitting next to me, gives me her undivided attention, and places her hand familiarly upon my knee. In defence I remove her hand. Then she says: 'But you have always had such beautiful eyes.'. . . . I then distinctly see something like two eyes as a sketch or as the contour of a spectacle lens. . . ."

This is the whole dream, or, at all events, all that I can remember. It appears to me not only obscure and meaningless, but more especially odd. Mrs. E. L. is a person with whom I am scarcely on visiting terms, nor to my knowledge have I ever desired any more cordial relationship. I have not seen her for a long time, and do not think there was any mention of her recently. No emotion whatever accompanied the dream process.

Reflecting upon this dream does not make it a bit clearer to my mind. I will now, however, present the ideas, without premeditation and without criticism, which introspection yielded. I soon notice that it is an advantage to break up the dream into its elements, and to search out the ideas which link themselves to each fragment.

Company; at table or table d'hote. The recollection of the slight event with which the evening of yesterday ended is at once called up. I left a small party in the company of a friend, who offered to drive me home in his cab. "I prefer a taxi," he said; "that gives one such a pleasant occupation; there is always something to look at." When we were in the cab, and the cab-driver turned the disc so that the first sixty hellers were visible, I continued the jest. "We have hardly got in and we already owe sixty hellers. The taxi always reminds me of the table d'hote. It makes me avaricious and selfish by continuously reminding me of my debt. It seems to me to mount up too quickly, and I am always afraid that I shall be at a disadvantage, just as I cannot resist at table d'hote the comical fear that I am getting too little, that I must look after myself." In far-fetched connection with this I quote:

> "To earth, this weary earth, ye bring us,
> To guilt ye let us heedless go."[14]

Another idea about the table d'hote. A few weeks ago I was very cross with my dear wife at the dinner-table at a Tyrolese health resort, because she was not sufficiently reserved with some neighbours with whom I wished to have absolutely nothing to do. I begged her to occupy herself rather with me than with the strangers. That is just as if I had been at a disadvantage at the table d'hote.

The contrast between the behavior of my wife at the table and that of Mrs. E. L. in the dream now strikes me: *"Addresses herself entirely to me."* Further, I now notice that the dream is the reproduction of a little scene which transpired between my wife and myself when I was secretly courting her. The caressing under cover of the tablecloth was an answer to a wooer's passionate letter. In the dream, however, my wife is replaced by the unfamiliar E. L.

Mrs. E. L. is the daughter of a man to whom I *owed money!* I cannot help noticing that here there is revealed an unsuspected connection between the dream content and my thoughts. If the chain of associations be followed up which proceeds from one element of the dream one is soon led back to another of its elements. The thoughts evoked by the dream stir up associations which were not noticeable in the dream itself.

Is it not customary, when some one expects others to look after his interests without any advantage to themselves, to ask the innocent question satirically: "Do you think this will be done *for the sake of your beautiful eyes?*" Hence Mrs. E. L.'s speech in the dream. "You have always had such beautiful eyes," means nothing but "people always do everything to you for love of you; you have had *everything for nothing.*" The contrary is, of course, the truth; I have always paid

---

14 Freud quotes the German poet Johann Wolfgang von Goethe.

dearly for whatever kindness others have shown me. Still, the fact that *I had a ride for nothing* yesterday when my friend drove me home in his cab must have made an impression upon me.

In any case, the friend whose guests we were yesterday has often made me his debtor. Recently I allowed an opportunity of requiting him to go by. He has had only one present from me, an antique shawl, upon which eyes are painted all round, a so-called Occhiale, as a charm against the *Malocchio*. Moreover, he is an *eye specialist*. That same evening I had asked him after a patient whom I had sent to him for *glasses*.

As I remarked, nearly all parts of the dream have been brought into this new connection. I still might ask why in the dream it was *spinach* that was served up. Because spinach called up a little scene which recently occurred at our table. A child, whose *beautiful eyes* are really deserving of praise, refused to eat spinach. As a child I was just the same; for a long time I loathed spinach, until in later life my tastes altered, and it became one of my favorite dishes. The mention of this dish brings my own childhood and that of my child's near together. "You should be glad that you have some spinach," his mother had said to the little gourmet. "Some children would be very glad to get spinach." Thus I am reminded of the parents' duties towards their children. Goethe's words—

> "To earth, this weary earth, ye bring us,
> To guilt ye let us heedless go"—

take on another meaning in this connection.

Here I will stop in order that I may recapitulate the results of the analysis of the dream. By following the associations which were linked to the single elements of the dream torn from their context, I have been led to a series of thoughts and reminiscences where I am bound to recognize interesting expressions of my psychical life. The matter yielded by an analysis of the dream stands in intimate relationship with the dream content, but this relationship is so special that I should never have been able to have inferred the new discoveries directly from the dream itself. The dream was passionless, disconnected, and unintelligible. During the time that I am unfolding the thoughts at the back of the dream I feel intense and well-grounded emotions. The thoughts themselves fit beautifully together into chains logically bound together with certain central ideas which ever repeat themselves. Such ideas not represented in the dream itself are in this instance the antitheses *selfish, unselfish, to be indebted, to work for nothing.* I could draw closer the threads of the web which analysis has disclosed, and would then be able to show how they all run together into a single knot; I am debarred from making this work public by considerations of a private, not of a scientific, nature. After having cleared up many things which I do not willingly acknowledge as mine, I should have much to reveal which had better remain my secret. Why, then, do not I choose another dream whose analysis would be more suitable for publication, so that I could awaken a fairer conviction of the sense and cohesion of the results disclosed by analysis? The answer is, because every dream which I investigate leads to the same difficulties and places me under the same need of discretion; nor should I forgo this difficulty any the more were I to analyze the dream of some one else. That could only be done when opportunity allowed all conceal-ment to be dropped without injury to those who trusted me.

The conclusion which is now forced upon me is that the dream is a *sort of substitution* for those emotional and intellectual trains of thought which I attained after complete analysis. I do not yet know the process by which the dream arose from those thoughts, but I perceive that it is wrong to regard the dream as psychically unim-portant, a purely physical process which has arisen from the activity of isolated cortical elements awakened out of sleep.

I must further remark that the dream is far shorter than the thoughts which I hold it replaces; whilst analysis discovered that the dream was provoked by an unimportant occurrence the evening before the dream.

Socrates

Phaedo
c. 375 BCE

Though the Greek philosopher Socrates (c. 470–399 BCE) never wrote a word, his words and wisdom were recounted by his pupil Plato, primarily in dialogues. Phaedo *tells of Socrates's last day, before he took the poison that ended his life.*

[. . .] Cebes said: "I am very glad indeed, Socrates, that you mentioned the name of Aesop. For that reminds me of a question which has been asked by others, and was asked of me only the day before yesterday by Evenus the poet, and as he will be sure to ask again, you may as well tell me what I should say to him, if you would like him to have an answer. He wanted to know why you who never before wrote a line of poetry, now that you are in prison are putting Aesop into verse, and also composing that hymn in honor of Apollo."

"Tell him, Cebes," he replied, "that I had no idea of rivalling him or his poems; which is the truth, for I knew that I could not do that. But I wanted to see whether I could purge away a scruple which I felt about certain dreams. In the course of my life I have often had intimations in dreams 'that I should make music.' The same dream came to me sometimes in one form, and sometimes in an other, but always saying the same or nearly the same words: Make and cultivate music, said the dream. And hitherto I had imagined that this was only intended to exhort and encourage me in the study of philosophy, which has always been the pursuit of my life, and is the noblest and best of music. The dream was bidding me to do what I was already doing, in the same way that the competitor in a race is bidden by the spectators to run when he is already running. But I was not certain of this, as the dream might have meant music in the popular sense of the word, and being under sentence of death, and the festival giving me a respite, I thought that I should be safer if I satisfied the scruple, and, in obedience to the dream, composed a few verses before I departed. And first I made a hymn in honor of the god of the festival, and then considering that a poet, if he is really to be a poet or maker, should not only put words together but make stories, and as I have no invention, I took some fables of Aesop, which I had ready at hand and knew, and turned them into verse. Tell Evenus this, and bid him be of good cheer; say that I would have him come after me if he be a wise man, and not tarry; and that today I am likely to be going, for the Athenians say that I must."

Voltaire

"Of Dreams"
c. 1764

The French wit and philosopher François-Marie Arouet (1694–1778), known as Voltaire, was one of the most learned people who ever walked the Earth. He was a do-gooder and provocateur, mocking kings, the Church, governments, and himself.

According to Petronius, dreams are not of divine origin, but self-formed:

> *Somnia qua mentes ludunt volitantibus umbris,*
> *Non delumbra deum nec ab æthere numina mittunt,*
> *Sed sibi quisque facit.*[15]

But how, all the senses being defunct in sleep, does there remain an internal one which retains consciousness? How is it, that while the eyes see not, the ears hear not, we notwithstanding understand in our dreams? The hound renews the chase in a dream: he barks, follows his prey, and is in at the kill. The poet composes verses in his sleep; the mathematician examines his diagram; and the metaphysician reasons well or ill; of all which there are striking examples.

Are they only the organs of the machine which act? Is it the pure soul, submitted to the empire of the senses, enjoying its faculties at liberty?

If the organs alone produce dreams by night, why not alone produce ideas by day? If the soul, pure and tranquil, acting for itself during the repose of the senses, is the sole cause of our ideas while we are sleeping, why are all these ideas usually irregular, unreasonable, and incoherent? What! at a time when the soul is least disturbed, it is so much disquieted in its imagination? Is it frantic when at liberty? If it was produced with metaphysical ideas, as so many sages assert who dream with their eyes open, its correct and luminous ideas of being, of infinity, and of all the primary principles, ought to be revealed in the soul with the greatest energy when the body sleeps. We should never be good philosophers except when dreaming.

Whatever system we embrace, whatever our vain endeavors to prove that the memory impels the brain, and that the brain acts upon the soul, we must allow that our ideas come, in sleep, independently of our will. It is therefore certain that we can think seven or eight hours running without the least intention of doing so, and even

---

15 Latin for "It is not the shrines of the gods, nor the powers of the air, that send the dreams which mock the mind with flitting shadows; each man makes dreams for himself." [Petronius. *Poems*. Translated by Michael Heseltine. London: Loeb Classical Library, 1913.]

without being certain that we think. Pause upon that, and endeavor to divine what there is in this which is animal.

Dreams have always formed a great object of superstition, and nothing is more natural. A man deeply affected by the sickness of his mistress dreams that he sees her dying; she dies the next day; and of course the gods have predicted her death.

The general of an army dreams that he shall gain a battle; he subsequently gains one; the gods had decreed that he should be a conqueror. Dreams which are accomplished are alone attended to. Dreams form a great part of ancient history, as also of oracles.

The "Vulgate" thus translates the end of Leviticus, xix, 26: "You shall not observe dreams." But the word "dream" exists not in the Hebrew; and it would be exceedingly strange, if attention to dreams was reproved in the same book in which it is said that Joseph became the benefactor of Egypt and his family, in consequence of his interpretation of three dreams.

The interpretation of dreams was a thing so common, that the supposed art had no limits, and the interpreter was sometimes called upon to say what another person had dreamed. Nebuchadnezzar, having forgotten his dream, orders his Magi to say what it was he had dreamed, and threatened them with death if they failed; but the Jew Daniel, who was in the school of the Magi, saved their lives by divining at once what the king had dreamed, and interpreting it. This history, and many others, may serve to prove that the laws of the Jews did not forbid oneiromancy, that is to say, the science of dreams.

Zhuangzi (also known as Chuang Tzŭ)

Zhuangzi
c. 400–300 BCE

The Daoist philosopher lived in China during its classical period. His reflections—known by his name, Master Zhuang—were collected centuries later.

Those who dream of the banquet, wake to lamentation and sorrow. Those who dream of lamentation and sorrow wake to join the hunt. While they dream, they do not know that they dream. Some will even interpret the very dream they are dreaming; and only when they awake do they know it was a dream. By and by comes the Great Awakening, and then we find out that this life is really a great dream. Fools think they are awake now, and flatter themselves they know if they are really princes or peasants. Confucius and you are both dreams; and I who say you are dreams,—I am but a dream myself. This is a paradox. Tomorrow a sage may arise to explain it; but that tomorrow will not be until ten thousand generations have gone by.

★ ★ ★

Once upon a time, I, Chuang Tzŭ, dreamt I was a butterfly, fluttering hither and thither, to all intents and purposes a butterfly. I was conscious only of following my fancies as a butterfly, and was unconscious of my individuality as a man. Suddenly, I awaked, and there I lay, myself again. Now I do not know whether I was then a man dreaming I was a butterfly, or whether I am now a butterfly dreaming I am a man.

IV. Poetry and Drama

Louisa May Alcott

"Mary's Dream"
1886

The author of the popular novel Little Women *and its sequels was also a poet. This poem of the drowned sailor—which appears in the* Jo's Boys *sequel—echoes, perhaps, Ovid's tale of Halcyone and Ceyx (see page 98).*

> The moon had climbed the eastern hill
> Which rises o'er the sands of Dee,
> And from its highest summit shed
> A silver light on tower and tree,
> When Mary laid her down to sleep
> (Her thoughts on Sandy far at sea);
> When soft and low a voice was heard,
> Saying, "Mary, weep no more for me."
>
> She from her pillow gently raised
> Her head, to see who there might be,
> And saw young Sandy, shivering stand
> With visage pale and hollow e'e.
> "Oh Mary dear, cold is my clay;
> It lies beneath the stormy sea;
> Far, far from thee, I sleep in death.
> Dear Mary, weep no more for me.

"Three stormy nights and stormy days
We tossed upon the raging main.
And long we strove our bark to save;
But all our striving was in vain.
E'en then, when terror chilled my blood,
My heart was filled with love of thee.
The storm is past, and I'm at rest;
So, Mary, weep no more for me.

"Oh maiden dear, yourself prepare;
We soon shall meet upon that shore
Where love is free from doubt and care,
And you and I shall part no more."
Loud crew the cock, the shadow fled;
No more her Sandy did she see;
But soft the passing spirit said,
"Sweet Mary, weep no more for me."

Matthew Arnold

"Longing"
1852

*The poet and critic was also a British school inspector. The poem's
original title was "Faded Leaves."*

Come to me in my dreams, and then
By day I shall be well again!
For then the night will more than pay
The hopeless longing of the day.

Come, as thou cam'st a thousand times,
A messenger from radiant climes,
And smile on thy new world, and be
As kind to all the rest as me.

Or, as thou never cam'st in sooth,
Come now, and let me dream it truth;

And part my hair, and kiss my brow,
And say: *My love! why suff'rest thou?*

Come to me in my dreams, and then
By day I shall be well again!
For then the night will more than pay
The hopeless longing of the day.

William Blake

"A Dream" and "The Land of Dreams"
1789 and c. 1801–03

Blake was a mystical painter and poet. The first poem is from his Songs of Innocence and of Experience. *The second is from* The Pickering Manuscript.

"A Dream"

Once a dream did weave a shade,
O'er my Angel-guarded bed,
That an emmet[16] lost its way
Where on grass methought I lay.

Troubled wilderd and forlorn
Dark benighted travel-worn,
Over many a tangled spray
All heart-broke I heard her say:

"O my children! do they cry
Do they hear their father sigh.
Now they look abroad to see,
Now return and weep for me."

---

16 An emmet is an ant.

Pitying I dropp'd a tear:
But I saw a glow-worm near:
Who replied: "What wailing wight
Calls the watchman of the night.

"I am set to light the ground,
While the beetle goes his round:
Follow now the beetles hum,
Little wanderer hie thee home."

★ ★ ★

"The Land of Dreams"

Awake, awake my little Boy!
Thou wast thy Mother's only joy:
Why dost thou weep in thy gentle sleep?
Awake! thy Father does thee keep.

"O, what land is the Land of Dreams?
What are its mountains, and what are its streams?
O Father, I saw my Mother there,
Among the lillies by waters fair.

Among the lambs clothed in white
She walked with her Thomas in sweet delight.
I wept for joy, like a dove I mourn—
O when shall I return again?"

Dear child, I also by pleasant streams
Have wandered all night in the Land of Dreams;
But though calm and warm the waters wide,
I could not get to the other side.

"Father, O Father, what do we here,
In this land of unbelief and fear?
The Land of Dreams is better far
Above the light of the Morning Star."

Samuel Taylor Coleridge

"Kubla Khan: or, A Vision in a Dream: A Fragment"
1816

The English poet and critic reflects on the details of how he wrote one of his most famous poems.

The following fragment is here published at the request of a poet of great and deserved celebrity [Lord Byron], and, as far as the Author's own opinions are concerned, rather as a psychological curiosity, than on the ground of any supposed poetic merits.

In the summer of the year 1797, the Author, then in ill health, had retired to a lonely farm-house between Porlock and Linton, on the Exmoor confines of Somerset and Devonshire. In consequence of a slight indisposition, an anodyne had been prescribed, from the effects of which he fell asleep in his chair at the moment that he was reading the following sentence, or words of the same substance, in Purchas's *Pilgrimage*: "Here the Khan Kubla commanded a palace to be built, and a stately garden thereunto. And thus ten miles of fertile ground were inclosed with a wall." The Author continued for about three hours in a profound sleep, at least of the external senses, during which time he has the most vivid confidence, that he could not have composed less than from two to three hundred lines; if that indeed can be called composition in which all the images rose up before him as things, with a parallel production of the correspondent expressions, without any sensation or consciousness of effort. On awakening he appeared to himself to have a distinct recollection of the whole, and taking his pen, ink, and paper, instantly and eagerly wrote down the lines that are here preserved. At this moment he was unfortunately called out by a person on business from Porlock, and detained by him above an hour, and on his return to his room, found, to his no small surprise and mortification, that though he still retained some vague and dim recollection of the general purport of the vision, yet, with the exception of some eight or ten scattered lines and images, all the rest had passed away like the images on the surface of a stream into which a stone has been cast, but, alas! without the after restoration of the latter!

> Then all the charm
> Is broken—all that phantom-world so fair
> Vanishes, and a thousand circlets spread,

And each mis-shape the other. Stay awile,
Poor youth! who scarcely dar'st lift up thine eyes—
The stream will soon renew its smoothness, soon
The visions will return! And lo, he stays,
And soon the fragments dim of lovely forms
Come trembling back, unite, and now once more
The pool becomes a mirror.

Yet from the still surviving recollections in his mind, the Author has frequently purposed to finish for himself what had been originally, as it were, given to him. Σαμερον αδιον ασω: but the tomorrow is yet to come.

As a contrast to this vision, I have annexed a fragment of a very different character, describing with equal fidelity the dream of pain and disease.

In Xanadu did Kubla Khan
A stately pleasure-dome decree:
Where Alph, the sacred river, ran
Through caverns measureless to man
Down to a sunless sea.
So twice five miles of fertile ground
With walls and towers were girdled round:
And there were gardens bright with sinuous rills,
Where blossomed many an incense-bearing tree;
And here were forests ancient as the hills,
Enfolding sunny spots of greenery.

But oh! that deep romantic chasm which slanted
Down the green hill athwart a cedarn cover!
A savage place! as holy and enchanted
As e'er beneath a waning moon was haunted
By woman wailing for her demon-lover!
And from this chasm, with ceaseless turmoil seething,
As if this earth in fast thick pants were breathing,
A mighty fountain momently was forced:
Amid whose swift half-intermitted burst
Huge fragments vaulted like rebounding hail,
Or chaffy grain beneath the thresher's flail:
And 'mid these dancing rocks at once and ever
It flung up momently the sacred river.

Five miles meandering with a mazy motion
Through wood and dale the sacred river ran,
Then reached the caverns measureless to man,
And sank in tumult to a lifeless ocean:
And 'mid this tumult Kubla heard from far
Ancestral voices prophesying war!
The shadow of the dome of pleasure
Floated midway on the waves;
Where was heard the mingled measure
From the fountain and the caves.
It was a miracle of rare device,
A sunny pleasure-dome with caves of ice!

A damsel with a dulcimer
In a vision once I saw:
It was an Abyssinian maid,
And on her dulcimer she played,
Singing of Mount Abora.
Could I revive within me
Her symphony and song,
To such a deep delight 'twould win me,
That with music loud and long,
I would build that dome in air,
That sunny dome! those caves of ice!
And all who heard should see them there,
And all should cry, Beware! Beware!
His flashing eyes, his floating hair!
Weave a circle round him thrice,
And close your eyes with holy dread,
For he on honey-dew hath fed,
And drunk the milk of Paradise.

Emily Dickinson

"In Winter in my Room" and "I Years had been from Home"
1886

America's premier poet of the nineteenth century was a sleepwalker, though this isn't noted in these untitled poems. The date of publication

*is given as Dickinson's year of death, as they were unpublished in her
lifetime. As she said elsewhere, "It's prudent—to dream."*

"In Winter in my Room"

In Winter in my Room
I came upon a Worm—
Pink, lank and warm—
But as he was a worm
And worms presume
Not quite with him at home—
Secured him by a string
To something neighboring
And went along.

A Trifle afterward
A thing occurred
I'd not believe it if I heard
But state with creeping blood—
A snake with mottles rare
Surveyed my chamber floor
In feature as the worm before
But ringed with power—

The very string with which
I tied him—too
When he was mean and new
That string was there—

I shrank—"How fair you are"!
Propitiation's claw—
"Afraid," he hissed
"Of me"?
"No cordiality"—
He fathomed me—
Then to a Rhythm Slim
Secreted in his Form
As Patterns swim
Projected him.

That time I flew
Both eyes his way

Lest he pursue
Nor ever ceased to run
Till in a distant Town
Towns on from mine
I set me down
This was a dream.

* * *

"I Years had been from Home"

I Years had been from Home
And now before the Door
I dared not enter, lest a Face
I never saw before

Stare solid into mine
And ask my Business there—
"My Business but a Life I left
Was such remaining there?"

I leaned upon the Awe—
I lingered with Before—
The Second like an Ocean rolled
And broke against my ear—

I laughed a crumbling Laugh
That I could fear a Door
Who Consternation compassed
And never winced before.

I fitted to the Latch
My Hand, with trembling care
Lest back the awful Door should spring
And leave me in the Floor—

Then moved my Fingers off
As cautiously as Glass
And held my ears, and like a Thief
Fled gasping from the House—

H.D. (Hilda Doolittle)

"At Baia"
1921

Hilda Doolittle was an American poet who evoked in her work the classical Greek poets.

I should have thought
in a dream you would have brought
some lovely, perilous thing,
orchids piled in a great sheath,
as who would say (in a dream),
"I send you this,
who left the blue veins
of your throat unkissed."

Why was it that your hands
(that never took mine),
your hands that I could see
drift over the orchid-heads
so carefully,
your hands, so fragile, sure to lift
so gently, the fragile flower-stuff—
ah, ah, how was it

You never sent (in a dream)
the very form, the very scent,
not heavy, not sensuous,
but perilous—perilous—
of orchids, piled in a great sheath,
and folded underneath on a bright scroll,
some word:

"Flower sent to flower;
for white hands, the lesser white,
less lovely of flower-leaf,"
or
"Lover to lover, no kiss,
no touch, but forever and ever this."

Amy Lowell

"I had made a kite"
1919

The proficient imagist Lowell published at the close of World War I a series called "Dreams in War Time," of which this is verse seven.

I had made a kite,
On it I had pasted golden stars
And white torches,
And the tail was spotted scarlet like a tiger-lily,
And very long.
I flew my kite,
And my soul was contented
Watching it flash against the concave of the sky.
My friends pointed at the clouds;
They begged me to take in my kite.
But I was happy
Seeing the mirror shock of it
Against the black clouds.
Then the lightning came
And struck the kite.
It puffed—blazed—fell.
But still I walked on,
In the drowning rain,
Slowly winding up the string.

Edgar Allan Poe

"Dream-Land" and "A Dream Within a Dream"
1844 and 1849

The American writer most famous for haunting stories and tales, Poe conjured up many dreams: "All that we see or seem/Is but a dream within a dream."

"Dream-Land"

By a route obscure and lonely,
Haunted by ill angels only,
Where an Eidolon, named NIGHT,
On a black throne reigns upright,
I have reached these lands but newly
From an ultimate dim Thule—
From a wild weird clime that lieth, sublime,
    Out of SPACE—Out of TIME.

Bottomless vales and boundless floods,
And chasms, and caves, and Titan woods,
With forms that no man can discover
For the tears that drip all over;
Mountains toppling evermore
Into seas without a shore;
Seas that restlessly aspire,
Surging, unto skies of fire;
Lakes that endlessly outspread
Their lone waters—lone and dead,—
Their still waters—still and chilly
With the snows of the lolling lily.

By the lakes that thus outspread
Their lone waters, lone and dead,—
Their sad waters, sad and chilly
With the snows of the lolling lily,—
By the mountains—near the river
Murmuring lowly, murmuring ever,—
By the grey woods,—by the swamp
Where the toad and the newt encamp,—
By the dismal tarns and pools
    Where dwell the Ghouls,—
By each spot the most unholy—
In each nook most melancholy,—
There the traveller meets, aghast,
Sheeted Memories of the Past—
Shrouded forms that start and sigh
As they pass the wanderer by—
White-robed forms of friends long given,
In agony, to the Earth—and Heaven.

For the heart whose woes are legion
'T is a peaceful, soothing region—
For the spirit that walks in shadow
'T is—oh, 't is an Eldorado!
But the traveller, travelling through it,
May not—dare not openly view it;
Never its mysteries are exposed
To the weak human eye unclosed;
So wills its King, who hath forbid
The uplifting of the fring'd lid;
And thus the sad Soul that here passes
Beholds it but through darkened glasses.

By a route obscure and lonely,
Haunted by ill angels only,
Where an Eidolon, named NIGHT,
On a black throne reigns upright,
I have wandered home but newly
From this ultimate dim Thule.

★ ★ ★

"A Dream Within a Dream"

Take this kiss upon the brow!
And, in parting from you now,
Thus much let me avow—
You are not wrong, who deem
That my days have been a dream;
Yet if hope has flown away
In a night, or in a day,
In a vision, or in none,
Is it therefore the less gone?
All that we see or seem
Is but a dream within a dream.

I stand amid the roar
Of a surf-tormented shore,
And I hold within my hand
Grains of the golden sand—
How few! yet how they creep
Through my fingers to the deep,

While I weep—while I weep!
O God! Can I not grasp
Them with a tighter clasp?
O God! can I not save
One from the pitiless wave?
Is all that we see or seem
But a dream within a dream?

Ezra Pound

"Το Καλὸν"
1916

Before his anti-Semitism and mental illness manifested themselves and overwhelmed him, Pound was a brilliant translator, poet, and literary advocate.

Even in my dreams you have denied yourself to me,
You have sent me only your handmaids.

William Shakespeare

Macbeth (Act V, Scene 1)
c. 1606

The most famous sleepwalker in literature is Lady Macbeth, tormented here by guilt for the murder of her and her husband's guest, Duncan, the king of Scotland. Her "infected" mind discharges its secrets.

[*Dunsinane. A Room in the Castle. Enter a Doctor of Physic and a Waiting-Gentlewoman.*]

DOCTOR. I have two nights watched with you, but can perceive no truth in your report. When was it she last walked?

GENTLEWOMAN. Since his Majesty went into the field, I have seen her rise from her bed, throw her nightgown upon her, unlock her closet, take forth paper, fold it, write upon't, read it, afterwards seal it, and again return to bed; yet all this while in a most fast sleep.

DOCTOR. A great perturbation in nature, to receive at once the benefit of sleep, and do the effects of watching. In this slumbery agitation, besides her walking and other actual performances, what, at any time, have you heard her say?

GENTLEWOMAN. That, sir, which I will not report after her.

DOCTOR. You may to me; and 'tis most meet you should.

GENTLEWOMAN. Neither to you nor anyone; having no witness to confirm my speech. [*Enter Lady Macbeth with a taper.*] Lo you, here she comes! This is her very guise; and, upon my life, fast asleep. Observe her; stand close.

DOCTOR. How came she by that light?

GENTLEWOMAN. Why, it stood by her: she has light by her continually; 'tis her command.

DOCTOR. You see, her eyes are open.

GENTLEWOMAN. Ay, but their sense are shut.

DOCTOR. What is it she does now? Look how she rubs her hands.

GENTLEWOMAN. It is an accustomed action with her, to seem thus washing her hands. I have known her continue in this a quarter of an hour.

LADY MACBETH. Yet here's a spot.

DOCTOR. Hark, she speaks. I will set down what comes from her, to satisfy my remembrance the more strongly.

LADY MACBETH. Out, damned spot! out, I say! One; two. Why, then 'tis time to do't. Hell is murky! Fie, my lord, fie! a soldier, and afeard? What need we fear who knows it, when none can call our power to account? Yet who would have thought the old man to have had so much blood in him?

DOCTOR. Do you mark that?

LADY MACBETH. The Thane of Fife had a wife. Where is she now?—What, will these hands ne'er be clean? No more o' that, my lord, no more o' that: you mar all with this starting.

DOCTOR. Go to, go to. You have known what you should not.

GENTLEWOMAN. She has spoke what she should not, I am sure of that: heaven knows what she has known.

LADY MACBETH. Here's the smell of the blood still: all the perfumes of Arabia will not sweeten this little hand. Oh, oh, oh!

DOCTOR. What a sigh is there! The heart is sorely charged.

GENTLEWOMAN. I would not have such a heart in my bosom for the dignity of the whole body.

DOCTOR. Well, well, well.

GENTLEWOMAN. Pray God it be, sir.

DOCTOR. This disease is beyond my practice: yet I have known
     those which have walked in their sleep, who have died holily in
     their beds.
LADY MACBETH. Wash your hands, put on your nightgown; look
     not so pale. I tell you yet again, Banquo's buried; he cannot come
     out on's grave.
DOCTOR. Even so?
LADY MACBETH. To bed, to bed. There's knocking at the gate.
     Come, come, come, come, give me your hand. What's done
     cannot be undone. To bed, to bed, to bed. [Exit.]
DOCTOR. Will she go now to bed?
GENTLEWOMAN. Directly.
DOCTOR. Foul whisp'rings are abroad. Unnatural deeds
          Do breed unnatural troubles: infected minds
          To their deaf pillows will discharge their secrets.
          More needs she the divine than the physician.—
          God, God, forgive us all! Look after her;
          Remove from her the means of all annoyance,
          And still keep eyes upon her. So, good night:
          My mind she has mated, and amaz'd my sight.
          I think, but dare not speak.
GENTLEWOMAN. Good night, good doctor.
[Exeunt.]

Arthur Symons

"Dreams"
1918

Symons was a British critic and poet.

To dream of love, and, waking, to remember you:
As though, being dead, one dreamed of heaven, and woke in hell.
At night my lovely dreams forget the old farewell:
Ah! wake not by his side, lest you remember too!

V. Memoirs and Essays

Ambrose Bierce

"Visions of the Night"
1887

Bierce was a particularly inventive author of fiction. His notable "An Occurrence at Owl Creek Bridge" dramatizes the imagination's incredible productivity. In this essay, he asserts the impossibility of accurately describing a dream but then vividly describes three hair-raising nightmares.

I hold the belief that the Gift of Dreams is a valuable literary endowment—that if by some art not now understood the elusive fancies that it supplies could be caught and fixed and made to serve we should have a literature "exceeding fair." [. . .]

Who can so relate a dream that it shall seem one? No poet has so light a touch. As well try to write the music of an aeolian harp. There is a familiar species of the genus Bore (*penetrator intolerabilis*) who having read a story—perhaps by some master of style—is at the pains elaborately to expound its plot for your edification and delight; then thinks, good soul, that now you need not read it. "Under substantially similar circumstances and conditions" (as the interstate commerce law hath it) I should not be guilty of the like offense; but I purpose herein to set forth the plots of certain dreams of my own, the "circumstance and conditions" being, as I conceive, dissimilar in this, that the dreams themselves are not accessible to the reader. In endeavoring to make record of their poorer part I do not indulge the hope of a higher success. I have no salt to put upon the tail of a dream's elusive spirit.

I was walking at dusk through a great forest of unfamiliar trees. Whence and whither I did not know. I had a sense of the vast extent of the wood, a consciousness that I was the only living thing in it. I was obsessed by some awful spell in expiation of a forgotten crime

149

committed, as I vaguely surmised, against the sunrise. Mechanically and without hope, I moved under the arms of the giant trees along a narrow trail penetrating the haunted solitudes of the forest. I came at length to a brook that flowed darkly and sluggishly across my path, and saw that it was blood. Turning to the right, I followed it up a considerable distance, and soon came to a small circular opening in the forest, filled with a dim, unreal light, by which I saw in the center of the opening a deep tank of white marble. It was filled with blood, and the stream that I had followed up was its outlet. All around the tank, between it and the enclosing forest—a space of perhaps ten feet in breadth, paved with immense slabs of marble— were dead bodies of men—a score; though I did not count them I knew that the number had some significant and portentous relation to my crime. Possibly they marked the time, in centuries, since I had committed it. I only recognized the fitness of the number, and knew it without counting. The bodies were naked and arranged symmetrically around the central tank, radiating from it like spokes of a wheel. The feet were outward, the heads hanging over the edge of the tank. Each lay upon its back, its throat cut, blood slowly dripping from the wound. I looked on all this unmoved. It was a natural and necessary result of my offense, and did not affect me; but there was something that filled me with apprehension and terror—a monstrous pulsation, beating with a slow, inevitable recurrence. I do not know which of the senses it addressed, or if it made its way to the consciousness through some avenue unknown to science and experience. The pitiless regularity of this vast rhythm was maddening. I was conscious that it pervaded the entire forest, and was a manifestation of some gigantic and implacable malevolence.

Of this dream I have no further recollection. Probably, overcome by a terror which doubtless had its origin in the discomfort of an impeded circulation, I cried out and was awakened at the sound of my own voice.

The dream whose skeleton I shall now present occurred in my early youth. I could not have been more than sixteen. I am considerably more now, yet I recall the incidents as vividly as when the vision was "of an hour's age" and I lay cowering beneath the bed-covering and trembling with terror from the memory.

I was alone on a boundless level in the night—in my bad dreams I am always alone and it is usually night. No trees were anywhere in sight, no habitations of men, no streams or hills. The earth seemed to be covered with a short, coarse vegetation that was black and stubbly, as if the plain had been swept by fire. My way was broken here and there as I went forward with I know not what purpose by small pools of water occupying shallow depressions, as if the fire had been succeeded by rain. These pools were on every side, and kept vanishing and appearing again, as heavy dark clouds drove athwart those parts of the sky which they reflected, and passing on disclosed again the steely glitter of the stars, in whose cold light the waters shone with a black luster. My course lay toward the west, where low along the horizon burned a crimson light beneath long strips of cloud, giving that effect of measureless distance that I have since learned to look for in Dore's pictures, where every touch of his hand has laid a portent and a curse. As I moved I saw outlined against this uncanny background a silhouette of battlements and towers which, expanding with every mile of my journey, grew at last to an unthinkable height and breadth, till the building subtended a wide angle of vision, yet seemed no nearer than before. Heartless and hopeless I struggled on over the blasted and forbidding plain, and still the mighty structure grew until I could no longer compass it with a look, and its towers shut out the stars directly overhead; then I passed in at an open portal, between columns of cyclopean masonry whose single stones were larger than my father's house.

Within all was vacancy; everything was coated with the dust of desertion. A dim light—the lawless light of dreams, sufficient unto itself—enabled me to pass from corridor to corridor, and from room to room, every door yielding to my hand. In the rooms it was a long walk from wall to wall; of no corridor did I ever reach an end. My footfalls gave out that strange, hollow sound that is never heard but in abandoned dwellings and tenanted tombs. For hours I wandered in the awful solitude, conscious of a seeking purpose, yet knowing not what I sought. At last, in what I conceived to be an extreme angle of the building, I entered a room of the ordinary dimensions, having a single window. Through this I saw the same crimson light still lying along the horizon in the measureless reaches of the west, like a visible doom, and knew it for the lingering fire of eternity. Looking upon the red menace of its sullen and sinister glare, there came to me the dreadful truth which years later as an extravagant fancy I endeavored to express in verse:

Man is long ages dead in every zone,
The angels all are gone to graves unknown;
The devils, too, are cold enough at last,
And God lies dead before the great white throne!

The light was powerless to dispel the obscurity of the room, and it was some time before I discovered in the farthest angle the outlines of a bed, and approached it with a prescience of ill. I felt that here somehow the bad business of my adventure was to end with some horrible climax, yet could not resist the spell that urged me to the fulfillment. Upon the bed, partly clothed, lay the dead body of a human being. It lay upon its back, the arms straight along the sides. By bending over it, which I did with loathing but no fear, I could see that it was dreadfully decomposed. The ribs protruded from the leathern flesh; through the skin of the sunken belly could be seen the protuberances of the spine. The face was black and shriveled and the lips, drawn away from the yellow teeth, cursed it with a ghastly grin. A fullness under the closed lids seemed to indicate that the eyes had survived the general wreck; and this was true, for as I bent above them they slowly opened and gazed into mine with a tranquil, steady regard. Imagine my horror how you can—no words of mine can assist the conception; the eyes were my own! That vestigial fragment of a vanished race—that unspeakable thing which neither time nor eternity had wholly effaced—that hateful and abhorrent scrap of mortality, still sentient after the death of God and the angels, was I!

There are dreams that repeat themselves. Of this class is one of my own, which seems sufficiently singular to justify its narration, though truly I fear the reader will think the realms of sleep are anything but a happy hunting-ground for my night-wandering soul. This is not true; the greater number of my incursions into dreamland, and I suppose those of most others, are attended with the happiest results. My imagination returns to the body like a bee to the hive, loaded with spoil which, reason assisting, is transmuted to honey and stored away in the cells of memory to be a joy forever. But the dream which I am about to relate has a double character; it is strangely dreadful in the experience, but the horror it inspires is so ludicrously disproportionate to the one incident producing it, that in retrospect the fantasy amuses.

I am passing through an open glade in a thinly wooded country. Through the belt of scattered trees that bound the irregular space there are glimpses of cultivated fields and the homes of strange intel- ligences. It must be near daybreak, for the moon, nearly at full, is low in the west, showing blood-red through the mists with which the landscape is fantastically freaked. The grass about my feet is heavy with dew, and the whole scene is that of a morning in early summer, glimmering in the unfamiliar light of a setting full moon. Near my path is a horse, visibly and audibly cropping the herbage. It lifts its head as I am about to pass, regards me motionless for a moment, then walks toward me. It is milk-white, mild of mien and amiable in look. I say to myself, "This horse is a gentle soul," and pause to caress it. It keeps its eyes fixed upon my own, approaches and speaks to me in a human voice, with human words. This does not surprise, but terrifies, and instantly I return to this our world.

The horse always speaks my own tongue, but I never know what it says. I suppose I vanish from the land of dreams before it finishes expressing what it has in mind, leaving it, no doubt, as greatly terrified by my sudden disappearance as I by its manner of accosting me. I would give value to know the purport of its communication.

Perhaps some morning I shall understand—and return no more to this our world.

G. K. Chesterton

"Dreams"
1901

The witty and prolific Gilbert Keith Chesterton was both naturally skeptical and deeply religious. A biographer, mystery novelist, reviewer, essayist, and editor, he scoffs at most fictional representations of dreams.

There can be comparatively little question that the place ordinarily occupied by dreams in literature is peculiarly unreal and unsatisfy- ing. When the hero tells us that "last night he dreamed a dream," we are quite certain from the perfect and decorative character of the dream that he made it up at breakfast. The dream is so reason- able that it is quite impossible. An angel came to him and opened before him a scroll inscribed with some tremendous moral truth; a knight in armour rode past him declaring some ideal quest; the phantom of his mother arose to warn him from some imminent sin. Dreams like these are (with occasional exceptions) practically unknown in the lawless kingdoms of the night. A dream is scarcely ever rounded to express faultlessly some faultless ideas. An angel might indeed open a scroll before the dreamer, but it would probably be inscribed with some remark about excursion trains to Brighton; a knight in armour might ride by him, but it would be impossible to deny that the most salient fact about that warrior was the fact that he was wearing three hats; his mother might indeed appear to the dreamer, and give him the tenderest and most elevated counsel, but it would be impossible for the loftiest ethical comfort to entirely obscure the fact that her nose was growing longer and longer every minute. Dreams have a kind of hellish ingenuity and energy in the pursuit of the inappropriate; the most omniscient and cunning artist never took so much trouble or achieved such success in finding exactly the word that was right or exactly the action that was significant, as this midnight lord of misrule can do in finding exactly the word that is wrong and exactly the action that is meaningless. The object of art is to subordinate the detail that is incidental to the tendency which is general. The object of a dream appears to be so to develop itself that some utterly futile and half-witted detail shall gradually devour all the other details of the vision. The flower upon the wall-paper just behind the head of Napoleon Buonaparte becomes brighter and brighter until we see nothing but a flower; the third waistcoat button of our best friend grows larger and larger until it is the great round sun of a revolving cosmos.

Thus at first sight it would seem that the lord of dreams was the eternal opponent of art. He seems to be to the aesthetic system what Satan is to the religious system, an unconquerable enemy, an irreducible minimum. The prigs of art who in this period erect their impeccable edifice, with even more than the gravity of the prigs of religion, have to deal with this mighty underworld of man in which their new rules are set as much at naught as the old ones, which is as careless of the modern canons of pleasure as of the ancient canons of pain. Asleep the artist is in the hands of an enchantress of ugliness who makes him love the discordant and hate the beautiful. In that realm the landscape painter paints monstrous landscapes, mingling scarlet and purple; in that realm the musician devises torturing melodies, and the architect top-heavy cathedrals.

So far as the forms and modes of art are concerned this is indeed true. The translucently allegorical dreams so often narrated in romance are essentially inconceivable. When the aged priest in a story narrates his dream, in which the imagery is dignified and the message plain, we are free to yield finally to a conviction that must have long been growing on us, and conclude that he is a somewhat distinguished liar. Dreams may have infinite meanings, but those meanings are not conveyed obviously by communicative mothers and candid angels. The Bible is an excellent place to look for a wisdom and morality older than mere words and ideals, and there is certainly far more truth in the old Biblical version of the nature of dreams which made them inscrutable and somewhat grotesque parables requiring particular persons to interpret them. If great spiritual truths are conveyed by dreams, they must certainly be conveyed as they were to Pharaoh or Nebuchadnezzar by farcical mysteries of clay-footed images and lean cows eating fat ones.

But there is another and far deeper manner in which dreams definitely correspond to art. Nothing is more remarkable in some of the great artistic masterpieces of the world than their startling deficiency in much of that sense of grace and proportion which goes nowadays by the name of art. If art were really what some contemporary critics represent it, a matter of the faultless arrangement of harmonies and transitions, Shakespeare would certainly not be anything like so great an artist as the last poetaster in Fleet Street who published a series of seven sonnets on seven varieties of grey sunset. Shakespeare often suffers from too much inventiveness; that which clogs us and trips us up in his masterpieces is not so much inferior work as irrelevant brilliancy; not so much failures as fragments of other masterpieces. Dickens was designless without knowing or caring; Sterne was designless by design. Yet these great works which mix up abstractions fit for an epic with fooleries not fit for a pantomime, which clash the sword with the red-hot poker, which present such a picture of literary chaos as might be produced if the characters in every book from *Paradise Lost* to *Pickwick* broke from their covers and mingled in one mad romance—these great works have assuredly a unity of their own or they would not be works of art. The unity which they have is a unity which when properly understood gives us the key of almost the whole of literary aesthetics: it is the same unity that we find in dreams. There is one unity which we do find in dreams. It binds together their brutal inconsequence and all their moonstruck anti-climaxes. It makes the unimaginable nocturnal farce which begins with a saint choosing parasols and ends with a policeman shelling peas, as rounded and single a harmony as some poet's roundel upon a passion flower. This unity is the absolute unity of emotion. If we wish to experience pure and naked feeling we can never experience it so really as in that unreal land. There the passions seem to live an outlawed and abstract existence, unconnected with any facts or persons. In dreams we have revenge without any injury, remorse without any sin, memory without any recollections, hope without any prospect. Love, indeed, almost proves itself a divine thing by the logic of dreams; for in a dream every material circumstance may alter, spectacles may grow on a baby, and moustaches on a maiden aunt, and yet the great sway of one tyrannical tenderness may never cease. Our dream may begin with the end of the world, and end with a picnic at Hampton Court, but the same rich and nameless mood will be expressed by the falling stars and by the crumbling sandwiches. In a dream daisies may glare at us like the eyes of demons. In a dream lightning and conflagration may warm and soothe us like our own fireside. In this sub-conscious world, in short, existence betrays itself; it shows that it is full of spiritual forces which disguise themselves as lions and lamp-posts, which can as easily disguise themselves as butterflies and Babylonian temples. The essential unity of a dream, which is never broken or impaired, is the unity of its attitude towards God, wistful or vacant, or grateful, or rebellious or assured.

Surely this unity of dreams was the unity which underlay the old wild masterpieces of literature. The plays of Shakespeare, for example, may be full of incidental discords, but not one of them ever fails to convey its aboriginal sentiment, that life is as black as the tempest or as green as the greenwood. It is said that art should represent life. So indeed it should, but it labours under the primary disadvantage that no man has seen life at any time. Long records of Whitechapel crime, long rows of Brixton villas, the words which one clerk says to another clerk, the despatches that one diplomatist writes to another diplomatist, none of these things even approach to being life. For life the man of science, even if he lives in the very heart of Brixton, is still searching with a microscope. Life dwells alone in our very heart of hearts, life is one and virgin and unconquered, and sometimes in the watches of the night speaks in its own terrible harmony.

Dante

The New Life (La Vita Nuova)
1295

Dante Alighieri (1265–1321) is most renowned for The Divine
Comedy. *In this excerpt from his earlier and lesser known yet extraor-
dinary work, he recounts the terrifying dream of the death of his beloved
Beatrice.*

[. . .] my body became afflicted with a painful infirmity, whereby
I suffered bitter anguish for many days, which at last brought me
unto such weakness that I could no longer move. And I remember
that on the ninth day, being overcome with intolerable pain, a thought
came into my mind concerning my lady: but when it had a little
nourished this thought, my mind returned to its brooding over mine
enfeebled body. And then perceiving how frail a thing life is, even
though health keep with it, the matter seemed to me so pitiful that
I could not choose but weep; and weeping I said within myself:
"Certainly it must some time come to pass that the very gentle
Beatrice will die." Then, feeling bewildered, I closed mine eyes; and
my brain began to be in travail as the brain of one frantic, and to
have such imaginations as here follow.

And at the first, it seemed to me that I saw certain faces of women
with their hair loosened, which called out to me, "Thou shalt surely
die"; after the which, other terrible and unknown appearances said
unto me, "Thou art dead." At length, as my phantasy held on in its
wanderings, I came to be I knew not where, and to behold a throng
of dishevelled ladies wonderfully sad, who kept going hither and
thither weeping. Then the sun went out, so that the stars showed
themselves, and they were of such a colour that I knew they must
be weeping: and it seemed to me that the birds fell dead out of the
sky, and that there were great earthquakes.

With that, while I wondered in my trance, and was filled with a
grievous fear, I conceived that a certain friend came unto me and
said: "Hast thou not heard? She that was thine excellent lady hath
been taken out of life." Then I began to weep very piteously; and
not only in mine imagination, but with mine eyes, which were wet
with tears. And I seemed to look towards Heaven, and to behold a
multitude of angels who were returning upwards, having before them
an exceedingly white cloud: and these angels were singing together

gloriously, and the words of their song were these: "*Osanna in excelsis*"; and there was no more that I heard. Then my heart that was so full of love said unto me: "It is true that our lady lieth dead"; and it seemed to me that I went to look upon the body wherein that blessed and most noble spirit had had its abiding-place. And so strong was this idle imagining, that it made me to behold my lady in death; whose head certain ladies seemed to be covering with a white veil; and who was so humble of her aspect that it was as though she had said, "I have attained to look on the beginning of peace." And therewithal I came unto such humility by the sight of her, that I cried out upon Death, saying: "Now come unto me, and be not bitter against me any longer: surely, there where thou hast been, thou hast learned gentleness. Wherefore come now unto me who do greatly desire thee: seest thou not that I wear thy colour already?" And when I had seen all those offices performed that are fitting to be done unto the dead, it seemed to me that I went back unto mine own chamber, and looked up towards Heaven. And so strong was my phantasy, that I wept again in very truth, and said with my true voice: "O excellent soul! how blessed is he that now looketh upon thee!"

And as I said these words, with a painful anguish of sobbing and another prayer unto Death, a young and gentle lady, who had been standing beside me where I lay, conceiving that I wept and cried out because of the pain of mine infirmity, was taken with trembling and began to shed tears. Whereby other ladies, who were about the room, becoming aware of my discomfort by reason of the moan that she made, (who indeed was of my very near kindred), led her away from where I was, and then set themselves to awaken me, thinking that I dreamed, and saying: "Sleep no longer, and be not disquieted."

Then, by their words, this strong imagination was brought suddenly to an end, at the moment that I was about to say, "O Beatrice! peace be with thee." And already I had said, "O Beatrice!" when being aroused, I opened mine eyes, and knew that it had been a deception. But albeit I had indeed uttered her name, yet my voice was so broken with sobs, that it was not understood by these ladies; so that in spite of the sore shame that I felt, I turned towards them by Love's counselling. And when they beheld me, they began to say, "He seemeth as one dead," and to whisper among themselves, "Let us strive if we may not comfort him." Whereupon they spake to me many soothing words, and questioned me moreover touching the cause of my fear.

Then I, being somewhat reassured, and having perceived that it was a mere phantasy, said unto them, "This thing it was that made me afeard"; and told them of all that I had seen, from the beginning even unto the end, but without once speaking the name of my lady. Also, after I had recovered from my sickness, I bethought me to write these things in rhyme; deeming it a lovely thing to be known. [. . .]

Thomas De Quincey

Confessions of an Opium-Eater
1821

Thomas De Quincey (1785–1859) was a poet and critic who befriended the older famous poets Samuel Taylor Coleridge and William Wordsworth. He attended Oxford University, where, perhaps in response to a painful neurological condition, he began his use of and eventual addiction to opium. In this excerpt from his most famous work, he discusses how disturbing his dreams were as a child and young person, and how we never actually forget anything: ". . . the dread book of account which the Scriptures speak of is in fact the mind itself of each individual. Of this at least I feel assured, that there is no such thing as forgetting possible to the mind; a thousand accidents may and will interpose a veil between our present consciousness and the secret inscriptions on the mind; accidents of the same sort will also rend away this veil; but alike, whether veiled or unveiled, the inscription remains for ever, just as the stars seem to withdraw before the common light of day, whereas in fact we all know that it is the light which is drawn over them as a veil, and that they are waiting to be revealed when the obscuring daylight shall have withdrawn."

I now pass to what is the main subject of these latter confessions, to the history and journal of what took place in my dreams, for these were the immediate and proximate cause of my acutest suffering.

The first notice I had of any important change going on in this part of my physical economy was from the reawakening of a state of eye generally incident to childhood, or exalted states of irritability. I know not whether my reader is aware that many children, perhaps most, have a power of painting, as it were upon the darkness, all sorts of phantoms. In some that power is simply a mechanical affection of the eye; others have a voluntary or semi-voluntary power to dismiss or to summon them; or, as a child once said to me when I questioned

him on this matter, "I can tell them to go, and they go—, but sometimes they come when I don't tell them to come." Whereupon I told
him that he had almost as unlimited a command over apparitions as
a Roman centurion over his soldiers.—In the middle of 1817, I think
it was, that this faculty became positively distressing to me: at night,
when I lay awake in bed, vast processions passed along in mournful
pomp; friezes of never-ending stories, that to my feelings were as sad
and solemn as if they were stories drawn from times before Oedipus
or Priam, before Tyre, before Memphis. And at the same time a
corresponding change took place in my dreams; a theatre seemed
suddenly opened and lighted up within my brain, which presented
nightly spectacles of more than earthly splendour. And the four
following facts may be mentioned as noticeable at this time:

1. That as the creative state of the eye increased, a sympathy seemed
to arise between the waking and the dreaming states of the brain in
one point—that whatsoever I happened to call up and to trace by a
voluntary act upon the darkness was very apt to transfer itself to my
dreams, so that I feared to exercise this faculty; for, as Midas turned
all things to gold that yet baffled his hopes and defrauded his human
desires, so whatsoever things capable of being visually represented
I did but think of in the darkness, immediately shaped themselves
into phantoms of the eye; and by a process apparently no less inevitable, when thus once traced in faint and visionary colours, like
writings in sympathetic ink, they were drawn out by the fierce
chemistry of my dreams into insufferable splendour that fretted my
heart.

2. For this and all other changes in my dreams were accompanied
by deep-seated anxiety and gloomy melancholy, such as are wholly
incommunicable by words. I seemed every night to descend, not
metaphorically, but literally to descend, into chasms and sunless
abysses, depths below depths, from which it seemed hopeless that
I could ever reascend. Nor did I, by waking, feel that I had reas-
cended. This I do not dwell upon; because the state of gloom which
attended these gorgeous spectacles, amounting at last to utter darkness,
as of some suicidal despondency, cannot be approached by words.

3. The sense of space, and in the end the sense of time, were both
powerfully affected. Buildings, landscapes, &c., were exhibited in
proportions so vast as the bodily eye is not fitted to receive. Space
swelled, and was amplified to an extent of unutterable infinity. This,
however, did not disturb me so much as the vast expansion of time;
I sometimes seemed to have lived for 70 or 100 years in one

night—nay, sometimes had feelings representative of a millennium passed in that time, or, however, of a duration far beyond the limits of any human experience.

4. The minutest incidents of childhood, or forgotten scenes of later years, were often revived: I could not be said to recollect them, for if I had been told of them when waking, I should not have been able to acknowledge them as parts of my past experience. But placed as they were before me, in dreams like intuitions, and clothed in all their evanescent circumstances and accompanying feelings, I recognised them instantaneously. I was once told by a near relative of mine, that having in her childhood fallen into a river, and being on the very verge of death but for the critical assistance which reached her, she saw in a moment her whole life, in its minutest incidents, arrayed before her simultaneously as in a mirror; and she had a faculty developed as suddenly for comprehending the whole and every part. This, from some opium experiences of mine, I can believe; I have indeed seen the same thing asserted twice in modern books, and accompanied by a remark which I am convinced is true; viz., that the dread book of account which the Scriptures speak of is in fact the mind itself of each individual. Of this at least I feel assured, that there is no such thing as forgetting possible to the mind; a thousand accidents may and will interpose a veil between our present consciousness and the secret inscriptions on the mind; accidents of the same sort will also rend away this veil; but alike, whether veiled or unveiled, the inscription remains for ever, just as the stars seem to withdraw before the common light of day, whereas in fact we all know that it is the light which is drawn over them as a veil, and that they are waiting to be revealed when the obscuring daylight shall have withdrawn. [. . .]

Charles Dickens

"Night Walks"
1860

In a meditation from one of his essays, Dickens tries to show that dream life and waking life do in fact overlap and that we continually confuse them. He asks, comparing his experience to those in an insane asylum, "Do we not nightly jumble events and personages and times and places?"

[. . .] I chose next to wander by Bethlehem Hospital; partly, because it lay on my road round to Westminster; partly, because I had a night fancy in my head which could be best pursued within sight of its walls and dome. And the fancy was this: Are not the sane and the insane equal at night as the sane lie a dreaming? Are not all of us outside this hospital, who dream, more or less in the condition of those inside it, every night of our lives? Are we not nightly persuaded, as they daily are, that we associate preposterously with kings and queens, emperors and empresses, and notabilities of all sorts? Do we not nightly jumble events and personages and times and places, as these do daily? Are we not sometimes troubled by our own sleeping inconsistencies, and do we not vexedly try to account for them or excuse them, just as these do sometimes in respect of their waking delusions? Said an afflicted man to me, when I was last in a hospital like this, "Sir, I can frequently fly." I was half ashamed to reflect that so could I—by night. Said a woman to me on the same occasion, "Queen Victoria frequently comes to dine with me, and her Majesty and I dine off peaches and macaroni in our night-gowns, and his Royal Highness the Prince Consort does us the honour to make a third on horseback in a Field-Marshal's uniform." Could I refrain from reddening with consciousness when I remembered the amazing royal parties I myself had given (at night), the unaccountable viands I had put on table, and my extraordinary manner of conducting myself on those distinguished occasions? I wonder that the great master who knew everything, when he called Sleep the death of each day's life, did not call Dreams the insanity of each day's sanity.

Ralph Waldo Emerson

"Demonology"
1877

In this wonderfully wandering essay, delivered first as a lecture in 1839–40, Emerson suggests that dreams can give us clues to what our dogs are thinking about: "Animals have been called 'the dreams of Nature.' Perhaps for a conception of their consciousness we may go to our own dreams." As for the title of his piece, he explains: "The name Demonology covers dreams, omens, coincidences, luck, sortilege, magic and other experiences which shun rather than court inquiry, and deserve notice chiefly because every man has usually in a lifetime two or three hints in this kind which are specially impressive to him. They also shed light on our structure."

> Night-dreams trace on Memory's wall
> Shadows of the thoughts of day,
> And thy fortunes as they fall
> The bias of thy will betray.[17]

[. . .] Dreams are jealous of being remembered; they dissipate instantly and angrily if you try to hold them. When newly awaked from lively dreams, we are so near them, still agitated by them, still in their sphere,—give us one syllable, one feature, one hint, and we should repossess the whole; hours of this strange entertainment would come trooping back to us; but we cannot get our hand on the first link or fibre, and the whole is lost. There is a strange wilfulness in the speed with which it disperses and baffles our grasp.

A dislocation seems to be the foremost trait of dreams. A painful imperfection almost always attends them. The fairest forms, the most noble and excellent persons, are deformed by some pitiful and insane circumstance. The very landscape and scenery in a dream seem not to fit us, but like a coat or cloak of some other person to overlap and encumber the wearer; so is the ground, the road, the house, in dreams, too long or too short, and if it served no other purpose would show us how accurately Nature fits man awake.

There is one memory of waking and another of sleep. In our dreams the same scenes and fancies are many times associated, and that too, it would seem, for years. In sleep one shall travel certain roads in stage-coaches or gigs, which he recognizes as familiar, and has dreamed that ride a dozen times; or shall walk alone in familiar fields and meadows, which road or which meadow in waking hours he never looked upon. This feature of dreams deserves the more attention from its singular resemblance to that obscure yet startling experience which almost every person confesses in daylight, that particular passages of conversation and action have occurred to him in the same order before, whether dreaming or waking; a suspicion that they have been with precisely these persons in precisely this room, and heard precisely this dialogue, at some former hour, they know not when.

---

17 The epigraph is from "Memory" (1867), one of Emerson's "Quatrains."

Animals have been called "the dreams of Nature." Perhaps for a conception of their consciousness we may go to our own dreams. In a dream we have the instinctive obedience, the same torpidity of the highest power, the same unsurprised assent to the monstrous as these metamorphosed men exhibit. Our thoughts in a stable or in a menagerie, on the other hand, may well remind us of our dreams. What compassion do these imprisoning forms awaken! You may catch the glance of a dog sometimes which lays a kind of claim to sympathy and brotherhood. What! somewhat of me down there? Does he know it? Can he too, as I, go out of himself, see himself, perceive relations? We fear lest the poor brute should gain one dreadful glimpse of his condition, should learn in some moment the tough limitations of this fettering organization. It was in this glance that Ovid got the hint of his metamorphoses; Calidasa of his transmigration of souls. For these fables are our own thoughts carried out. What keeps those wild tales in circulation for thousands of years? What but the wild fact to which they suggest some approximation of theory? [. . .]

Dreams have a poetic integrity and truth. This limbo and dust-hole of thought is presided over by a certain reason, too. Their extravagance from nature is yet within a higher nature. They seem to us to suggest an abundance and fluency of thought not familiar to the waking experience. They pique us by independence of us, yet we know ourselves in this mad crowd, and owe to dreams a kind of divination and wisdom. My dreams are not me; they are not Nature, or the Not-me: they are both. They have a double consciousness, at once sub- and ob-jective. We call the phantoms that rise, the creation of our fancy, but they act like mutineers, and fire on their commander; showing that every act, every thought, every cause, is bipolar, and in the act is contained the counteraction. If I strike, I am struck; if I chase, I am pursued.

Wise and sometimes terrible hints shall in them be thrown to the man out of a quite unknown intelligence. He shall be startled two or three times in his life by the justice as well as the significance of this phantasmagoria. Once or twice the conscious fetters shall seem to be unlocked, and a freer utterance attained. A prophetic character in all ages has haunted them. They are the maturation often of opinions not consciously carried out to statements, but whereof we already possessed the elements. Thus, when awake, I know the character of Rupert, but do not think what he may do. In dreams I see him engaged in certain actions which seem preposterous,—out of all fitness. He is hostile, he is cruel, he is frightful, he is a poltroon. It turns out prophecy a year later. But it was already in my mind as character, and the sibyl dreams merely embodied it in fact. Why then should not symptoms, auguries, forebodings be, and, as one said, the moanings of the spirit?

We are let by this experience into the high region of Cause, and acquainted with the identity of very unlike-seeming effects. We learn that actions whose turpitude is very differently reputed proceed from one and the same affection. Sleep takes off the costume of circumstance, arms us with terrible freedom, so that every will rushes to a deed. A skilful man reads his dreams for his self-knowledge; yet not the details, but the quality. What part does he play in them,—a cheerful, manly part, or a poor drivelling part? However monstrous and grotesque their apparitions, they have a substantial truth. The same remark may be extended to the omens and coincidences which may have astonished us. Of all it is true that the reason of them is always latent in the individual. Goethe said: "These whimsical pictures, inasmuch as they originate from us, may well have an analogy with our whole life and fate."

The soul contains in itself the event that shall presently befall it, for the event is only the actualizing of its thoughts. It is no wonder that particular dreams and presentiments should fall out and be prophetic. The fallacy consists in selecting a few insignificant hints when all are inspired with the same sense. As if one should exhaust his astonishment at the economy of his thumb-nail, and overlook the central causal miracle of his being a man. Every man goes through the world attended with innumerable facts prefiguring (yes, distinctly announcing) his fate, if only eyes of sufficient heed and illumination were fastened on the sign. The sign is always there, if only the eye were also; just as under every tree in the speckled sunshine and shade no man notices that every spot of light is a perfect image of the sun, until in some hour the moon eclipses the luminary; and then first we notice that the spots of light have become crescents, or annular, and correspond to the changed figure of the sun. Things are significant enough, Heaven knows; but the seer of the sign,—where is he? We doubt not a man's fortune may be read in the lines of his hand, by palmistry; in the lines of his face, by physiognomy; in the outlines of the skull, by craniology: the lines are all there, but the reader waits. The long waves indicate to the instructed mariner that there is no near land in the direction from which they come. Belzoni describes the three marks which led him to dig for a door to the pyramid of Ghizeh. What thousands had beheld the same spot for so many ages, and seen no three marks. [. . .]

"There is one world common to all who are awake, but each sleeper betakes himself to one of his own."[18] Dreams retain the infirmities of our character. The good genius may be there or not, our evil genius is sure to stay. The Ego partial makes the dream; the Ego total the interpretation. Life is also a dream on the same terms.

Johann Wolfgang von Goethe and Johann Peter Eckermann

Conversations with Goethe
1836

Eckermann was the personal secretary of the German author Goethe and recounted in diary and memoir format their conversations on many topics.

March 12, 1828

After I had quitted Goethe yesterday evening, the important conversation I had carried on with him remained constantly in my mind. The discourse had also been upon the sea and sea air; and Goethe had expressed the opinion, that he considered all islanders and inhabitants of the sea-shore in temperate climates far more productive, and possessed of more active force, than the people in the interior of large continents.

Whether or not it was that I had fallen asleep with these thoughts, and with a certain longing for the inspiring powers of the sea; suffice it to say, I had in the night the following pleasant, and to me very remarkable, dream:—

I saw myself in an unknown region, amongst strange men, thoroughly cheerful and happy. The most beautiful summer day surrounded me in a charming scene, such as might be witnessed somewhere on the shores of the Mediterranean, in the south of Spain or France, or in the neighbourhood of Genoa. We had been drinking at noon

---

18 Emerson is citing the Greek philosopher Heraclitus.

round a merry table, and I went with some others, rather young people, to make another party for the afternoon.

We had loitered along through bushy and pleasant low lands, when we suddenly found ourselves in the sea, upon the smallest of islands, on a jutting rock, where there was scarcely room for five or six men, and where one could not stir for fear of slipping into the water. Behind us, whence we had come, there was nothing to be seen but sea; but before us lay the shore at about a quarter of an hour's distance, spread out most invitingly. The shore was in some places flat, in others rocky and somewhat elevated; and one might observe, between green leaves and white tents, a crowd of joyous men in light-coloured clothes, recreating themselves with music, which sounded from the tents. "There is nothing else to be done," said one of us to the other, "we must undress and swim over." "It is all very well to say so," said I, "you are young, handsome fellows, and good swimmers; but I swim badly, and I do not possess a shape fine enough to appear, with pleasure and comfort, before the strange people on shore." "You are a fool," said one of the handsomest, "undress yourself, give me your form, and you shall have mine."

At these words I undressed myself quickly, and was soon in the water, and immediately found myself in the body of the other as a powerful swimmer. I soon reached the shore, and, naked and dripping, stepped with the most easy confidence amongst the men. I was happy in the sensation of these fine limbs; my deportment was unconstrained, and I at once became intimate with the strangers, at a table before an arbour, where there was a great deal of mirth. My comrades had now reached land one by one, and had joined us, and the only one missing was the youth with my form, in whose limbs I found myself so comfortable. At last he also approached the shore, and I was asked if I was not glad to see my former self? At these words I experienced a certain discomfort, partly because I did not expect any great joy from myself, and partly because I feared that my young friend would ask for his own body back again. However, I turned to the water, and saw my second self swimming close up to me, and laughing at me with his head turned a little on one side. "There is no swimming with those limbs of yours," exclaimed he, "I have had a fine struggle against waves and breakers, and it is not to be wondered at that I have come so late, and am last of all." I at once recognized the countenance; it was my own, but grown young, and rather fuller and broader, with the freshest complexion. He now came to land, and whilst he raised himself, and first stepped along the sand, I had a view of his back and legs, and was delighted with the perfection of the form. He came up the rocky shore to us, and as he came up to me he had completely my new stature.

"How is it," thought I to myself, "that your little body has grown so handsome. Have the primeval powers of the sea operated so wonderfully upon it, or is it because the youthful spirit of my friend has penetrated the limbs?" Whilst we enjoyed ourselves together for some time, I silently wondered that my friend did not show any inclination to resume his own body. "Truly," thought I, "he looks bravely, and it may be a matter of indifference to him in which body he is placed, but it is not the same thing to me; for I am not sure whether in that body I may not shrink and become as diminutive as before." In order to satisfy myself on this point, I took my friend aside, and asked him how he felt in my limbs? "Perfectly well," said he; "I have the same sensation of my own natural power as before; I do not know what you have to complain of in your limbs. They are quite right with me; and you see one only has to make the best of oneself. Remain in my body as long as you please; for I am perfectly contented to remain in yours through all futurity." I was much pleased by this explanation, and as in all my sensations, thoughts, and recollections, I felt quite as usual, my dream gave me the impression of a perfect independence of the soul, and the possibility of a future existence in another body.

"That is a very pretty dream," said Goethe, when, after dinner today, I imparted to him the principal features. "We see," continued he, "that the muses visit you even in sleep, and, indeed, with particular favour; for you must confess that it would be difficult for you to invent anything so peculiar and pretty in your waking moments."

"I can scarcely conceive how it happened to me," returned I; "for I had felt so dejected all day, that the contemplation of so fresh a life was far from my mind."

"Human nature possesses wonderful powers," returned Goethe, "and has something good in readiness for us when we least hope for it. There have been times in my life when I have fallen asleep in tears; but in my dreams the most charming forms have come to console and to cheer me, and I have risen the next morning fresh and joyful. [. . .]"

Maxim Gorky

Reminiscences of Tolstoy
1920

When Gorky first met Russia's most famous author, Leo Tolstoy, in 1900, Gorky's own fame as a writer was on the rise. His memoirs about Tolstoy and Chekhov are vivid, candid, and touching.

"What is the most terrible dream you have ever had?" Tolstoy asked me.

I rarely have dreams and remember them badly, but two have remained in my memory and probably will for the rest of my life.

I dreamt once that I saw the sky scrofulous, putrescent, greenish-yellow, and the stars in it were round, flat, without rays, without lustre, like scabs on the skin of a diseased person. And there glided across this putrescent sky slowly reddish forked lightning, rather like a snake, and when it touched a star the star swelled up into a ball and burst noiselessly, leaving behind it a darkish spot, like a little smoke; and then the spot vanished quickly in the bleared and liquid sky. Thus all the stars one after another burst and perished, and the sky, growing darker and more horrible, at last whirled upwards, bubbled and bursting into fragments began to fall on my head in a kind of cold jelly, and in the spaces between the fragments there appeared a shiny blackness as though of iron. Leo Nikolayevich said: "Now that comes from a learned book; you must have read something on astronomy; hence the nightmare. And the other dream?"

The other dream: a snowy plain, smooth like a sheet of paper; no hillock, no tree, no bush anywhere, only—barely visible—a few rods poked out from under the snow. And across the snow of this dead desert from horizon to horizon there stretched a yellow strip of a hardly distinguishable road, and over the road there marched slowly a pair of grey felt top boots—empty.

He raised his shaggy, were-wolf eyebrows, looked at me intently and thought for a while.

"That's terrible. Did you really dream that, you didn't invent it? But there's something bookish in it also."

And suddenly he got angry, and said, irritably, sternly, rapping his knee with his finger: "But you're not a drinking man? It's unlikely that you ever drank much. And yet there's something drunken in these dreams. There was a German writer, [E. T. A.] Hoffmann, who dreamt that card tables ran about the street, and all that sort of thing, but then he was a drunkard—a 'calaholic,' as our literate coachmen say. Empty boots marching—that's really terrible. Even if you did invent it, it's good. Terrible."

Suddenly he gave a broad smile, so that even his cheek bones beamed.

"And imagine this: suddenly, in the Tverskaya street, there runs a card table with its curved legs, its boards clap, clap, raising a chalky dust, and you can even still see the numbers on the green cloth—excise clerks playing whist on it for three days and nights on end—the table could not bear it any longer and ran away."

He laughed, and then, probably noticing that I was a little hurt by his distrust of me:

"Are you hurt because I thought your dreams bookish? Don't be annoyed; sometimes, I know, one invents something without being aware of it, something which one cannot believe, which can't possibly be believed, and then one imagines that one dreamt it and did not invent it at all. There was a story which an old landowner told. He dreamt that he was walking in a wood and came out of it on to a steppe. On the steppe he saw two hills, which suddenly turned into a woman's breasts, and between them rose up a black face which, instead of eyes, had two moons like white spots. The old man dreamt that he was standing between the woman's legs, in front of him a deep, dark ravine, which sucked him in. After the dream his hair began to grow grey and his hands to tremble, and he went abroad to Doctor Kneip to take a water cure. But, really, he must have seen something of the kind—he was a dissolute fellow."

He patted me on the shoulder.

"But you are neither a drunkard nor dissolute—how do you come to have such dreams?"

"I don't know."

"We know nothing about ourselves."

He sighed, screwed up his eyes, thought for a bit, and then added in a low voice: "We know nothing."

This evening, during our walk, he took my arm and said:

"The boots are marching—terrible, eh? Quite empty—*tiop, tiop*—and the snow scrunching. Yes, it's good; but you are very bookish, very. Don't be cross, but it's bad and will stand in your way."

I am scarcely more bookish than he, and at the time I thought him a cruel rationalist despite all his pleasant little phrases.

William Hazlitt

"On Dreams"
1823

*The English essayist Hazlitt discusses in his lively, ever-personal way
a wide range of dream phenomena, from sleepwalking to the unconscious:
"Let any one call you at any time, however fast asleep you may be, you
make out their voice in the first surprise to be like some one's you were
thinking of in your sleep. Let an accidental noise, the falling of something
in the next room, rouse you up, you constantly find something to associate it with, or translate it back into the language of your slumbering
thoughts. You are never taken completely at a* nonplus—*summoned,
as it were, out of a state of non-existence."*

[. . .] I myself am (or used some time ago to be) a sleep-walker; and
know how the thing is. In this sort of disturbed, unsound sleep, the
eyes are not closed, and are attracted by the light. I used to get up
and go towards the window, and make violent efforts to throw it
open. The air in some measure revived me, or I might have tried to
fling myself out. I saw objects indistinctly, the houses, for instance,
facing me on the opposite side of the street; but still it was some time
before I could recognise them or recollect where I was: that is, I was
still asleep, and the dimness of my senses (as far as it prevailed) was
occasioned by the greater numbness of my memory. This phenomenon is not astonishing, unless we chuse in all such cases to put the
cart before the horse. For in fact, it is the mind that sleeps, and
the senses (so to speak) only follow the example. The mind dozes,
and the eye-lids close in consequence: we do not go to sleep, because
we shut our eyes. I can, however, speak to the fact of the eyes being
open, when their sense is shut; or rather, when we are unable to
draw just inferences from it. It is generally in the night-time indeed,
or in a strange place, that the circumstance happens; but as soon as
the light dawns on the recollection, the obscurity and perplexity
of the senses clear up. The external impression is made before, much
in the same manner as it is after we are awake; but it does not lead
to the usual train of associations connected with that impression; *e.g.* the name of the street or town where we are, who lives at
the opposite house, how we came to sleep in the room where we are,
&c.; all which are ideas belonging to our waking experience, and are
at this time cut off or greatly disturbed by sleep. It is just the same as

when persons recover from a swoon, and fix their eyes unconsciously on those about them, for a considerable time before they recollect where they are.

Would any one but a German physiologist think it necessary to assure us that at this time they see, but with their eyes open, or pretend that though they have lost all memory or understanding during their fainting fit, their minds act then more vigorously and freely than ever, because they are not distracted by outward impressions? The appeal is made to the outward sense, in the instances we have seen; but the mind is deaf to it, because its functions are for the time gone. It is ridiculous to pretend with this author, that in sleep some of the organs of the mind rest, while others are active: it might as well be pretended that in sleep one eye watches while the other is shut.

The stupor is general: the faculty of thought itself is impaired; and whatever ideas we have, instead of being confined to any particular faculty or the impressions of any one sense, and invigorated thereby, float at random from object to object, from one class of impressions to another, without coherence or control. The *conscious* or connecting link between our ideas, which forms them into separate groups or compares different parts and views of a subject together, seems to be that which is principally wanting in sleep; so that any idea that presents itself in this anarchy of the mind is lord of the ascendant for the moment, and is driven out by the next straggling notion that comes across it. The bundles of thought are, as it were, untied, loosened from a common centre, and drift along the stream of fancy as it happens. Hence the confusion (not the concentration of the faculties) that continually takes place in this state of half-perception. The mind takes in but one thing at a time, but one part of a subject, and therefore cannot correct its sudden and heterogeneous transitions from one momentary impression to another by a larger grasp of understanding. Thus we confound one person with another, merely from some accidental coincidence, the name or the place where we have seen them, or their having been concerned with us in some particular transaction the evening before. They lose and regain their proper identity perhaps half a dozen times in this rambling way; nor are we able (though we are somewhat incredulous and surprised at these compound creations) to detect the error, from not being prepared to trace the same connected subject of thought to a number of varying and successive ramifications, or to form the idea of a *whole*. We think that Mr. Such-a-one did so and so: then, from a second face coming across us, like the sliders of a magic lantern, it was not he, but another; then some one calls him by his right name, and he is himself again. We are little shocked at these gross contradictions; for if the mind was capable of perceiving them in all their absurdity, it would not be liable to fall into them. It runs into them for the same reason that it is hardly conscious of them when made.

> "——That which was now a horse, a bear, a cloud,
> Even with a thought the rack dislimns,
> And makes it indistinct as water is in water."

The difference, so far then, between sleeping and waking seems to be that in the latter we have a greater range of conscious recollections, a larger discourse of reason, and associate ideas in longer trains and more as they are connected one with another in the order of nature; whereas in the former, any two impressions, that meet or are alike, join company, and then are parted again, without notice, like the froth from the wave. So in madness, there is, I should apprehend, the same tyranny of the imagination over the judgment; that is, the mind has slipped its cable, and single images meet, and jostle, and unite suddenly together, without any power to arrange or compare them with others, with which they are connected in the world of reality. There is a continual phantasmagoria: whatever shapes and colours come together are by the heat and violence of the brain referred to external nature, without regard to the order of time, place, or circumstance. From the same want of continuity, we often forget our dreams so speedily: if we cannot catch them as they are passing out at the door, we never set eyes on them again. There is no clue or thread of imagination to trace them by. In a morning sometimes we have had a dream that we try in vain to recollect; it is gone, like the rainbow from the cloud. At other times (so evanescent is their texture) we forget that we have dreamt at all; and at these times the mind seems to have been a mere blank, and sleep presents only an image of death.

Hence has arisen the famous dispute, *Whether the soul thinks always?*—on which Mr. Locke and different writers have bestowed so much tedious and unprofitable discussion; some maintaining that the mind was like a watch that goes continually, though more slowly and irregularly at one time than another; while the opposite party contended that it often stopped altogether, bringing the example of sound sleep as an argument, and desiring to know what proof we could have of thoughts passing through the mind, of which it was itself perfectly unconscious, and retained not the slightest recollection. I grant, we often sleep so sound, or have such faint imagery passing through the brain, that if we awake by degrees, we forget it altogether: we recollect our first waking, and perhaps some imperfect suggestions of fancy just before; but beyond this, all is mere oblivion. But I have observed that whenever I have been waked up suddenly, and not left to myself to recover from this state of mental torpor, I have been always dreaming of something, *i.e.* thinking, according to the tenor of the question.

Let any one call you at any time, however fast asleep you may be, you make out their voice in the first surprise to be like some one's you were thinking of in your sleep. Let an accidental noise, the falling of something in the next room, rouse you up, you constantly find something to associate it with, or translate it back into the language of your slumbering thoughts. You are never taken completely at a *nonplus*—summoned, as it were, out of a state of non-existence. It is easy for any one to try the experiment upon himself; that is, to examine every time he is waked up suddenly, so that his waking and sleeping state are brought into immediate contact, whether he has not in all such cases been dreaming of something, and not fairly *caught napping*. For myself, I think I can speak with certainty. It would indeed be rather odd to awake out of such an absolute privation and suspense of thought as is contended for by the partisans of the contrary theory. It would be a peep into the grave, a consciousness of death, an escape from the world of non-entity!

The vividness of our impressions in dreams, of which so much has been said, seems to be rather apparent than real; or, if this mode of expression should be objected to as unwarrantable, rather physical than mental. It is a vapour, a fume, the effect of the "heat-oppressed brain." The imagination gloats over an idea, and doats at the same time. However warm or brilliant the colouring of these changing appearances, they vanish with the dawn. They are put out by our waking thoughts, as the sun puts out a candle. It is unlucky that we sometimes remember the heroic sentiments, the profound discoveries, the witty repartees we have uttered in our sleep. The one turn to bombast, the others are mere truisms, and the last absolute nonsense. Yet we clothe them certainly with a fancied importance at the moment. This seems to be merely the effervescence of the blood or of the brain, physically acting. It is an odd thing in sleep, that we not only fancy we see different persons, and talk to them, but that we hear them make answers, and startle us with an observation or a piece of news; and though we of course put the answer into their mouths, we have no idea beforehand what it will be, and it takes us as much by surprise as it would in reality. This kind of successful ventriloquism which we practise upon ourselves may perhaps be in some measure accounted for from the short-sightedness and incomplete consciousness which were remarked above as the peculiar characteristics of sleep.

The power of prophesying or foreseeing things in our sleep, as from a higher and more abstracted sphere of thought, need not be here argued upon. There is, however, a sort of profundity in sleep; and it may be usefully consulted as an oracle in this way. It may be said, that the voluntary power is suspended, and things come upon us as unexpected revelations, which we keep out of our thoughts at other times. We may be aware of a danger, that yet we do not chuse, while we have the full command of our faculties, to acknowledge to ourselves: the impending event will then appear to us as a dream, and we shall most likely find it verified afterwards. Another thing of no small consequence is, that we may sometimes discover our tacit, and almost unconscious sentiments, with respect to persons or things in the same way. We are not hypocrites in our sleep. The curb is taken off from our passions, and our imagination wanders at will. When awake, we check these rising thoughts, and fancy we have them not. In dreams, when we are off our guard, they return securely and unbidden. We may make this use of the infirmity of our sleeping metamorphosis, that we may repress any feelings of this sort that we disapprove in their incipient state, and detect, ere it be too late, an unwarrantable antipathy or fatal passion. Infants cannot disguise their thoughts from others; and in sleep we reveal the secret to ourselves.

It should appear that I have never been in love, for the same reason. I never dream of the face of any one I am particularly attached to. I have thought almost to agony of the same person for years, nearly without ceasing, so as to have her face always before me, and to be haunted by a perpetual consciousness of disappointed passion, and yet I never in all that time dreamt of this person more than once or twice, and then not vividly. I conceive, therefore, that this perseverance of the imagination in a fruitless track must have been owing to mortified pride, to an intense desire and hope of good in the abstract, more than to love, which I consider as an individual and involuntary passion, and which therefore, when it is strong, must predominate over the fancy in sleep.

William Dean Howells

"I Talk of Dreams"
1896

*Howells's comic rant against telling one's dreams is chock-full of his
recounting of his own often humorous dreams.*

[. . .] Every one knows how delightful the dreams are that one dreams
one's self, and how insipid the dreams of others are. I had an illustration of the fact, not many evenings ago, when a company of us
got telling dreams. I had by far the best dreams of any; to be quite
frank, mine were the only dreams worth listening to; they were richly
imaginative, delicately fantastic, exquisitely whimsical, and humorous
in the last degree; and I wondered that when the rest could have
listened to them they were always eager to cut in with some silly,
senseless, tasteless thing, that made me sorry and ashamed for them.
I shall not be going too far if I say that it was on their part the grossest
betrayal of vanity that I ever witnessed.

But the egotism of some people concerning their dreams is almost
incredible. They will come down to breakfast and bore everybody
with a recital of the nonsense that has passed through their brains
in sleep, as if they were not bad enough when they were awake;
they will not spare the slightest detail; and if, by the mercy of
Heaven, they have forgotten something, they will be sure to recollect
it, and go back and give it all over again with added circumstance.
Such people do not reflect that there is something so purely and
intensely personal in dreams that they can rarely interest any one
but the dreamer, and that to the dearest friend, the closest relation
or connection, they can seldom be otherwise than tedious and
impertinent. The habit husbands and wives have of making one
another listen to their dreams is especially cruel. They have each
other quite helpless, and for this reason they should all the more
carefully guard themselves from abusing their advantage. Parents
should not afflict their offspring with the rehearsal of their mental
maunderings in sleep, and children should learn that one of the first
duties a child owes its parents is to spare them the anguish of hearing
what it has dreamed about overnight. A like forbearance in regard
to the community at large should be taught as the first trait of
good manners in the public schools, if we ever come to teach good
manners there.

I.

Certain exceptional dreams, however, are so imperatively significant, so vitally important, that it would be wrong to withhold them from the knowledge of those who happened not to dream them, and I feel some such quality in my own dreams so strongly that I could scarcely forgive myself if I did not, however briefly, impart them. It was only the last week, for instance, that I found myself one night in the company of the Duke of Wellington, the great Duke, the Iron one, in fact; and after a few moments of agreeable conversation on topics of interest among gentlemen, his Grace said that now, if I pleased, he would like a couple of those towels. We had not been speaking of towels, that I remember, but it seemed the most natural thing in the world that he should mention them in the connection, whatever it was, and I went at once to get them for him. At the place where they gave out towels, and where I found some very civil people, they told me that what I wanted was not towels, and they gave me instead two bath-gowns, of rather scanty measure, butternut in color and Turkish in texture. The garments made somehow a very strong impression upon me, so that I could draw them now, if I could draw anything, as they looked when they were held up to me. At the same moment, for no reason that I can allege, I passed from a social to a menial relation to the Duke, and foresaw that when I went back to him with these bath-gowns he would not thank me as one gentleman would another, but would offer me a tip as if I were a servant. This gave me no trouble, for I at once dramatized a little scene between myself and the Duke, in which I should bring him the bath-gowns, and he should offer me the tip, and I should refuse it with a low bow, and say that I was an American. What I did not dramatize, or what seemed to enter into the dialogue quite without my agency, was the Duke's reply to my proud speech. It was foreshown me that he would say, He did not see why that should make any difference. I suppose it was in the hurt I felt at this wound to our national dignity that I now instantly invented the society of some ladies, whom I told of my business with those bath-gowns (I still had them in my hands), and urged them to go with me and call upon the Duke. They expressed, somehow, that they would rather not, and then I urged that the Duke was very handsome. This seemed to end the whole affair, and I passed on to other visions, which I cannot recall.

I have not often had a dream of such international import, in the offence offered through me to the American character, and its well-known superiority to tips, but I have had others quite as humiliating to me personally. In fact, I am rather in the habit of having such dreams, and I think I may not unjustly attribute to them the disciplined modesty which the reader will hardly fail to detect in the present essay. It has more than once been my fate to find myself during sleep in battle, where I behave with so little courage as to bring discredit upon our flag and shame upon myself. In these circumstances I am not anxious to make even a showing of courage; my one thought is to get away as rapidly and safely as possible. It is said that this is really the wish of all novices under fire, and that the difference between a hero and a coward is that the hero hides it, with a duplicity which finally does him honor, and that the coward frankly runs away. I have never really been in battle, and if it is anything like a battle in dreams, I would not willingly qualify myself to speak by the card on this point. Neither have I ever really been upon the stage, but in dreams I have often been there, and always in a great trouble of mind at not knowing my part. It seems a little odd that I should not sometimes be prepared, but I never am, and I feel that when the curtain rises I shall be disgraced beyond all reprieve. I dare say it is the suffering from this that awakens me in time, or changes the current of my dreams so that I have never yet been actually hooted from the stage.

II.

But I do not so much object to these ordeals as to some social experiences which I have in dreams. I cannot understand why one should dream of being slighted or snubbed in society, but this is what I have done more than once, though never perhaps so signally as in the instance I am about to give. I found myself in a large room, where people were sitting at lunch or supper around small tables, as is the custom, I am told, at parties in the houses of our nobility and gentry. I was feeling very well; not too proud, I hope, but in harmony with the time and place. I was very well dressed, for me; and as I stood talking to some ladies at one of the tables I was saying some rather brilliant things, for me; I lounged easily on one foot, as I have observed men of fashion do, and as I talked, I flipped my gloves, which I held in one hand, across the other; I remember thinking that this was a peculiarly distinguished action. Upon the whole I comported myself like one in the habit of such affairs, and I turned to walk away to another table, very well satisfied with myself and with the effect of my splendor upon the ladies. But I had got only a few paces off when I perceived (I could not see with my back turned) one of the ladies lean forward, and heard her say to the rest in a tone of killing condescension and patronage, "*I* don't see why that person isn't as well as another."

I say that I do not like this sort of dreams, and I never would have them if I could help. They make me ask myself if I am really such a snob when I am waking, and this in itself is very unpleasant. If I am, I cannot help hoping that it will not be found out; and in my dreams I am always less sorry for the misdeeds I commit than for their possible discovery. I have done some very bad things in dreams which I have no concern for whatever, except as they seem to threaten me with publicity, or bring me within the penalty of the law; and I believe this is the attitude of most other criminals, remorse being a fiction of the poets, according to the students of the criminal class. It is not agreeable to bring this home to one's self, but the fact is not without its significance in another direction. It implies that both in the case of the dream-criminal and the deed-criminal there is perhaps the same taint of insanity; only in the deed-criminal it is active. and in the dream-criminal it is passive. In both, the inhibitory clause that forbids evil is off, but the dreamer is not bidden to do evil as the maniac is, or as the malefactor often seems to be. The dreamer is purely unmoral; good and bad are the same to his conscience; he has no more to do with right and wrong than the animals; he is reduced to the state of the merely natural man; and perhaps the primitive men were really like what we all are now in our dreams. Perhaps all life to them was merely dreaming, and they never had anything like our waking consciousness, which seems to be the offspring of conscience, or else the parent of it. Until men passed the first stage of being, perhaps that which we call the soul, for want of a better name, or a worse, could hardly have existed, and perhaps in dreams the soul is mostly absent now. The soul, or the principle that we call the soul, is the supernal criticism of the deeds done in the body, which goes perpetually on in the waking mind. While this watches, and warns or commands, we go right; but when it is off duty we go neither right nor wrong, but are as the beasts that perish. [. . .]

III.

It is very strange, in the matter of dreadful dreams, how the body of the terror is, in the course of often dreaming, reduced to a mere convention. For a long time I was tormented with a nightmare of burglars, and at first I used to dramatize the whole affair in detail, from the time the burglars approached the house, till they mounted the stairs, and the light of their dark-lanterns shone under the door into my room. Now I have blue-pencilled all that introductory detail; I have a light shining in under my door at once; I know that it is my old burglars; and I have the effect of nightmare without further ceremony. There are other nightmares that still cost me a great deal of trouble in their construction, as for instance the nightmare of clinging to the face of a precipice or the eaves of a lofty building; I have to take as much pains with the arrangement of these as if I were now dreaming them for the first time, and were hardly more than an apprentice in the business. Perhaps the most universal dream of all is that disgraceful dream of appearing in public places, and in society, with very little or nothing on. This dream spares neither age nor sex, I believe, and I dare say the innocency of wordless infancy is abused by it, and dotage pursued to the tomb. I have not the least doubt Adam and Eve had it in Eden; though up to the moment the fig-leaf came in, it is difficult to imagine just what plight they found themselves in that seemed improper; probably there was some plight. The most amusing thing about this dream is the sort of defensive process that goes on in the mind, in search of self-justification or explanation. Is there not some peculiar circumstance or special condition, in whose virtue it is wholly right and proper for one to come to a fashionable assembly clad simply in a towel, or to go about the street in nothing but a pair of kid gloves, or of pyjamas at the most? This, or something like it, the mind of the dreamer struggles to establish, with a good deal of anxious appeal to the bystanders and a final sense of the hopelessness of the cause. One may easily laugh off this sort of dream in the morning, but there are other shameful dreams, whose inculpation projects itself far into the day, and whose infamy often lingers about one till lunch-time. Every one, nearly, has had them, but it is not the kind of dream that any one is fond of telling: the gross vanity of the most besotted dream-teller keeps that sort back. During the forenoon, at least, the victim goes about with the dim question whether he is not really that kind of man harassing him, and a sort of remote fear that he may be. I fancy that as to his nature and as to his mind, he is so, and that but for the supernal criticism, but for his soul, he might be that kind of man in very act and deed.

The dreams we sometimes have about other people are not without a curious suggestion; and the superstitious (of those superstitious who like to invent their own superstitions) might very well imagine that the persons dreamed of had a witting complicity in their facts, as well as the dreamer. This is a conjecture that must of course not be forced to any conclusion. One must not go to one of these persons and ask, however much one would like to ask, "Sir, have you no recollection of such and such a thing, at such and such a time and place, which happened to us in my dream?" Any such person would be fully justified in not answering the question. It would be, of all interviewing, the most intolerable species. Yet a singular interest, a curiosity not altogether indefensible, will attach to these persons in the dreamer's mind, and he will not be without the sense, ever after, that he and they have a secret in common. This is dreadful, but the only thing that I can think to do about it is to urge people to keep out of other people's dreams by every means in their power. [. . .]

VI.

[. . .] As we grow older, I think we are less and less able to remember our dreams. This is perhaps because the experience of youth is less dense, and the empty spaces of the young consciousness are more hospitable to these airy visitants. A few dreams of my later life stand out in strong relief, but for the most part they blend in an indistinguishable mass, and pass away with the actualities into a common oblivion. I should say that they were more frequent with me than they used to be; it seems to me that now I dream whole nights through, and much more about the business of my waking life than formerly. As I earn my living by weaving a certain sort of dreams into literary form, it might be supposed that I would sometime dream of the personages in these dreams, but I cannot remember that I have ever done so. The two kinds of inventing, the voluntary and the involuntary, seem absolutely and finally distinct. Of the prophetic dreams which people sometimes have I have mentioned the only one of mine which had any dramatic interest, but I have verified in my own experience the theory of Ribot that approaching disease sometimes intimates itself in dreams of the disorder impending, before it is otherwise declared in the organism. In actual sickness I think that I dream rather less than in health. I had a malarial fever when I was a boy, and I had a sort of continuous dream in it that distressed me greatly. It was of gliding down the school-house stairs without touching my feet to the steps, and this was indescribably appalling. The anguish of mind that one suffers from the imaginary dangers of dreams is probably of the same quality as that inspired by real peril in waking. A curious proof of this happened within my knowledge not many years ago. One of the neighbor's children was coasting down a long hill with a railroad at the foot of it, and as he neared the bottom an express train rushed round the curve. The flag-man ran forward and shouted to the boy to throw himself off his sled, but he kept on, and ran into the locomotive, and was so hurt that he died. His injuries, however, were to the spine, and they were of a kind that rendered him insensible to pain while he lived. He talked very clearly and calmly of his accident, and when he was asked why he did not throw himself off his sled, as the flag-man bade him, he said, "*I thought it was a dream.*" The reality had, through the mental stress, no doubt transmuted itself to the very substance of dreams, and he had felt the same kind and quality of suffering as he would have done if he had been dreaming.

The Norwegian poet and novelist, Björnstjerne Björnson, was at my house shortly after this happened, and he was greatly struck by the psychological implications of the incident; it seemed to mean for him all sorts of possibilities in the obscure realm where it cast a fitful light. But such a glimmer soon fades, and the darkness thickens round us again. It is not with the blindfold sense of sleep that we shall ever find out the secret of life, I fancy, either in the dreams which seem personal to us each one, or those universal dreams which we apparently share with the whole race. Of the race-dream, as I may call it, there is one hardly less common than that dream of going about insufficiently clad, which I have already mentioned, and that is the dream of suddenly falling from some height, and waking with a start. The experience before the start is extremely dim, and latterly I have condensed this dread almost as much as the preliminary passages of my burglar-dream. I am aware of nothing but an instant of danger, and then comes the jar or jolt that wakens me. Upon the whole, I find this a great saving of emotion, and I do not know but there is a tendency, as I grow older, to shorten up the detail of what may be styled the conventional dream, the dream which we have so often that it is like a story read before. Indeed, the plots of dreams are not much more varied than the plots of romantic novels, which are notoriously stale and hackneyed. It would be interesting, and possibly important, if some observer would note the recurrence of this sort of dreams, and classify their varieties. I think we should all be astonished to find how few and slight the variations were.

VII.

If I come to speak of dreams concerning the dead, it must be with a tenderness and awe that all who have had them will share with me.

Nothing is more remarkable in them than the fact that the dead, though they are dead, yet live, and are, to our commerce with them, quite like all other living persons. We may recognize, and they may recognize, that they are no longer in the body, but they are as verily living as we are. This may be merely an effect from the doctrine of immortality which we all hold or have held, and yet I would fain believe that it may be something like proof of it. No one really knows, or can know, but one may at least hope, without offending science, which indeed no longer frowns so darkly upon faith. This persistence of life in those whom we mourn as dead, may not it be a witness of the fact that the consciousness cannot accept the notion of death at all, and,

"Whatever crazy sorrow saith,"

that we have never truly felt them lost? Sometimes those who have died come back in dreams as parts of a common life which seems never to have been broken; the old circle is restored without a flaw; but whether they do this, or whether it is acknowledged between them and us that they have died, and are now disembodied spirits, the effect of life is the same. Perhaps in those dreams they and we are alike disembodied spirits, and the soul of the dreamer, which so often seems to abandon the body to the animal, is then the conscious entity, the thing which the dreamer feels to be himself, and is mingling with the souls of the departed on something like the terms which shall hereafter be constant.

[. . .] I have heard people say they have sometimes dreamed of a thing, and awakened from their dream, and then fallen asleep and dreamed of the same thing; but I believe that this is all one continuous dream; that they did not really awaken, but only dreamed that they awakened. I have never had any such dream, but at one time I had a recurrent dream, which was so singular that I thought no one else had ever had a recurrent dream till I proved that it was rather common by starting the inquiry in the Contributors' Club in the *Atlantic Monthly*, when I found that great numbers of people have recurrent dreams. My own recurrent dreams began to come during the first year of my consulate at Venice, where I had hoped to find the same kind of poetic dimness on the phases of American life, which I wished to treat in literature, as the distance in time would have given. I should not wish any such dimness now; but those were my romantic days, and I was sorely baffled by its absence. The disappointment began to haunt my nights as well as my days, and a dream repeated itself from week to week for a matter of eight or ten months to one effect.

I dreamed that I had gone home to America, and that people met me and said, "Why, you have given up your place!" and I always answered: "Certainly not; I haven't done at all what I mean to do there, yet. I am only here on my ten days' leave." I meant the ten days which a consul might take each quarter without applying to the Department of State; and then I would reflect how impossible it was that I should make the visit in that time. I saw that I should be found out, and dismissed from my office and publicly disgraced. Then, suddenly, I was not consul at Venice, and had not been, but consul at Delhi in India; and the distress I felt would all end in a splendid Oriental phantasmagory of elephants and native princes, with their retinues in procession, which I suppose was mostly out of my reading of De Quincey. This dream, with no variation that I can recall, persisted till I broke it up by saying, in the morning after it had recurred, that I had dreamed that dream again; and so it began to fade away, coming less and less frequently, and at last ceasing altogether.

I am rather proud of that dream; it is really my battle-horse among dreams, and I think I will ride away on it.

Jerome K. Jerome

"Dreams"
1891

The English humorist and novelist appreciates dreams for their deadpan comedy: "Nothing does surprise one in a dream."

The most extraordinary dream I ever had was one in which I fancied that, as I was going into a theater, the cloak-room attendant stopped me in the lobby and insisted on my leaving my legs behind me.

I was not surprised; indeed, my acquaintanceship with theater harpies would prevent my feeling any surprise at such a demand, even in my waking moments; but I was, I must honestly confess, considerably annoyed. It was not the payment of the cloak-room fee that I so much minded—I offered to give that to the man then and there. It was the parting with my legs that I objected to.

I said I had never heard of such a rule being attempted to be put in force at any respectable theater before, and that I considered it a most absurd and vexatious regulation. I also said I should write to *The Times* about it.

The man replied that he was very sorry, but that those were his instructions. People complained that they could not get to and from their seats comfortably, because other people's legs were always in the way; and it had, therefore, been decided that, in future, everybody should leave their legs outside.

It seemed to me that the management, in making this order, had clearly gone beyond their legal right; and, under ordinary circumstances, I should have disputed it. Being present, however, more in the character of a guest than in that of a patron, I hardly like to make a disturbance; and so I sat down and meekly prepared to comply with the demand.

I had never before known that the human leg did unscrew. I had always thought it was a fixture. But the man showed me how to undo them, and I found that they came off quite easily.

The discovery did not surprise me any more than the original request that I should take them off had done. Nothing does surprise one in a dream.

I dreamed once that I was going to be hanged; but I was not at all surprised about it. Nobody was. My relations came to see me off, I thought, and to wish me "Good-by!" They all came, and were all very pleasant; but they were not in the least astonished—not one of them. Everybody appeared to regard the coming tragedy as one of the most-naturally-to-be-expected things in the world.

They bore the calamity, besides, with an amount of stoicism that would have done credit to a Spartan father. There was no fuss, no scene. On the contrary, an atmosphere of mild cheerfulness prevailed.

Yet they were very kind. Somebody—an uncle, I think—left me a packet of sandwiches and a little something in a flask, in case, as he said, I should feel peckish on the scaffold.

It is "those twin-jailers of the daring" thought, Knowledge and Experience, that teach us surprise. We are surprised and incredulous when, in novels and plays, we come across good men and women, because Knowledge and Experience have taught us how rare and problematical is the existence of such people. In waking life, my friends and relations would, of course, have been surprised at hearing that I had committed a murder, and was, in consequence, about to be hanged, because Knowledge and Experience would have taught them that, in a country where the law is powerful and the police alert, the Christian citizen is usually pretty successful in withstanding the voice of temptation, prompting him to commit crime of an illegal character.

But into Dreamland, Knowledge and Experience do not enter. They stay without, together with the dull, dead clay of which they form a part; while the freed brain, released from their narrowing tutelage, steals softly past the ebon gate, to wanton at its own sweet will among the mazy paths that wind through the garden of Persephone.

Nothing that it meets with in that eternal land astonishes it because, unfettered by the dense conviction of our waking mind, that nought outside the ken of our own vision can in this universe be, all things to it are possible and even probable. In dreams, we fly and wonder not—except that we never flew before. We go naked, yet are not ashamed, though we mildly wonder what the police are about that they do not stop us. We converse with our dead, and think it was unkind that they did not come back to us before. In dreams, there happens that which human language cannot tell. In dreams, we see "the light that never was on sea or land," we hear the sounds that never yet were heard by waking ears.

It is only in sleep that true imagination ever stirs within us. Awake, we never imagine anything; we merely alter, vary, or transpose. We give another twist to the kaleidoscope of the things we see around us, and obtain another pattern; but not one of us has ever added one tiniest piece of new glass to the toy. [. . .]

I dreamed a dream once. (It is the sort of thing a man would dream. You cannot very well dream anything else, I know. But the phrase sounds poetical and biblical, and so I use it.) I dreamed that I was in a strange country—indeed, one might say an extraordinary country. It was ruled entirely by critics.

The people in this strange land had a very high opinion of critics—nearly as high an opinion of critics as the critics themselves had, but not, of course, quite—that not being practicable—and they had agreed to be guided in all things by the critics. I stayed some years in that land. But it was not a cheerful place to live in, so I dreamed. [. . .]

But I never finished telling you about the dream in which I thought I left my legs behind me when I went into a certain theater.

I dreamed that the ticket the man gave me for my legs was No. 19, and I was worried all through the performance for fear No. 61 should get hold of them, and leave me his instead. Mine are rather a fine pair of legs, and I am, I confess, a little proud of them—at all events, I prefer them to anybody else's. Besides, number sixty-one's might be a skinny pair, and not fit me.

It quite spoiled my evening, fretting about this.

Another extraordinary dream I had was one in which I dreamed that I was engaged to be married to my Aunt Jane. That was not, however, the extraordinary part of it; I have often known people to dream things like that. I knew a man who once dreamed that he was actually married to his own mother-in-law! He told me that never in his life had he loved the alarm clock with more deep and grateful tenderness than he did that morning. The dream almost reconciled him to being married to his real wife. They lived quite happily together for a few days, after that dream.

No; the extraordinary part of my dream was, that I knew it was a dream. "What on earth will uncle say to this engagement?" I thought to myself, in my dream. "There's bound to be a row about it. We shall have a deal of trouble with uncle, I feel sure." And this thought quite troubled me until the sweet reflection came: "Ah! well, it's only a dream."

And I made up my mind that I would wake up as soon as uncle found out about the engagement, and leave him and Aunt Jane to fight the matter out between themselves.

It is a very great comfort, when the dream grows troubled and alarming, to feel that it is only a dream, and to know that we shall awake soon and be none the worse for it. We can dream out the foolish perplexity with a smile then.

Sometimes the dream of life grows strangely troubled and perplexing, and then he who meets dismay the bravest is he who feels that the fretful play is but a dream—a brief, uneasy dream of three score years and ten, or thereabouts, from which, in a little while, he will awake—at least, he dreams so.

Samuel Johnson

Life of Johnson by James Boswell
1791

England's greatest man of the century, the poet, biographer, dictionary maker, and wit Samuel Johnson thought about and remarked upon seemingly everything—prompted at times by his biographer, James Boswell.

He related, that he had once in a dream a contest of wit with some other person, and that he was very much mortified by imagining that his opponent had the better of him. "Now, (said he,) one may mark here the effect of sleep in weakening the power of reflection; for had not my judgement failed me, I should have seen, that the wit of this supposed antagonist, by whose superiority I felt myself depressed, was as much furnished by me, as that which I thought I had been uttering in my own character."

Helen Keller

The World I Live In
1909

Keller (1880–1968) was one of the most famous women in the world in the 1900s. Deaf and blind since the age of nineteen months, Keller learned how to speak at nine years old. She read by braille and raised-letter texts, and she wrote by hand and composed several books on regular and special typewriters. For decades she gave lectures around the world. In Chapters 13–14 of her memoir, she discusses her experiences of "The Dream World": "My dreams do not seem to differ very much from the dreams of other people. Some of them are coherent and safely hitched to an event or a conclusion. Others are inconsequent and fantastic. All attest that in Dreamland there is no such thing as repose. We are always up and doing with a mind for any adventure."

Everybody takes his own dreams seriously, but yawns at the breakfast-table when somebody else begins to tell the adventures of the night before. I hesitate, therefore, to enter upon an account of my dreams; for it is a literary sin to bore the reader, and a scientific sin to report the facts of a far country with more regard to point and brevity than to complete and literal truth. The psychologists have trained a pack of theories and facts which they keep in leash, like so many bulldogs, and which they let loose upon us whenever we depart from the straight and narrow path of dream probability. One may not even tell an entertaining dream without being suspected of having liberally edited it,—as if editing were one of the seven deadly sins, instead of a useful and honourable occupation! Be it understood, then, that I am discoursing at my own breakfast-table, and that no scientific man is present to trip the autocrat.

I used to wonder why scientific men and others were always asking me about my dreams. But I am not surprised now, since I have discovered what some of them believe to be the ordinary waking experience of one who is both deaf and blind. They think that I can know very little about objects even a few feet beyond the reach of my arms. Everything outside of myself, according to them, is a hazy blur. Trees, mountains, cities, the ocean, even the house I live in are but fairy fabrications, misty unrealities. Therefore it is assumed that my dreams should have peculiar interest for the man of science. In some undefined way it is expected that they should reveal the world I dwell in to be flat, formless, colourless, without perspective, with little thickness and less solidity—a vast solitude of soundless space. But who shall put into words limitless, visionless, silent void? One should be a disembodied spirit indeed to make anything out of such insubstantial experiences. A world, or a dream for that matter, to be comprehensible to us, must, I should think, have a warp of substance woven into the woof of fantasy. We cannot imagine even in dreams an object which has no counterpart in reality. Ghosts always resemble somebody, and if they do not appear themselves, their presence is indicated by circumstances with which we are perfectly familiar.

During sleep we enter a strange, mysterious realm which science has thus far not explored. Beyond the border-line of slumber the investigator may not pass with his common-sense rule and test. Sleep with softest touch locks all the gates of our physical senses and lulls to rest the conscious will—the disciplinarian of our waking thoughts. Then the spirit wrenches itself free from the sinewy arms of reason and like a winged courser spurns the firm green earth and speeds away upon wind and cloud, leaving neither trace nor footprint by which science may track its flight and bring us knowledge of the distant, shadowy country that we nightly visit. When we come back from the dream-realm, we can give no reasonable report of what we met there. But once across the border, we feel at home as if we had always lived there and had never made any excursions into this rational daylight world.

My dreams do not seem to differ very much from the dreams of other people. Some of them are coherent and safely hitched to an event or a conclusion. Others are inconsequent and fantastic. All attest that in Dreamland there is no such thing as repose. We are always up and doing with a mind for any adventure. We act, strive, think, suffer and are glad to no purpose. We leave outside the portals of Sleep all troublesome incredulities and vexatious speculations as to probability. I float wraith-like upon clouds in and out among the winds, without the faintest notion that I am doing anything unusual. In Dreamland I find little that is altogether strange or wholly new to my experience. No matter what happens, I am not astonished, however extraordinary the circumstances may be. I visit a foreign land where I have not been in reality, and I converse with peoples whose language I have never heard. Yet we manage to understand each other perfectly. Into whatsoever situation or society my wanderings bring me, there is the same homogeneity. If I happen into Vagabondia, I make merry with the jolly folk of the road or the tavern.

I do not remember ever to have met persons with whom I could not at once communicate, or to have been shocked or surprised at the doings of my dream-companions. In its strange wanderings in those dusky groves of Slumberland my soul takes everything for granted and adapts itself to the wildest phantoms. I am seldom confused. Everything is as clear as day. I know events the instant they take place, and wherever I turn my steps, Mind is my faithful guide and interpreter.

I suppose every one has had in a dream the exasperating, profitless experience of seeking something urgently desired at the moment, and the aching, weary sensation that follows each failure to track the thing to its hiding-place. Sometimes with a singing dizziness in my head I climb and climb, I know not where or why. Yet I cannot quit the torturing, passionate endeavour, though again and again I reach out blindly for an object to hold to. Of course according to the perversity of dreams there is no object near. I clutch empty air, and then I fall downward, and still downward, and in the midst of the fall I dissolve into the atmosphere upon which I have been floating so precariously.

Some of my dreams seem to be traced one within another like a series of concentric circles. In sleep I think I cannot sleep. I toss about in the toils of tasks unfinished. I decide to get up and read for a while. I know the shelf in my library where I keep the book I want. The book has no name, but I find it without difficulty. I settle myself comfortably in the morris-chair, the great book open on my knee. Not a word can I make out, the pages are utterly blank. I am not surprised, but keenly disappointed. I finger the pages, I bend over them lovingly, the tears fall on my hands. I shut the book quickly as the thought passes through my mind, "The print will be all rubbed out if I get it wet." Yet there is no print tangible on the page!

This morning I thought that I awoke. I was certain that I had overslept. I seized my watch, and sure enough, it pointed to an hour after my rising time. I sprang up in the greatest hurry, knowing that breakfast was ready. I called my mother, who declared that my watch must be wrong. She was positive it could not be so late. I looked at my watch again, and lo! the hands wiggled, whirled, buzzed and disappeared. I awoke more fully as my dismay grew, until I was at the antipodes of sleep. Finally my eyes opened actually, and I knew that I had been dreaming. I had only waked into sleep. What is still more bewildering, there is no difference between the consciousness of the sham waking and that of the real one.

It is fearful to think that all that we have ever seen, felt, read, and done may suddenly rise to our dream-vision, as the sea casts up objects it has swallowed. I have held a little child in my arms in the midst of a riot and spoken vehemently, imploring the Russian soldiers not to massacre the Jews. I have re-lived the agonizing scenes of the Sepoy Rebellion and the French Revolution. Cities have burned before my eyes, and I have fought the flames until I fell exhausted. Holocausts overtake the world, and I struggle in vain to save my friends.

Once in a dream a message came speeding over land and sea that winter was descending upon the world from the North Pole, that the Arctic zone was shifting to our mild climate. Far and wide the message flew. The ocean was congealed in midsummer. Ships were held fast in the ice by thousands, the ships with large, white sails were held fast. Riches of the Orient and the plenteous harvests of the Golden West might no more pass between nation and nation. For some time the trees and flowers grew on, despite the intense cold. Birds flew into the houses for safety, and those which winter had overtaken lay on the snow with wings spread in vain flight. At last the foliage and blossoms fell at the feet of Winter. The petals of the flowers were turned to rubies and sapphires. The leaves froze into emeralds. The trees moaned and tossed their branches as the frost pierced them through bark and sap, pierced into their very roots. I shivered myself awake, and with a tumult of joy I breathed the many sweet morning odours wakened by the summer sun.

One need not visit an African jungle or an Indian forest to hunt the tiger. One can lie in bed amid downy pillows and dream tigers as terrible as any in the pathless wild. I was a little girl when one night I tried to cross the garden in front of my aunt's house in Alabama. I was in pursuit of a large cat with a great bushy tail. A few hours before he had clawed my little canary out of its cage and crunched it between his cruel teeth. I could not see the cat. But the thought in my mind was distinct: "He is making for the high grass at the end of the garden. I'll get there first!" I put my hand on the box border and ran swiftly along the path. When I reached the high grass, there was the cat gliding into the wavy tangle. I rushed forward and tried to seize him and take the bird from between his teeth. To my horror a huge beast, not the cat at all, sprang out from the grass, and his sinewy shoulder rubbed against me with palpitating strength! His ears stood up and quivered with anger. His eyes were hot. His nostrils were large and wet. His lips moved horribly. I knew it was a tiger, a real live tiger, and that I should be devoured—my little bird and I. I do not know what happened after that. The next important thing seldom happens in dreams.

Some time earlier I had a dream which made a vivid impression upon me. My aunt was weeping because she could not find me. But I took an impish pleasure in the thought that she and others were searching for me, and making great noise which I felt through my feet. Suddenly the spirit of mischief gave way to uncertainty and fear. I felt cold. The air smelt like ice and salt. I tried to run; but the long grass tripped me, and I fell forward on my face. I lay very still, feeling with all my body. After a while my sensations seemed to be concentrated in my fingers, and I perceived that the grass blades were sharp as knives, and hurt my hands cruelly. I tried to get up cautiously, so as not to cut myself on the sharp grass. I put down a tentative foot, much as my kitten treads for the first time the primeval forest in the backyard. All at once I felt the stealthy patter of something creeping, creeping, creeping purposefully toward me. I do not know how at that time the idea was in my mind; I had no words for intention or purpose. Yet it was precisely the evil intent, and not the creeping animal that terrified me. I had no fear of living creatures. I loved my father's dogs, the frisky little calf, the gentle cows, the horses and mules that ate apples from my hand, and none of them had ever harmed me. I lay low, waiting in breathless terror for the creature to spring and bury its long claws in my flesh. I thought, "They will feel like turkey-claws." Something warm and wet touched my face. I shrieked, struck out frantically, and awoke. Something was still struggling in my arms. I held on with might and main until I was exhausted, then I loosed my hold. I found dear old Belle, the setter, shaking herself and looking at me reproachfully. She and I had gone to sleep together on the rug, and had naturally wandered to the dream-forest where dogs and little girls hunt wild game and have strange adventures. We encountered hosts of elfin foes, and it required all the dog tactics at Belle's command to acquit herself like the lady and huntress that she was. Belle had her dreams too. We used to lie under the trees and flowers in the old garden, and I used to laugh with delight when the magnolia leaves fell with little thuds, and Belle jumped up, thinking she had heard a partridge. She would pursue the leaf, point it, bring it back to me and lay it at my feet with a humorous wag of her tail as much as to say, "This is the kind of bird that waked me." I made a chain for her neck out of the lovely blue Paulownia flowers and covered her with great heart-shaped leaves.

Dear old Belle, she has long been dreaming among the lotus-flowers and poppies of the dogs' paradise. [. . .]

In my dreams I have sensations, odours, tastes and ideas which I do not remember to have had in reality. Perhaps they are the glimpses which my mind catches through the veil of sleep of my earliest babyhood. I have heard "the trampling of many waters." Sometimes a wonderful light visits me in sleep. Such a flash and glory as it is! I gaze and gaze until it vanishes. I smell and taste much as in my waking hours; but the sense of touch plays a less important part. In sleep I almost never grope. No one guides me. Even in a crowded street I am self-sufficient, and I enjoy an independence quite foreign to my physical life. Now I seldom spell on my fingers, and it is still rarer for others to spell into my hand. My mind acts independent of my physical organs. I am delighted to be thus endowed, if only in sleep; for then my soul dons its winged sandals and joyfully joins the throng of happy beings who dwell beyond the reaches of bodily sense. [. . .]

Perhaps I feel more than others the analogy between the world of our waking life and the world of dreams because before I was taught, I lived in a sort of perpetual dream. The testimony of parents and friends who watched me day after day is the only means that I have of knowing the actuality of those early, obscure years of my childhood. The physical acts of going to bed and waking in the morning alone mark the transition from reality to Dreamland. As near as I can tell, asleep or awake I only felt with my body. I can recollect no process which I should now dignify with the term of thought. It is true that my bodily sensations were extremely acute; but beyond a crude connection with physical wants they are not associated or directed. They had little relation to each other, to me or the experience of others. Idea—that which gives identity and continuity to experience—came into my sleeping and waking existence at the same moment with the awakening of self-consciousness. Before that moment my mind was in a state of anarchy in which meaningless sensations rioted, and if thought existed, it was so vague and inconsequent, it cannot be made a part of discourse. Yet before my education began, I dreamed. I know that I must have dreamed because I recall no break in my tactual experiences. Things fell suddenly, heavily. I felt my clothing afire, or I fell into a tub of cold water. Once I smelt bananas, and the odour in my nostrils was so vivid that in the morning, before I was dressed, I went to the sideboard to look for the bananas. There were no bananas, and no odour of bananas anywhere! My life was in fact a dream throughout.

The likeness between my waking state and the sleeping one is still marked. In both states I see, but not with my eyes. I hear, but not with my ears. I speak, and am spoken to, without the sound of a voice. I am moved to pleasure by visions of ineffable beauty which I have never beheld in the physical world. Once in a dream I held in my hand a pearl. The one I saw in my dreams must, therefore, have been a creation of my imagination. It was a smooth, exquisitely moulded crystal. As I gazed into its shimmering deeps, my soul was flooded with an ecstasy of tenderness, and I was filled with wonder as one who should for the first time look into the cool, sweet heart of a rose. My pearl was dew and fire, the velvety green of moss, the soft whiteness of lilies, and the distilled hues and sweetness of a thousand roses. It seemed to me, the soul of beauty was dissolved in its crystal bosom. This beauteous vision strengthens my conviction that the world which the mind builds up out of countless subtle experiences and suggestions is fairer than the world of the senses. The splendour of the sunset my friends gaze at across the purpling hills is wonderful. But the sunset of the inner vision brings purer delight because it is the worshipful blending of all the beauty that we have known and desired.

Charles Lamb

"Witches, and Other Night-Fears"
1823

Lamb was one of the most notable English essayists. He reflects here on his own childhood terrors: "Parents do not know what they do when they leave tender babes alone to go to sleep in the dark. The feeling about for a friendly arm—the hoping for a familiar voice—when they wake screaming—and find none to soothe them—what a terrible shaking it is to their poor nerves!"

In my father's book-closet, the History of the Bible, by Stackhouse, occupied a distinguished station. The pictures with which it abounds—one of the ark, in particular, and another of Solomon's temple, delineated with all the fidelity of ocular admeasurement, as if the artist had been upon the spot—attracted my childish attention. There was a picture, too, of the Witch raising up Samuel, which I wish that I had never seen. [. . .]

That detestable picture! I was dreadfully alive to nervous terrors. The night-time solitude, and the dark, were my hell. The sufferings I endured in this nature would justify the expression. I never laid my head on my pillow, I suppose, from the fourth to the seventh or eighth year of my life—so far as memory serves in things so long ago—without an assurance, which realized its own prophecy, of seeing some frightful spectre. Be old Stackhouse then acquitted in part, if I say, that to his picture of the Witch raising up Samuel—(O that old man covered with a mantle!) I owe—not my midnight terrors, the hell of my infancy—but the shape and manner of their visitation. It was he who dressed up for me a hag that nightly sate upon my pillow—a sure bed-fellow, when my aunt or my maid was far from me. All day long, while the book was permitted me, I dreamed waking over his delineation, and at night (if I may use so bold an expression) awoke into sleep, and found the vision true. I durst not, even in the day-light, once enter the chamber where I slept, without my face turned to the window, aversely from the bed where my witch-ridden pillow was.—Parents do not know what they do when they leave tender babes alone to go to sleep in the dark. The feeling about for a friendly arm—the hoping for a familiar voice—when they wake screaming—and find none to soothe them—what a terrible shaking it is to their poor nerves! The keeping them up till midnight, through candle-light and the unwholesome hours, as they are called,—would, I am satisfied, in a medical point of view, prove the better caution.—That detestable picture, as I have said, gave the fashion to my dreams—if dreams they were—for the scene of them was invariably the room in which I lay. Had I never met with the picture, the fears would have come self-pictured in some shape or other—but, as it was, my imaginations took that form.—It is not book, or picture, or the stories of foolish servants, which create these terrors in children. They can at most but give them a direction. Dear little T. H. who of all children has been brought up with the most scrupulous exclusion of every taint of superstition—who was never allowed to hear of goblin or apparition, or scarcely to be told of bad men, or to read or hear of any distressing story—finds all this world of fear, from which he has been so rigidly excluded *ab extra*, in his own "thick-coming fancies"; and from his little midnight pillow, this nurse-child of optimism will start at shapes, unborrowed of tradition, in sweats to which the reveries of the cell-damned murderer are tranquillity.

Gorgons, and Hydras, and Chimæras—dire stories of Celæno and the Harpies—may reproduce themselves in the brain of superstition— but they were there before. They are transcripts, types—the archetypes are in us, and eternal. How else should the recital of that, which we know in a waking sense to be false, come to affect us at all?—or

> —Names, whose sense we see not,
> Fray us with things that be not?[19]

Is it that we naturally conceive terror from such objects, considered in their capacity of being able to inflict upon us bodily injury?—O, least of all! These terrors are of older standing. They date beyond body—or, without the body, they would have been the same. All the cruel, tormenting, defined devils in Dante—tearing, mangling, choking, stifling, scorching demons—are they one half so fearful to the spirit of a man, as the simple idea of a spirit unembodied following him—

> Like one that on a lonesome road
> Doth walk in fear and dread,
> And having once turn'd round, walks on,
> And turns no more his head;
> Because he knows a frightful fiend
> Doth close behind him tread.[20]

That the kind of fear here treated of is purely spiritual—that it is strong in proportion as it is objectless upon earth—that it predomi-

---

19 From Edmund Spenser's "Epithalamion" (1597).
20 From Samuel Taylor Coleridge's "The Rime of the Ancient Mariner."

nates in the period of sinless infancy—are difficulties, the solution of which might afford some probable insight into our antemundane condition, and a peep at least into the shadow-land of pre-existence.

My night-fancies have long ceased to be afflictive. I confess an occasional night-mare; but I do not, as in early youth, keep a stud of them. Fiendish faces, with the extinguished taper, will come and look at me; but I know them for mockeries, even while I cannot elude their presence, and I fight and grapple with them. For the credit of my imagination, I am almost ashamed to say how tame and prosaic my dreams are grown. They are never romantic, seldom even rural. They are of architecture and of buildings—cities abroad, which I have never seen, and hardly have hope to see. I have traversed, for the seeming length of a natural day, Rome, Amsterdam, Paris, Lisbon—their churches, palaces, squares, market-places, shops, suburbs, ruins, with an inexpressible sense of delight—a map-like distinctness of trace—and a day-light vividness of vision, that was all but being awake.—I have formerly travelled among the Westmoreland fells—my highest Alps,—but they are objects too mighty for the grasp of my dreaming recognition; and I have again and again awoke with ineffectual struggles of the inner eye, to make out a shape in any way whatever, of Helvellyn. Methought I was in that country, but the mountains were gone. The poverty of my dreams mortifies me. There is Coleridge, at his will can conjure up icy domes, and pleasure-houses for Kubla Khan, and Abyssinian maids, and songs of Abara, and caverns,

> Where Alph, the sacred river, runs,

to solace his night solitudes—when I cannot muster a fiddle. Barry Cornwall has his tritons and his nereids gamboling before him in nocturnal visions, and proclaiming sons born to Neptune—when my stretch of imaginative activity can hardly, in the night season, raise up the ghost of a fish-wife. To set my failures in somewhat a mortifying light—it was after reading the noble Dream of this poet, that my fancy ran strong upon these marine spectra; and the poor plastic power, such as it is, within me set to work, to humour my folly in a sort of dream that very night. Methought I was upon the ocean billows at some sea nuptials, riding and mounted high, with the customary train sounding their conchs before me, (I myself, you may be sure, the *leading god*,) and jollily we went careering over the main, till just where Ino Leucothea should have greeted me (I think it was

Ino) with a white embrace, the billows gradually subsiding, fell from a sea-roughness to a sea-calm, and thence to a river-motion, and that river (as happens in the familiarization of dreams) was no other than the gentle Thames, which landed me, in the wafture of a placid wave or two, alone, safe and inglorious, somewhere at the foot of Lambeth palace.

The degree of the soul's creativeness in sleep might furnish no whimsical criterion of the quantum of poetical faculty resident in the same soul waking. An old gentleman, a friend of mine, and a humorist, used to carry this notion so far, that when he saw any stripling of his acquaintance ambitious of becoming a poet, his first question would be,—"Young man, what sort of dreams have you?" I have so much faith in my old friend's theory, that when I feel that idle vein returning upon me, I presently subside into my proper element of prose, remembering those eluding nereids, and that inauspicious inland landing.

Michel de Montaigne

Essays
1580

Montaigne's writings remain the model for personal essays: ever developing, ever thoughtful, modest, candid, and conversational. He was not a big dreamer, but he had occasional thoughts about them.

(From "Apology for Raimond de Sebonde")

They who have compared our life to a dream were, peradventure, more in the right than they were aware of. When we dream, the soul lives, works, exercises all its faculties, neither more nor less than when awake; but if more gently and obscurely, yet not so much certainly, that the difference should be as great as betwixt night and the meridional brightness of the sun; nay, as betwixt night and shade; there she sleeps, here she slumbers, but whether more or less, 'tis still dark and Cimmerian darkness. We wake sleeping, and sleep waking. I do not see so clearly in my sleep; but as to my being awake, I never find it clear enough and free from clouds: moreover, sleep, when it is profound, sometimes rocks even dreams themselves asleep;

but our awaking is never so sprightly that it rightly and thoroughly purges and dissipates those reveries which are waking dreams, and worse than dreams. Our reason and soul receiving those fancies and opinions that come in dreams, and authorising the actions of our dreams, in like manner as they do those of the day, why do we not doubt whether our thought and action is not another sort of dreaming, and our waking a certain kind of sleep?

★ ★ ★

(From "On Experience")

I have no reason to complain of my imagination; I have had few thoughts in my life that have so much as broken my sleep, except those of desire, which have awakened without afflicting me. I dream but seldom, and then of chimæras and fantastic things, commonly produced from pleasant thoughts, and rather ridiculous than sad; and I believe it to be true that dreams are faithful interpreters of our inclinations; but there is art required to sort and understand them:

> *Res, quæ in vita usurpant homines, cogitant, curant, vident,*
> *Quæque agunt vigilantes, agitantque, ea si cui in somno accidunt,*
> *Minus mirandum est.*[21]

Plato, moreover, says, that 'tis the office of prudence to draw instructions of divination of future things from dreams: I don't know about this, but there are wonderful instances of it that Socrates, Xenophon, and Aristotle, men of irreproachable authority, relate. Historians say that the Atlantes never dream; who also never eat any animal food, which I add, forasmuch as it is, peradventure, the reason why they never dream, for Pythagoras ordered a certain preparation of diet to beget appropriate dreams. Mine are very gentle, without any agitation of body or expression of voice. I have seen several of my time wonderfully disturbed by them. Theon, the philosopher, walked in his sleep, and so did Pericles' servant, and that upon the tiles and top of the house.

---

21 Montaigne quotes the Roman poet Lucius Accius, or Attius (170–c. 86 BCE). Charles Cotton translates the verses: " 'Tis no wonder if what men practise, think, care for, see, and do when waking, should also run in their heads and disturb them when they are asleep."

John Ruskin

"On Carpaccio's Dream of Saint Ursula"
1872

In the second half of the nineteenth century, Ruskin was England's most renowned art critic. In this conversational analysis of the Italian Renaissance painter Vittore Carpaccio's work, he appreciatively evokes Saint Ursula's dreaming thoughts: "It is very pretty of Carpaccio to make her dream out the angel's dress so particularly, and notice the slashed sleeves; and to dream so little an angel—very nearly a doll angel,—bringing her the branch of palm, and message. But the lovely characteristic of all is the evident delight of her continual life. Royal power over herself, and happiness in her flowers, her books, her sleeping and waking, her prayers, her dreams, her earth, her heaven."

In the year 1869, just before leaving Venice I had been carefully looking at a picture by Victor Carpaccio, representing the dream of a young princess. Carpaccio has taken much pain to explain to us, as far as he can, the kind of life she leads, by completely painting her little bedroom in the light of dawn, so that you can see everything in it. It is lighted by two doubly-arched windows, the arches being painted crimson round their edges, and the capitals of the shafts that bear them, gilded. They are filled at the top with small round panes of glass; but beneath, are open to the blue morning sky, with a low lattice across them; and in the one at the back of the room are set two beautiful white Greek vases with a plant in each; one having rich dark and pointed green leaves, the other crimson flowers, but not of any species known to me, each at the end of a branch like a spray of heath.

These flower-pots stand on a shelf which runs all round the room, and beneath the window, at about the height of the elbow, and serves to put things on anywhere: beneath it, down to the floor, the walls are covered with green cloth; but above are bare and white. The second window is nearly opposite the bed, and in front of it is the princess's reading-table, some two feet and a half square, covered by a red cloth with a white border and dainty fringe; and beside it her seat, not at all like a reading chair in Oxford, but a very small three-legged stool like a music stool, covered with crimson cloth. On the table are a book, set up at a slope fittest for reading, and an hour-glass. Under the shelf near the table so as to be easily reached by the outstretched arm, is a press full of books. The door of this has been left open, and the books, I am grieved to say, are rather in disorder, having been pulled about before the princess went to bed, and one left standing on its side.

Opposite this window, on the white wall, is a small shrine or picture (I can't see which, for it is in sharp retiring perspective), with a lamp before it, and a silver vessel hung from the lamp, looking like one for holding incense.

The bed is a broad four-poster, the posts being beautifully wrought golden or gilded rods, variously wreathed and branched, carrying a canopy of warm red. The princess's shield is at the head of it, and the feet are raised entirely above the floor of the room, on a dais which projects at the lower end so as to form a seat, on which the child has laid her crown. Her little blue slippers lie at the side of the bed,—her white dog beside them, the coverlid is scarlet, the white sheet folded half way back over it; the young girl lies straight, bending neither at waist nor knee, the sheet rising and falling over her in a narrow unbroken wave, like the shape of the coverlid of the last sleep, when the turf scarcely rises. She is some seventeen or eighteen years old, her head is turned towards us on the pillow, the cheek resting on her hand, as if she were thinking, yet utterly calm in sleep, and almost colourless. Her hair is tied with a narrow riband, and divided into two wreaths, which encircle her head like a double crown. The white nightgown hides the arm raised on the pillow, down to the wrist.

At the door of the room an angel enters (the little dog, though lying awake, vigilant, takes no notice). He is a very small angel, his head just rises a little above the shelf round the room, and would only reach as high as the princess's chin, if she were standing up. He has soft grey wings, lustreless; and his dress, of subdued blue, has violet sleeves, open above the elbow, and showing white sleeves below. He comes in without haste, his body, like a mortal one, casting shadow from the light through the door behind, his face perfectly quiet; a palm-branch in his right hand—a scroll in his left.

So dreams the princess, with blessed eyes, that need no earthly dawn. It is very pretty of Carpaccio to make her dream out the angel's dress so particularly, and notice the slashed sleeves; and to dream so little an angel—very nearly a doll angel,—bringing her the branch of palm, and message. But the lovely characteristic of all is the evident delight of her continual life. Royal power over herself, and happiness in her flowers, her books, her sleeping and waking, her prayers, her dreams, her earth, her heaven. . . .

"How do I know the princess is industrious?"

Partly by the trim state of her room,—by the hour-glass on the table,—by the evident use of all the books she has (well bound, every one of them, in stoutest leather or velvet, and with no dog's-ears), more distinctly from another picture of her, not asleep. In that one a prince of England has sent to ask her in marriage: and her father, little liking to part with her, sends for her to his room to ask her what she would do. He sits, moody and sorrowful; she, standing before him in a plain house-wifely dress, talks quietly, going on with her needlework all the time.

A work-woman, friends, she, no less than a princess; and princess most in being so. In like manner, is a picture by a Florentine, whose mind I would fain have you know somewhat, as well as Carpaccio's— Sandro Botticelli—the girl who is to be the wife of Moses, when he first sees her at the desert well, has fruit in her left hand, but a distaff in her right.

"To do good work, whether you live or die," it is the entrance to all Princedoms; and if not done, the day will come, and that infallibly, when you must labour for evil instead of good.

Robert Louis Stevenson

"A Chapter on Dreams"
1888

Stevenson relates his experience of finding plots for his famous stories, among them The Strange Case of Dr. Jekyll and Mr. Hyde, *from his dreams: "When he lay down to prepare himself for sleep, he no longer sought amusement, but printable and profitable tales."*

The past is all of one texture—whether feigned or suffered—whether acted out in three dimensions, or only witnessed in that small theatre of the brain which we keep brightly lighted all night long, after the jets are down, and darkness and sleep reign undisturbed in the remainder of the body. There is no distinction on the face of our experiences; one is vivid indeed, and one dull, and one pleasant, and another agonising to remember; but which of them is what we call true, and which a dream, there is not one hair to prove. The past stands on a precarious footing [. . .] among the treasures of memory that all men review for their amusement, these count in no second place the harvests of their dreams. There is one of this kind whom I have in my eye, and whose case is perhaps unusual enough to be described. He was from a child an ardent and uncomfortable dreamer. When he had a touch of fever at night, and the room swelled and shrank, and his clothes, hanging on a nail, now loomed up instant to the bigness of a church, and now drew away into a horror of infinite distance and infinite littleness, the poor soul was very well aware of what must follow, and struggled hard against the approaches of that slumber which was the beginning of sorrows.

But his struggles were in vain; sooner or later the night-hag would have him by the throat, and pluck him strangling and screaming, from his sleep. His dreams were at times commonplace enough, at times very strange, at times they were almost formless: he would be haunted, for instance, by nothing more definite than a certain hue of brown, which he did not mind in the least while he was awake, but feared and loathed while he was dreaming; at times, again, they took on every detail of circumstance, as when once he supposed he must swallow the populous world, and awoke screaming with the horror of the thought. The two chief troubles of his very narrow existence—the practical and everyday trouble of school tasks and the ultimate and airy one of hell and judgment—were often confounded together into one appalling nightmare. He seemed to himself to stand before the Great White Throne; he was called on, poor little devil, to recite some form of words, on which his destiny depended; his tongue stuck, his memory was blank, hell gaped for him; and he would awake, clinging to the curtain-rod with his knees to his chin.

These were extremely poor experiences, on the whole; and at that time of life my dreamer would have very willingly parted with his power of dreams. But presently, in the course of his growth, the cries and physical contortions passed away, seemingly for ever; his visions were still for the most part miserable, but they were more constantly supported; and he would awake with no more extreme symptom than a flying heart, a freezing scalp, cold sweats, and the speechless midnight fear. His dreams, too, as befitted a mind better stocked with particulars, became more circumstantial, and had more the air and continuity of life. The look of the world beginning to take hold on his attention, scenery came to play a part in his sleeping as well as in his waking thoughts, so that he would take long, uneventful journeys and see strange towns and beautiful places as he lay in bed. And, what is more significant, an odd taste that he had for the Georgian costume and for stories laid in that period of English history, began to rule the features of his dreams; so that he masqueraded there in a three-cornered hat and was much engaged with Jacobite conspiracy between the hour for bed and that for breakfast. About the same time, he began to read in his dreams—tales, for the most part, and for the most part after the manner of G. P. R. James, but so incredibly more vivid and moving than any printed book, that he has ever since been malcontent with literature.

And then, while he was yet a student, there came to him a dream-adventure which he has no anxiety to repeat; he began, that is to say, to dream in sequence and thus to lead a double life—one of the day, one of the night—one that he had every reason to believe was the true one, another that he had no means of proving to be false. I should have said he studied, or was by way of studying, at Edinburgh College, which (it may be supposed) was how I came to know him. Well, in his dream-life, he passed a long day in the surgical theatre, his heart in his mouth, his teeth on edge, seeing monstrous malformations and the abhorred dexterity of surgeons. In a heavy, rainy, foggy evening he came forth into the South Bridge, turned up the High Street, and entered the door of a tall LAND, at the top of which he supposed himself to lodge. All night long, in his wet clothes, he climbed the stairs, stair after stair in endless series, and at every second flight a flaring lamp with a reflector. All night long, he brushed by single persons passing downward—beggarly women of the street, great, weary, muddy labourers, poor scarecrows of men, pale parodies of women—but all drowsy and weary like himself, and all single, and all brushing against him as they passed. In the end, out of a northern window, he would see day beginning to whiten over the Firth, give up the ascent, turn to descend, and in a breath be back again upon the streets, in his wet clothes, in the wet, haggard dawn, trudging to another day of monstrosities and operations. Time went quicker in the life of dreams, some seven hours (as near as he can guess) to one; and it went, besides, more intensely, so that the gloom of these fancied experiences clouded the day, and he had not shaken off their shadow ere it was time to lie down and to renew them. I cannot tell how long it was that he endured this discipline; but it was long enough to leave a great black blot upon his memory, long enough to send him, trembling for his reason, to the doors of a certain doctor; whereupon with a simple draught he was restored to the common lot of man.

The poor gentleman has since been troubled by nothing of the sort; indeed, his nights were for some while like other men's, now blank, now chequered with dreams, and these sometimes charming, sometimes appalling, but except for an occasional vividness, of no extraordinary kind. I will just note one of these occasions, ere I pass on to what makes my dreamer truly interesting. It seemed to him that he was in the first floor of a rough hill-farm. The room showed some poor efforts at gentility, a carpet on the floor, a piano, I think, against the wall; but, for all these refinements, there was no mistaking he was in a moorland place, among hillside people, and set in miles of heather. He looked down from the window upon a bare farmyard, that seemed to have been long disused. A great, uneasy stillness lay upon the world. There was no sign of the farm-folk or of any live stock, save for an old, brown, curly dog of the retriever breed, who sat close in against the wall of the house and seemed to be dozing. Something about this dog disquieted the dreamer; it was quite a nameless feeling, for the beast looked right enough—indeed, he was so old and dull and dusty and broken-down, that he should rather have awakened pity; and yet the conviction came and grew upon the dreamer that this was no proper dog at all, but something hellish. A great many dozing summer flies hummed about the yard; and presently the dog thrust forth his paw, caught a fly in his open palm, carried it to his mouth like an ape, and looking suddenly up at the dreamer in the window, winked to him with one eye. The dream went on, it matters not how it went; it was a good dream as dreams go; but there was nothing in the sequel worthy of that devilish brown dog. And the point of interest for me lies partly in that very fact: that having found so singular an incident, my imperfect dreamer should prove unable to carry the tale to a fit end and fall back on indescribable noises and indiscriminate horrors. It would be different now; he knows his business better!

For, to approach at last the point: This honest fellow had long been in the custom of setting himself to sleep with tales, and so had his father before him; but these were irresponsible inventions, told for the teller's pleasure, with no eye to the crass public or the thwart reviewer: tales where a thread might be dropped, or one adventure quitted for another, on fancy's least suggestion. So that the little people who manage man's internal theatre had not as yet received a very rigorous training; and played upon their stage like children who should have slipped into the house and found it empty, rather than like drilled actors performing a set piece to a huge hall of faces. But presently my dreamer began to turn his former amusement of story-telling to (what is called) account; by which I mean that he began to write and sell his tales. Here was he, and here were the little people who did that part of his business, in quite new conditions. The stories must now be trimmed and pared and set upon all fours, they must run from a beginning to an end and fit (after a manner) with the laws of life; the pleasure, in one word, had become a business; and that not only for the dreamer, but for the little people of his theatre. These understood the change as well as he. When he lay down to prepare himself for sleep, he no longer sought amusement, but printable and profitable tales; and after he had dozed off in his box-seat, his little people continued their evolutions with the same mercantile designs. All other forms of dream deserted him but two: he still occasionally reads the most delightful books, he still visits at times the most delightful places; and it is perhaps worthy of note that to these same places, and to one in particular, he returns at intervals of months and years, finding new field-paths, visiting new neighbours, beholding that happy valley under new effects of noon and dawn and sunset. But all the rest of the family of visions is quite lost to him: the common, mangled version of yesterday's affairs, the raw-head-and-bloody-bones nightmare, rumoured to be the child of toasted cheese—these and their like are gone; and, for the most part, whether awake or asleep, he is simply occupied—he or his little people—in consciously making stories for the market. This dreamer (like many other persons) has encountered some trifling vicissitudes of fortune. When the bank begins to send letters and the butcher to linger at the back gate, he sets to belabouring his brains after a story, for that is his readiest money-winner; and, behold! at once the little people begin to bestir themselves in the same quest, and labour all night long, and all night long set before him truncheons of tales upon their lighted theatre. No fear of his being frightened now; the flying heart and the frozen scalp are things by-gone; applause, growing applause, growing interest, growing exultation in his own cleverness (for he takes all the credit), and at last a jubilant leap to wakefulness, with the cry, "I have it, that'll do!" upon his lips: with such and similar emotions he sits at these nocturnal dramas, with such outbreaks, like Claudius in the play, he scatters the performance in the midst. Often enough the waking is a disappointment: he has been too deep asleep, as I explain the thing; drowsiness has gained his little people, they have gone stumbling and maundering through their parts; and the play, to the awakened mind, is seen to be a tissue of absurdities. And yet how often have these sleepless Brownies done him honest service, and given him, as he sat idly taking his pleasure in the boxes, better tales than he could fashion for himself.

Here is one, exactly as it came to him. It seemed he was the son of a very rich and wicked man, the owner of broad acres and a most damnable temper. The dreamer (and that was the son) had lived much abroad, on purpose to avoid his parent; and when at length he returned to England, it was to find him married again to a young wife, who was supposed to suffer cruelly and to loathe her yoke. Because of this marriage (as the dreamer indistinctly understood) it was desirable for father and son to have a meeting; and yet both being proud and both angry, neither would condescend upon a visit. Meet they did accordingly, in a desolate, sandy country by the sea; and there they quarrelled, and the son, stung by some intolerable insult, struck down the father dead. No suspicion was aroused; the dead man was found and buried, and the dreamer succeeded to the broad estates, and found himself installed under the same roof with his father's widow, for whom no provision had been made. These two lived very much alone, as people may after a bereavement, sat down to table together, shared the long evenings, and grew daily better friends; until it seemed to him of a sudden that she was prying about dangerous matters, that she had conceived a notion of his guilt, that she watched him and tried him with questions. He drew back from her company as men draw back from a precipice suddenly discovered; and yet so strong was the attraction that he would drift again and again into the old intimacy, and again and again be startled back by some suggestive question or some inexplicable meaning in her eye. So they lived at cross purposes, a life full of broken dialogue, challenging glances, and suppressed passion; until, one day, he saw the woman slipping from the house in a veil, followed her to the station, followed her in the train to the seaside country, and out over the sandhills to the very place where the murder was done. There she began to grope among the bents, he watching her, flat upon his face; and presently she had something in her hand—I cannot remember what it was, but it was deadly evidence against the dreamer—and as she held it up to look at it, perhaps from the shock of the discovery, her foot slipped, and she hung at some peril on the brink of the tall sand-wreaths. He had no thought but to spring up and rescue her; and there they stood face to face, she with that deadly matter openly in her hand—his very presence on the spot another link of proof. It was plain she was about to speak, but this was more than he could bear—he could bear to be lost, but not to talk of it with his destroyer; and he cut her short with trivial conversation.

Arm in arm, they returned together to the train, talking he knew not what, made the journey back in the same carriage, sat down to dinner, and passed the evening in the drawing-room as in the past. But suspense and fear drummed in the dreamer's bosom. "She has not denounced me yet"—so his thoughts ran—"when will she denounce me? Will it be tomorrow?" And it was not tomorrow, nor the next day, nor the next; and their life settled back on the old terms, only that she seemed kinder than before, and that, as for him, the burthen of his suspense and wonder grew daily more unbearable, so that he wasted away like a man with a disease. Once, indeed, he broke all bounds of decency, seized an occasion when she was abroad, ransacked her room, and at last, hidden away among her jewels, found the damning evidence. There he stood, holding this thing, which was his life, in the hollow of his hand, and marvelling at her inconsequent behaviour, that she should seek, and keep, and yet not use it; and then the door opened, and behold herself. So, once more, they stood, eye to eye, with the evidence between them; and once more she raised to him a face brimming with some communication; and once more he shied away from speech and cut her off. But before he left the room, which he had turned upside down, he laid back his death-warrant where he had found it; and at that, her face lighted up. The next thing he heard, she was explaining to her maid, with some ingenious falsehood, the disorder of her things. Flesh and blood could bear the strain no longer; and I think it was the next morning (though chronology is always hazy in the theatre of the mind) that he burst from his reserve. They had been breakfasting together in one corner of a great, parqueted, sparely-furnished room of many windows; all the time of the meal she had tortured him with sly allusions; and no sooner were the servants gone, and these two pro-tagonists alone together, than he leaped to his feet. She too sprang up, with a pale face; with a pale face, she heard him as he raved out his complaint: Why did she torture him so? she knew all, she knew he was no enemy to her; why did she not denounce him at once? what signified her whole behaviour? why did she torture him? and yet again, why did she torture him? And when he had done, she fell upon her knees, and with outstretched hands: "Do you not under-stand?" she cried. "I love you!"

Hereupon, with a pang of wonder and mercantile delight, the dreamer awoke. His mercantile delight was not of long endurance; for it soon became plain that in this spirited tale there were unmar-ketable elements; which is just the reason why you have it here so briefly told. But his wonder has still kept growing; and I think the reader's will also, if he consider it ripely. For now he sees why I speak of the little people as of substantive inventors and performers. To the end they had kept their secret. I will go bail for the dreamer (having excellent grounds for valuing his candour) that he had no guess whatever at the motive of the woman—the hinge of the whole well-invented plot—until the instant of that highly dramatic decla-ration. It was not his tale; it was the little people's! And observe: not only was the secret kept, the story was told with really guileful craftsmanship. The conduct of both actors is (in the cant phrase) psychologically correct, and the emotion aptly graduated up to the surprising climax. I am awake now, and I know this trade; and yet I cannot better it. I am awake, and I live by this business; and yet I could not outdo—could not perhaps equal—that crafty artifice (as of some old, experienced carpenter of plays, some Dennery or Sardou) by which the same situation is twice presented and the two actors twice brought face to face over the evidence, only once it is in her hand, once in his—and these in their due order, the least dramatic first. The more I think of it, the more I am moved to press upon the world my question: Who are the Little People? They are near connections of the dreamer's, beyond doubt; they share in his financial worries and have an eye to the bank-book; they share plainly in his training; they have plainly learned like him to build the scheme of a considerate story and to arrange emotion in progressive order; only I think they have more talent; and one thing is beyond doubt, they can tell him a story piece by piece, like a serial, and keep him all the while in ignorance of where they aim. Who are they, then? and who is the dreamer?

Well, as regards the dreamer, I can answer that, for he is no less a person than myself;—as I might have told you from the beginning, only that the critics murmur over my consistent egotism;—and as I am positively forced to tell you now, or I could advance but little farther with my story. And for the Little People, what shall I say they are but just my Brownies, God bless them! who do one-half my work for me while I am fast asleep, and in all human likelihood, do the rest for me as well, when I am wide awake and fondly suppose I do it for myself.

Selected Bibliography

Borges, Jorge Luis. *Collected Fictions*. Edited by Andrew Hurley. New York: Viking, 1998.

Borges, Jorge Luis. *Selected Nonfictions*. Edited by Eliot Weinberger. New York: Viking, 1999.

Borges, Jorge Luis. *Selected Poems*. Edited by Alexander Coleman. New York: Viking, 1999.

Dickinson Electronic Archives. Accessed February 9, 2023. https://www.emilydickinson.org/.

Dickson, Melissa. "Dickens's Nightmare: Dreams, Memory and Trauma." Published April 17, 2020. The Royal Society Publishing. https://doi.org/10.1098/rsfs.2019.0076.

Freud, Sigmund. *The Interpretation of Dreams*. Mineola, NY: Dover Publications, 2015.

Haase, Fee-Alexandra, ed. *Words Made Out of Dreams: An Anthology of Dreams in English Literature with an Introduction on Readings of Dreams in Non-Interpretative Ways*. Tübingen, Germany: Universitätsbibliothek Tübingen, 2007.

Kosmos Society, The. "Dreams | Part 2: Dreams in Later Greek Texts." Published March 6, 2020. https://kosmossociety.chs.harvard.edu/dreams-part-2-dreams-in-later-greek-texts/.

Lawrence, D. H. *Fantasia of the Unconscious*. New York: Thomas Seltzer, 1922.

Perseus Digital Library. Accessed February 9, 2023. https://www.perseus.tufts.edu/hopper/.

Prescott, F. C. *Poetry and Dreams*. Boston: Four Seas Co., 1919.

Rogers, L. W. *Dreams and Premonitions*. Los Angeles: Theosophical Book Concern, 1916.

Stekel, William. *Sex and Dreams: The Language of Dreams*. Boston: Richard G. Badger, The Gorham Press, 1922.

Trilling, Lionel. "Freud and Literature." In *The Liberal Imagination: Essays on Literature and Society*. New York: Viking, 1950.

Woods, Ralph. *The World of Dreams*. New York: Random House, 1947.

Zweifel, Philip Lee. "Escape into Reality: The Role of Dreams in the Writings of Mark Twain." PhD diss., University of Wisconsin–Madison, 1975. ProQuest Dissertations Publishing (7518207).